THE FEUD AT GLENCOE

And Other Adventures

A John and Mary Braemhor Mystery

by

Owen Magruder

For information, email **Cozy Cat Press**, cozycatpress@aol.com or visit our website at: www.cozycatpress.com

COZY CAT
P R E S S

ISBN: 978-1-939816-19-1
Printed in the United States of America

Cover by Laura Redmond
http://lauraredmondpicsnpoems.blogspot.com/

1 2 3 4 5 6 7 8 9 10

To Nellie

Prologue

The day dawned grey and ashen with just a hint of mist in the air. The smells of the wet fields crept into Dunmoor Cottage. Scottish mornings often begin this way and rarely progress beyond a dismal, rainy day. But the peat fire near the two overstuffed settees facing one another in the common room cut the dampness and gave the interior of the cottage the kind of warm glow expected of cozy Scottish hospitality in the heart of the lowlands. On colder evenings the peat fire was supplemented with two small electric fires.

John and Mary Braemhor had lived here for almost two years and welcomed the constant companionship of the rain in Scotland after enduring the dry seasons of Rhodesia. Dunmoor Cottage, set back from the Daraichburn to Melrose road on a side lane of dirt and stone ribbed by streamlets from the almost daily showers, was named for Mary's ancestral home, Dunmoor Castle, near Blanefield north of Glasgow. Even the old keep—built in the fifteenth century—was maintained on the family's 4500 acres for occasional large parties of the remaining aristocracy of Scotland. Theirs was a match of opposites, or so Mary's family thought. Her family—which traced its ancestry back to Robert the Bruce of fourteenth century fame—was appalled when Mary and her new husband no longer included even a touch of wine with dinner. Elevenses at Dunmoor Castle had always meant a Chablis for the ladies and a whiskey and soda for the men. Once when John informed Mary's grandfather, late of the

Queen's Own Royal Grenadiers, that he did not drink, the old gentleman responded, "Good heavens, how do you manage?" This lack of participation in a family tradition only confirmed further Mary's parents' conviction that John had corrupted her away from the traditional values of the jodhpurs and riding crop set.

Only one of Mary's family clan saw what she saw in John—Aunt Rita, her mother's maiden sister. Rita, like Mary, was small of build. Her hair was a premature white, her full lips often puckered as if she were contemplating a deep, dark puzzle of which only she was aware. Her eyes sparkled and twinkled with hidden wit and intelligence. The family enjoyed her strange, at times downright odd, behaviors—such as the time she tried to get the whole family to drink a daily cup of hot water "to cleanse the liver." She was known for her verbal non sequiturs. Once, in the middle of a family discussion about the taxes on their estate she announced: "King Tut died of AIDS." And so they lovingly referred to her as the "peculiar aunt in the tower." When John became aware of this particular characterization, he likened it to the Americans' phrase: "the crazy aunt in the attic." But her eccentricities endeared her to the family, though they did not agree with her assessment of John as a mate for their oldest offspring.

Her encouragement of Mary in her choice of mate was what cemented Mary's break with the family traditions on matters of matrimony. "Mary, he's a fine young man, intelligent, witty, principled. He'll make you a fine husband and helpmate. You have made an excellent choice," Rita told Mary in the privacy of the family library one dreary, rainy morning, when Mary was feeling most depressed by the family's assessment of John. Rita saw what most of the clan did not. Beneath John Braemhor's serious, introverted, almost austere exterior was a man of enormous intelligence and wit—a man who could see and appreciate the dry humor and satire behind even the most dismal and depressing events. He was an equal match for Mary's insightful and intelligent thoughtfulness—a match Aunt Rita thought would lead to many, many years of shared happiness in the Braemhor abode. She was right, for as the years passed, John and Mary built a relationship not only on love, but on mutual respect, friendship and common interests. Both were avid readers of history and of classic literature like Tolstoy and James.

But the main thorn in Mary's family's collective side was the fact that John was not of noteworthy bloodlines. Worse yet, he had been a civil servant in Africa, first as a member of the constabulary in Rhodesia for twenty-five years followed by ten in civil service in South Africa. Though his origins were on the Island of Mull, he spent his early childhood in South Africa with his civil servant father and his mother. As things heated up on the tip of Africa, John's parents thought it best for him to be schooled in Edinburgh. And so at the age of seven he and his mother left for Scotland and eventual domicile with his mother's unmarried sister, Emma, until he returned to Africa to become an officer in the Rhodesian constabulary twelve years later. In short order he rose to DCI in recognition of his many investigative skills and uncanny insight into the criminal mind. Only one case in his long career escaped resolution. It involved a series of unusual deaths by asphyxiation, which, except for the cause of death, seemed totally unrelated. After months of frustration and no success, John and his fellow DCI, Nigel Bowen, relegated the case to the file marked "unsolved." "Maybe some mysteries aren't meant to be solved," Nigel had mused, but John was not so sure and the case continued to this day to eat at John's need for completion.

Mary's background, however, was quite different. Reared at Dunmoor Castle, her life through the teen years was a model of genteel upbringing—public schooling, a constant whirl of social events, rubbing elbows with the upper crust of English and Scottish society. One would have thought that social snobbery would have been well-ingrained by the time she met John while on holiday in Rhodesia with her aunt and uncle. But, no, her aristocratic upbringing could not blind her to a highly intelligent "commoner," the DI who helped her aunt recover a purse snatched by a street gang in the capital city. Correspondence ensued and in a little over a year she returned to Rhodesia to become Mrs. John Braemhor.

Mary was the oldest and also the smallest of her generation. But her bird-like, sixty-four inch frame had not deterred her from dominating, both physically and intellectually, her younger brothers. Steel grey had replaced the chestnut hair of her youth, but she, like John, had maintained the trimness of bygone days.

Now, back in Scotland, the Braemhor's lives were far more sedentary than the days in Rhodesia. John had still not come fully to grips with the life of an innkeeper. He was improving though, what with tending his apple trees and passing the evenings round the fire with traveling guests. The American guests were so different from the Scottish or European visitors, so much more outgoing. Mary found them fascinating, but John on the other hand found them boorish and a bit too loud. Once when one couple insisted on smoking surreptitiously in their room—they thought no one would know—John got into quite a row with the husband, who first insisted they had not been smoking and then took umbrage at John's attitude toward smoking in general.

But John Braemhor was not to be confronted, not in his own home. Although he was but five feet ten inches, his frame was square and he tipped the scales at close to twelve stone. His auburn hair had yet to show even a sprinkle of grey around the temples and his hazel eyes were singularly disarming. In conversations, whether with old or new acquaintances, he always gave his full and focused attention. Fifty-eight years looked more like an over-athletic forty-five, and the Americans left at eleven p.m. with loud protests and threats to "notify the authorities." Mary had smiled a secret smile of pride.

Occasionally, John had managed to re-hone his investigative skills as when he helped Nigel Bowen's nephew, London DCI Peter Killmart, solve a particularly gruesome murder at Hadrian's Wall, a case which morphed into a plutonium smuggling operation in the isolated coastal village of Point Dread, Nova Scotia. It was during the latter part of that investigation that he first met and worked with Charlie MacLaine, a FBI investigator on loan to Interpol. Then, not long ago, on holiday visiting their son and his family in New Boston in the United States, the Braemhors were involved in investigating a case of corporate crime and the smuggling of Chinese workers into the U.S. So, despite the more sedentary life of operating a small B&B, John Braemhor had managed to stay in the game. His retirement was an active one.

Chapter 1

It was after nine and the knock was so light, so hesitant that Mary was not quite sure that she had heard a knock at all.

"Is that someone at the door, John?" she asked her husband.

"I'll see." John Braemhor got up from the overstuffed settee in front of the peat fire and put his book on the coffee table. The small peat fire was just the thing to counter the late fall chill of this November evening. John recognized the inefficiency of peat as a heating fuel, but he and Mary did so enjoy the glow in the fireplace and the aroma with which it filled the room. Now that the leaves of John's apple trees had turned and fallen and the first few frosts had added to the coziness of Dunmoor Cottage, it was time to enjoy stay-at-home warmth and hominess.

"It is rather late for a traveler," he remarked as he entered the front hall and opened the door. "Yes?" A burst of November frost-laden air greeted him, as did a tall stranger.

He was a giant of a man, well over six feet tall, with broad shoulders, and a massive shock of light brown hair topping his boyish, freckled face. He was dressed in a light overcoat beneath which he wore a dark business suit, a white button-down shirt and a blood red four-in-hand tie. His face reminded Braemhor of a Halloween mask, deadly white—matching his shirt—and without a hint of animation, neither a smile nor a glower. "Room? Do you have a room?" his voice matched the lack of animation of his face, little inflection and conveying no emotion.

"Yes, we do. Come in, won't you?" This was the off-season at Dunmoor Cottage and travelers, except for the few Americans trying to take advantage of shoulder season prices, were infrequent.

"You seem surprised," the stranger monotoned as he looked down at Braemhor, ducked slightly, and entered the cottage.

"We don't have many guests at this time of year. And the few we have don't usually arrive this late, unless they've booked ahead, that's all. Can I get your bags?" John started to go out to the car park in the front of the cottage.

"No, I have all I need here." He raised the small black leather briefcase he had in his left hand. "I travel lightly," he remarked as he surveyed the hall and peered through to the peat-warmed sitting room. "Nice," he observed, as Braemhor called to Mary.

"We have a guest. Which room should I show him?"

"Number three will be fine," Mary said as she came in from the breakfast room which lay to the left of the front door and behind which the Braemhor's had their quarters and the kitchen. "Mr.?" she extended her hand.

The stranger avoided her gesture and said, "Oh, sorry. Montgomery, Mort Montgomery. And you must be Mrs. Braemhor." Turning then to John, "Mr. Braemhor?" He avoided John's extended hand as well.

"You must be chilled through with just that light coat. Would you like to warm yourself by the fire after John shows you your room? I'll bring in some tea, too." Mary turned back into the breakfast room while John led Mr. Montgomery down the hall to his room. The Braemhors had no other guests that night.

****

"He seems a bit odd," John said to Mary as he entered the kitchen where she was preparing the tea. "He certainly didn't bring much luggage, and that light coat he's wearing wouldn't suit for one of our September evenings let alone November." John thought for a moment. "Somehow he seems vaguely familiar to me. I feel like I've seen him before."

"And did you notice his face? He was as pale as this serviette. He must be terribly cold. Well, some hot tea and the peat fire will warm him." Mary picked up the tea service and went into the sitting room where the strange Mr. Montgomery was already seated in front of the fire rubbing his hands together as if to restart his circulation.

"Ah," he looked up as John and Mary entered, "this is most kind."

Mary smiled as she poured the tea. "Sugar? Cream?"

"Neither, thanks." He leaned forward in his chair.

"What are you doing in this part of Scotland this late in November? You're obviously from America." John was quite direct.

"I guess it shows. Well, let me introduce myself." He fixed Braemhor with his pewter-grey eyes. "As I said, I am Mort Montgomery. A year ago I became Headmaster at The Styx School in Stirling. Before that I was the President of Edwards College in Massachusetts, and before that a Professor of Physics at Harwell University in New York. I give you this brief history, Mr. Braemhor, because it is intimately tied to the reason I have sought you out. My showing up here tonight is not happenstance. I desperately need to discuss a very troubling matter with you. I have sought you out specifically because I am given to understand that you engage in private investigation work."

"From time to time." Braemhor's eyes narrowed as he gave their strange guest his full attention, but

Montgomery's narrative faltered as he turned his glance to Mary.

"You can speak freely. Mary and I share much of my work." Mary had participated in each of John's adventures from their early days in Rhodesia. Especially, she took an equal part in the quiet meditations and mullings that followed a day of John's footwork. Only on rare occasions would he knowingly let her be in danger's way, but he highly valued her deductive input as information and clues mounted. Once, in Nova Scotia, Mary had briefly disappeared while John was following up a lead in the case of Mr. Nobody. John was so terror stricken at the thought that harm might have come to her that that incident served as a potent reminder to limit Mary's involvement in his cases as much as possible to the deductive phases of the investigations. She, also, especially enjoyed the shared intellectual challenge of his cases and through the years there had developed a mutual, symbiotic investigative life together.

"Well then, some years ago, as a fairly young Assistant Professor of Physics at Harwell University, I and a colleague were working on experiments on negative matter and parallel universes. These concepts can only be measured indirectly, not directly. In fact, there is a real question that they exist at all, although they provide a convenient theoretical explanation for some of the data of physics.

"My colleague, Nicholas Estinto, was absolutely brilliant. Some have called him a modern day Einstein when it comes to theoretical physics, and particularly when it comes to understanding the ramifications of negative matter. Except for one thing. When he was sober, he was brilliant, but in his cups he spouted sheer gibberish about moving among parallel universes and things like multiple incarnations. Poor Nick had a severe alcohol problem that not only blunted his theoretical musings, but left him completely incapacitated when it came to putting his thoughts into action. He could devise the most astounding experiments to investigate negative matter, but was unable—because of his heavy drinking—to bring them to fruition. Those of us who tried to encourage him to develop his ideas and experiments were completely frustrated. We could see the possibility of moving the world of physics dramatically forward, but could do little about it because of Nick's addiction.

"Finally frustrated, a few years back I took the initiative to take Nick's ideas and develop them on my own. Nick's ideas and some of his plans for experimentation became my own, and I wrote a series of theoretical papers on the subject and presented them to an international conference on physics. The reception of my papers by the profession was unbelievable. Men thirty years my senior—men I had always looked up to with great admiration, men who were the recognized leaders in the field—heaped unrestricted praise on me and *my* work. Professional association accolades followed, and soon I was the darling of modern physics. And I must admit to you, I bathed in the glory, though deep down I recognized that most of the praise and awards belonged to Nick, not to me.

"As you can imagine, my career blossomed. I was advanced to Dean at Harwell University. I received unsolicited offers from Princeton, Harvard, MIT. All the while my former friend and colleague, Nick, smoldered in the background. We never spoke, but I knew he hated me for what I had done. And, if I admit it, I was not totally comfortable with myself for my actions. Yet, I rationalized, he was doing nothing with his brilliant ideas, and the world of physics, in fact, the world at large, was missing a quantum stride forward in understanding our universe. Instead of being the brilliant physicist he was, Nick was sinking further and further into an alcoholic fog. What was I to do? Let that wealth of cerebration go fallow, never to see the light of publication?

"Well, I digress...I decided I had to get away from Harwell University and Nick's smoldering presence. I chose not Harvard or Princeton but a small, excellent liberal arts college—Edwards College, in the western mountains of Massachusetts—as a place of refuge. I even stopped working in the field of physics and moved instead into administration. I became the president of Edwards.

"But even there I was not happy. Oh, yes, my colleagues in the Physics Department continued their adulation—only reminding me of my fraudulent accolades. But I had problems as an administrator as well, run-ins with the town's people over a road through the campus, with the faculty over tenure guidelines and with the Board of Trustees over intercollegiate athletics. But these confrontations were not the reason I left Edwards and came to The Styx School." Montgomery put his head down and sighed audibly. "It was Nicholas Estinto."

"How so?" Braemhor asked.

Montgomery hesitated, then began again. "During my last years at Harwell University, I saw Nick from time to time, though, as I said, we never spoke. Almost by unspoken mutual consent we avoided each other whenever possible. Occasionally we both attended the same professional meetings, but if we ended up at the same paper session either he or I would leave. Professional meeting confrontations dwindled as time went on, I assumed because Nick's alcoholism prevented him from traveling far.

"I thought my moving to Edwards College would put an end to Nick's and my meetings, but a strange thing happened. Shortly after I took up tenure at

Edwards, I thought I saw Nick in the quad outside the building that housed the President's office. I was looking out of the window one morning—a foggy mist had not yet burned off of the lawn in front—and there stood Nick, looking up at me in his old, wistful way, dressed in the dark grey raincoat he used to wear at Harwell. He just stood there and stared. Even when, in exasperation, I gave a slight wave to him from my window, he showed no recognition. When I turned to answer the buzzer on my phone momentarily and then turned back, he was gone.

"These encounters—that's the only name I can accord them—continued and, if anything, became more frequent. I would be giving a lecture to the Science Colloquium and look up and there in the middle of the audience was Nick, oddly enough in his grey raincoat. No flicker of emotion on his face, just staring."

"He wore a raincoat inside in a lecture hall?" Braemhor interjected.

"Yes, I know it sounds odd, but there he was. Then more and more around campus and even in the village, I would see him. He made no move to speak to me or come up to me. Always just staring. Always in his grey raincoat." Montgomery paused as if recomposing himself.

"The last time I saw him was my going-away dinner the night before leaving Edwards. It was held in a local, posh restaurant and was hosted by the Board of Trustees—I think they were glad to be rid of me. After dinner there were the usual toasts people say at occasions like that. I stood to acknowledge and offer my gratitude for the kind words, knowing that most of them were not really sincere, and there he was...again...sitting in the back of the room, silently staring.

"I quickly finished my remarks, excused myself and made a direct line for where he sat. I was going to confront him once and for all. The back of the room was dark and by the time I got there, he was gone. I assumed he had slipped out of the door before I could get there."

"And now? Is it the same here in Scotland?" Braemhor asked.

"Now? Yes, yes, now here in Scotland. It's still the same. I had thought by moving over here I would be rid of his harassing presence. But no, it has continued to this day! I can't get away from him. I see him across the lawns at The Styx; I see him in the town of Stirling, at small shops, the pubs, touring Stirling Castle. I even saw him at Bannockburn near the Bruce statue. And then tonight—tonight as I ate dinner at the Inn up the road—I saw him in a dark corner of the pub." Montgomery paused for an extended period.

"And what exactly do you want me to do?" Braemhor finally broke the silence.

"I want you to find Nicolas Estinto for me. Bring him to me so that we can resolve this thing. Nick and I need to sit down and talk."

"I will need a complete description of him and as much as you know about him, his habits, his mannerisms, anything at all you can provide. Of course, I will need to know how I can contact you when I locate Mr. Estinto."

"Of course. Here is my address and phone at The Styx." He handed Braemhor some papers and a photo from his briefcase. "There is also a picture of Nick. Do you need anything else?"

"Not for the present," Braemhor said as he looked at the Montgomery papers and the photo.

The three of them, John, Mary and Mr. Montgomery, sat in silence, watching the peat slowly smolder to ashes. "Perhaps it's time to turn in," John offered as he rose to indicate that the interview was at an end.

"Breakfast will be ready by eight." Mary rose also.

With that, Montgomery thanked the Braemhors and went down the hall to his room, leaving John and Mary to contemplate what they had just heard.

****

"What a strange man," Mary said after John had finished looking through the packet Montgomery had given him.

"He did seem a bit odd, but the puzzle he posed, Nick Estinto, fascinates me. How and why does someone appear in so many places and then quickly disappear before Montgomery can confront him? Hmmm...." Braemhor thought for a few minutes while Mary cleaned up the tea service. "Well, I'd better check the car park gate before we turn in."

"Check the front door, too. Are you sure you closed it when Mr. Montgomery arrived? The house seems unusually chilly," Mary called after him.

When he returned, Mary noticed a puzzled, almost worried look on his face.

"What's wrong, John?"

"The door was closed, but there's no car out there."

"No car?"

"That's right, no car," John repeated. "How did he get here?"

"Maybe he left his car at the Inn and walked over. He did say he had supper at the Inn."

"True, but it's a mile and a half walk. It's cold and he was dressed very lightly." He thought for a minute. "Well, let's get to bed. We can ask him about it in the morning."

"Are you going to take the case?"

"I think so. I found his story interesting, but we may be dealing more with a case of an over-stressed conscience than one of a missing, or should I say, bashful physicist."

****

John entered the breakfast room as Mary was completing the table setting and putting three soft-boileds into their cups next to a rack of burnt toast, marmalade and a dish of baked beans. He kissed her on the cheek and asked, "Sleep well?"

"I had a little trouble going to sleep. I was awake until about midnight, and you know, John, an odd thing. You remember when we went to bed, the house was chilly? Well, by midnight it had warmed up again."

"Maybe the peat caught up," Braemhor offered absentmindedly.

"Maybe so." Mary smiled at John. "Coffee will be up in a minute or two. Why don't you let our guest know?"

John went down the hall to Room Three and returned a moment later with an even more puzzled look on his face than the night before.

"What's wrong?" Mary was setting the coffeepot out.

"He's not there."

"Not there? Where could he have gone?" Mary thought for a moment. "Maybe he decided to take a walk before breakfast."

"I doubt it. I rapped on the door and when I got no response, I cracked the door and peered in. He's gone and the bed has not been slept in!"

"How odd. Now, are you still going to try to find Mr.... what was it?...Estinto for him?" Mary clearly thought that Braemhor should not.

"Yes, I am. I find the whole developing set of circumstances even more fascinating. And another thing. It occurred to me when I woke up this morning. I've seen this Mr. Montgomery before, but I just cannot place him. Something about his face...and size."

"A previous case," Mary offered.

"I don't think so and yet I have the feeling I've seen him in a large room, a courtroom or a lecture hall, maybe. But I can't pin it down. Well, maybe as things develop, his identity will come to me. Meanwhile, I'll be off to Stirling after breakfast."

"Stirling?"

"That's where Montgomery said he last saw Estinto, and The Styx School is there. It shouldn't take me more than an hour or so." Braemhor sat there contemplating the whole sequence of events since Mr. Montgomery's arrival.

"John," Mary chided, "your egg is getting cold."

****

Braemhor turned his Vauxhall on to the A703 to Edinburgh and began to plan his approach to the elusive Mr. Estinto. *Montgomery had said that Estinto has a severe alcohol problem so the pubs near The Styx School will be my first stop. At least I have a picture of Estinto to go on.*

From Edinburgh it was on to Stirling and The Styx School area. He began a systematic search of the pubs nearest the school and then worked his way out block by block. In each pub he showed the picture Montgomery had given him of Estinto to the owner or head barkeep, but to no avail. No one had seen anyone even resembling the elusive Mr. Estinto. Then the barkeep in the sixth pub, the Golden Pheasant, said he thought maybe, maybe he had seen an individual who looked like the person in the photo, but he was not sure.

"Yah. Maybe. Comes in 'bout eight in the evening and sits over there." The barkeep nodded toward a dark corner between the door and the end of the large, mahogany bar. "It's dark there, so I can't be sure, but like I say, maybe. He's been a regular for the past couple of weeks. Never buys anything. Never talks to anyone. Just sits for a while, then leaves. Like he's waiting for someone. What do you want to know for?" The barkeep eyed Braemhor skeptically. "You a copper?"

"No, no, not a copper. Just looking for an old friend."

"You gonna buy anything or you gonna be like him?" It was hardly a welcoming question.

"Not now, thank you, but I'll be back later for a meal." Braemhor smiled.

"Not bloody likely!" the barkeep scowled and returned to wiping the glassware.

Once outside, Braemhor decided to call Mary to let her know that he would not be home until later that night.

"I'm glad you called, John. Mr. Montgomery called and said he needed to talk with you. Something he failed to tell us last night. He sounded urgent."

"He didn't say what?"

"No, just that he needed to contact you."

"Did you ask him why he wasn't in his room this morning?"

"I really didn't have a chance. His call was very brief and sounded as if he were calling from a great distance, like he was speaking through a hollow tube," Mary responded. "He said he'd call back later."

That will at least save me the trouble of tracking Montgomery down at the school, Braemhor thought, and then said, "Well, tell him to meet me at the Golden Pheasant here in Stirling tonight about eight. Tell him I may have some information for him."

"You found Mr. Estinto, then?"

"No, but I found someone who may have seen him. The barkeep here thinks he may have, but he's not sure. If Montgomery can get here, we may be able to clear up the whole matter this evening. I'll call you back later."

****

Mary hung up and was about to go make up one of the guest rooms when there was a light tapping at the front door. Opening the door, she was completely caught off guard, for there on the stoop stood Aunt Rita.

"Ah...ah...Aunt Rita! What a pleasant surprise!" she stammered.

"Hello, Mary, I've come down from Blanefield." The small woman with a head of pure white hair greeted her.

"Ah...So I see. But what is that you have in your hand?"

"It's my suitcase, dear."

"No. No, the other hand." Mary asked.

"Why, it's a vacuum cleaner, can't you see?" Rita raised the upright cleaner she was clutching and nodded slightly.

"Yes...but what I mean is, why do you have a vacuum cleaner?" Mary was truly perplexed.

"Why, to vacuum rugs and carpet, of course."

"Of course, but why did you bring it here with you all the way from Blanefield?"

"I thought you could use it. It's a 1934 Hoover. Best ever made. I don't need it anymore. My housemaid brings her own. And there is no sense letting a good Hoover go to waste, do you think?" All the while a playful smile was on her face so that Mary was not quite sure whether Rita was playing some kind of joke or was serious.

"Well that's very nice, Aunt Rita. Why don't you come inside. Here let me take your case." Rita wrapped her arm around the cleaner and carried it as one would a child and entered the Cottage. Her face was lit up with a delightfully vacant smile, the one Mary remembered Aunt Rita wearing when she had too many Chablis at Elevenses at Dunmoor Castle.

She hardly got inside the door when she plugged the vacuum in, turned it on, and began to demonstrate its capabilities.

"Aunt Rita! Aunt Rita!" Mary shouted over the din of the machine. "That's enough for now. Turn it off and you can tell me all about your trip." It was clear now to Mary that Rita was quite into her cups. She took Rita to the far guest room, put her suitcase on the bed and the vacuum in the closet. Then she guided her slightly unstable Aunt to the kitchen and put on a pot of strong Scottish coffee.

"Now, about your trip."

"Oh, it was a wonderful trip. I met the most delightful gentleman. And would you believe, he was a vacuum salesman. We sat in the club car. He told me all about his line of vacuums, and he insisted on buying me cocktails all the way down."

"And you couldn't refuse, could you?"

"Oh, my dear, that would have been terribly impolite." Rita smiled impishly.

"And so you sat in the club car for the whole trip?"

"Of course, otherwise," Rita started and then Mary and Rita spoke simultaneously, "it would have been terribly impolite."

"I see. Well, when you finish your coffee I want you to go to your room and take a nap. The trip must have been very exhausting."

"You're right. I am a little tired." And so Mary took her aunt to her room, saw her into bed, quietly closed the door, and shook her head in loving exasperation.

****

Several hours later, Braemhor rang up Mary again. Montgomery had called back and agreed to meet him at eight at the Golden Pheasant.

"Before you go, John, I think you should know that Aunt Rita showed up this afternoon. I opened the door and there she stood, her suitcase in one hand and a vacuum cleaner in the other."

"She had what in her other hand?" John thought he had misheard Mary.

"A vacuum cleaner. You know, to clean rugs and carpets with."

"Good Heavens, why?" John was incredulous.

"She just said she doesn't need it and thought we ought to have it. And, John, it's a 1934 machine."

"Does it still run or did she bring it for parts?" John snickered.

"And, John, she spent the whole trip down in the club car."

"I see." John shook his head in tolerant recognition that he did not need an inebriated relative in the midst of an investigation. "Well, fill her with coffee and keep her busy—maybe doing our rugs and carpets."

Mary laughed. "I put her to bed. She was exhausted from the trip."

****

Braemhor arrived at the Golden Pheasant about half past seven, seated himself at the dark corner table and ordered a light meal. He positioned himself so that he could see both the extent of the bar and the front door. *I wonder if he'll really show up?"*

But just as the clock above the center of the bar struck eight tinny, high-pitched twangs, in walked Montgomery, wearing the same light topcoat he wore when he first appeared at Dunmoor Cottage the night before. He appeared flustered and highly agitated, his blondish hair uncombed and looking like a disheveled dish mop. Not the neat and well-groomed academic exterior one would expect of a Headmaster.

Braemhor motioned him to a chair across the table and extended his hand in greeting. Montgomery declined both Braemhor's offered handshake and the chair he had indicated. He sat instead next to Braemhor where he, too, could see the front door.

"I want to see him when he comes in," Montgomery explained.

"Of course," Braemhor nodded, "Mary said you had something more to tell me?"

"Yes...but this is very embarrassing." Montgomery lowered his head and began to fidget with a gold pen he had taken out of his pocket. "You see, what I didn't tell you last night was that...that Nick Estinto hung himself two years ago." He emitted an audible sigh and stared down at the tabletop and Braemhor's empty dinner plate.

"He's been dead for two years? You've had me searching for a dead man, a...a...ghost?" Braemhor was incredulous. He started to rise and leave.

"Wait! Wait! Don't you see? If I had told you, you would never have helped me. You would have thought I was... was...crazy. And I need help! Maybe I need psychiatric help, yes, but more than that I need your help to find my own sanity. Don't you see? If someone else could find Nick, then I'm not insane, and furthermore, my—Nick's—theories about parallel universes might have some substance. We, together, could prove that parallel universes and negative matter actually exist. Don't you see...?"

"Mr. Montgomery, I am neither a psychiatrist nor a ghost chaser. I deal with the real world as I—as we—know it. I'm sure that your theories are very important to you, but I am not about to...." Braemhor's words hung in the air for Montgomery's face suddenly froze in a countenance mixed with fear, horror, relief and exuberance. He stared toward the door through which had come a burst of cold autumn air.

"He's here," his voice rasped.

Just as Braemhor turned to confront what Montgomery claimed to see, a barmaid came to Braemhor's side. "Mr. Braemhor? You have a phone call."

Distractedly, Braemhor responded, "Yes, yes, where?"

"At the end of the bar, Sir. The lady said it was urgent." She smiled sweetly.

Braemhor turned to Montgomery. "I'll be right back." And he walked quickly to the phone on the near end of the bar. "Yes, what is it?" He virtually shouted into the receiver.

Nothing. On the other end was a dial tone—nothing more.

Braemhor, exasperated, turned back to the table where he had left Montgomery. There was no one there! He looked quickly out of the front door. An empty street. *Where could he, they—have gone?*

Back at the table he slumped into his chair. The table had been cleared, except for a gold-filled pen, the one that had occupied Montgomery when he first arrived.

Chapter 2

The drive back to Daraichburn gave Braemhor time to think about what had just happened at the Golden Pheasant. Time cleared his irritation and he could now think more clearly about Mr. Montgomery and what he had told him about Estinto. *Either Montgomery is hallucinating or he has a major guilt complex...or both. Maybe he just wanted someone to talk to, to lift the burden of guilt for stealing another man's ideas and publishing them as his own. But why me? Surely, he didn't need a private investigator. He needed a good friend. Or a good psychiatrist.* Then Braemhor paused in his efforts to understand Montgomery's coming to him for help. *Maybe this has all been a dream. Maybe I'm asleep and soon I'll wake up in Dunmoor Cottage and wonder why I have such strange dreams.* However, an unfilled pothole dispelled that idea as the Vauxhall shuddered with the sudden unevenness of the roadway.

An hour and a half later, Braemhor parked in the small car park in front of the Cottage, locked the doors and went in to tell Mary of the evening's escapade.

****

"So you see, all today I have been chasing a will-o-the-wisp, Montgomery's guilt-provoked ghost," he said as he and Mary sat in front of the smoldering peat.

"But, John, why us? Why did he pick us to come to?"

"I've asked myself that question a dozen different ways, but I always, at least so far, come up blank.

Well...," he shrugged his shoulders, "maybe a good night's sleep will help unravel the mystery." Braemhor had long been an advocate of letting problems fester toward solutions in a night's sleep.

"By-the-by, did you ring me up at the Golden Pheasant a little after eight?"

"No, why?"

He told her about the distracting call he received as Estinto was entering the Golden Pheasant and then mused, "Just another piece of this strange odyssey of the last twenty-four hours."

****

"Dreamed up a solution yet?" Mary asked the next morning, as she set out two soft boileds. Rita was still asleep.

"Not quite yet, but I've decided to go back to Stirling. Probably should have stayed there overnight. I need to see Montgomery again." He showed her the pen Montgomery had left at the Golden Pheasant. "Maybe when I return this to him, I'll get some answers."

****

The Styx School was not far from the Golden Pheasant, a massive half-timbered structure with a vast inner court. *Reminds me a bit of Oxford, only smaller,* Braemhor thought as he sought out the Headmaster's quarters. He entered the massive oak door simply stenciled with the word, *Headmaster,* in gold.

"I'd like to speak with Headmaster Montgomery," Braemhor informed the receptionist.

There was a pause. Then, "Mr. Montgomery is no longer with us. Would you like to speak with Headmaster O'Malley?"

"No, where is Mr. Montgomery? How can I reach him?"

Another, longer pause. "Oh, Sir, you must not know. Mr. Montgomery committed suicide two months ago! I'm sorry."

Braemhor was momentarily stunned. Had he really been dealing with ghosts? Was there really something to Estinto's ideas of parallel universes? Had he, John Braemhor, actually entered another universe? No, that idea he rejected as rapidly as it had entered his mind. *Reality, John, reality,* he thought. *So, Montgomery's been dead for two months. Yet I spent time in the Golden Pheasant with him. And others in the pub saw and interacted with him as well. A ghost? I hardly think so. But what...? Another universe? No, I think not. Wait! I've got it.* "So am I. Do you have a picture of Mr. Montgomery?" Braemhor asked calmly.

"That's him," the receptionist said, pointing to the photographs on the wall behind her desk. "He's the one on the right, next to Headmaster O'Malley."

Just as I thought. No ghosts. No parallel universes. The photograph was not of the man that had come to Dunmoor Cottage two evenings ago. "I see," Braemhor said, "that's not the Mr. Montgomery I was looking for. I'm sorry to have troubled you." He paused. "Was Mr. Montgomery headmaster long?"

"Oh, yes, quite some time. Over fifteen years. We were so sorry to lose him."

"I'm sure that must have been very devastating. Well, I won't trouble you anymore. Thank you very much," he said as he let himself out. *Next stop the Golden Pheasant,* and he headed down the street towards the pub.

Braemhor entered and looked quickly around. *I'm in luck. That's the same barmaid as last night.* He approached her, "Got a moment?"

"Sure, dearie," she replied, looking up from wiping off the bar top. "Oh, you was one of the gentl'men what was in last night. Can I help?"

"The other man I was with...."

"The big 'un with the blondish hair?"

"That's the one. Do you know where I might find him?"

"Never seen 'im 'for last night. He was a nice 'un, though."

"In what way?"

"Big tipper, he was. Gave me a fiver."

"Really. Tell me about it." He knew that Montgomery had not tipped her while he was in the pub.

The woman looked skeptical and made no effort to continue the conversation.

"Could be another fiver in it for you." Braemhor smiled.

"That's different, then. Well, the other gent came in 'bout half-five, said he wanted to play a joke on his friend he was meetin' here. Wanted me to call his friend—you—away from the table for a phone call a little after eight. Then he gave me a fiver."

"Ever seen him before?" Braemhor asked as he handed her a five pound note.

"Never, but I'd sure like to see more like him. They don't pay me much for this job, you know," she said as she placed Braemhor's bill in her apron pocket.

"I'm sure they don't." Braemhor smiled again and took his leave.

As he walked to his car he thought, *Now we're getting somewhere. No ghosts, no other universes. Just a vaguely familiar stranger who says he's someone he's not and leads me on a chase to nowhere. And all I have to show for it is a gold-filled pen.* He paused. *The pen! My God, the pen.* He hurriedly got out his mobile.

"Mary, Mary," he tried to make his voice sound calm. "Where is the gold pen Montgomery left at the Golden Pheasant?"

"On the writing table, I think. Do you want me to get it?"

"No, no, leave it alone. Don't touch it! I'll explain everything when I get home, but whatever you do, don't handle that pen!"

"All right, John, but what's wrong?"

"The pen. I think it may be an incendiary device. Just don't touch it. I'll be there as soon as I can. All right...? Better still, you and Rita walk down to the Inn and I'll meet you there in about an hour. That will be safer."

****

In a little over an hour Braemhor strode quickly into the Inn, looked hastily around, and found Mary and Rita sitting at a small table in a corner of the barroom.

"Good," he said as he took a seat next to Mary and smiled at Aunt Rita and asked her how her trip was.

"What is this all about, John?" Mary interjected.

He quickly told her of his discoveries in Stirling—that Montgomery was not the same Montgomery who had been the Headmaster at Styx, and that Montgomery had bribed the barmaid to distract him at the crucial moment of Estinto's arrival in the Golden Pheasant. "It was then that I realized that the pen had been left deliberately—for me to take with me. Why? I asked myself. It wasn't a kind gesture so that I could write him a letter of thanks. No, it had some more sinister import. At that moment a host of forgotten memories came flooding back. Do you remember the case we helped Charlie MacLaine with in New Boston some time ago?"

"Of course, the smuggling of Chinese workmen into America," Mary responded.

"Precisely. And you'll remember that the lead lawyer for the corporation doing the smuggling—Wilhelm Steinmutter—had murdered the CEO and then committed suicide?"

"Yes?"

"Well, at the inquest into Steinmutter's suicide, Montgomery, or whoever he is, was there—remember I said that he looked vaguely familiar when he first came to the Cottage two days ago? Why it has taken me this long to remember him I'll never know, but that's the man. And another thing, at the inquest I noticed he was taking copious notes—with a gold pen—and seemed at times to be taking particular notice of me. I caught him several times staring at me, then he diverted his eyes when I tried to meet his gaze. I thought little of it at the time, but putting it all together now, I'm sure this whole adventure was carefully planned by him to see that I received—and I think used—the gold pen he left at the Golden Pheasant."

"But to what end, John?" Mary was intrigued by her husband's developing narrative.

"Let's assume—and it's only an assumption, I know—that the Montgomery of the inquest was a relative of Steinmutter, a brother, say. A brother who took from the inquest that I was a cause of his brother's suicide. If he had as many psychological problems as his brother, he could well develop in his own mind such a narrative. In his mind that would be reason enough for avenging his brother's death—on someone he thought drove his brother to end his life."

"But you didn't do that, John."

"Not directly. No. But indirectly, by being part of Charlie's investigation. To the deranged mind I was as culpable as the whole FBI team that closed down the smuggling operation and pushed Steinmutter over the edge. You see?"

Through all of this conversation Rita sat quietly listening, spellbound by what she was hearing. She was utterly entranced by John's story and her eyes bulged with excitement as the tale unfolded.

"So what do we do now?" Mary asked.

"First I want to have the pen assessed, see if it really is what I suspect. If it is some sort of miniature bomb or incendiary, then we have to locate Montgomery and force his hand. I doubt he will leave the area until he has ascertained that his plan has worked and I—and you—have been eliminated."

"We won't have to look far, John. I thought I saw him in the lobby when I arrived. It was just a fleeting image—like a ghost," she said, "but I do think it was he."

"Ah ha! Just as I suspected. The criminal seldom leaves the scene until he is sure his crime has been completed." With that, he got up, went to the call box outside and called his friend, DCI James Sinclair in Edinburgh.

****

For some years Sinclair had headed a special units subdivision and was an old friend of Braemhor's since his days in South Africa. A man of slight build with a fringe of white hair surrounding his otherwise bald head, Sinclair looked more like a fine art antique dealer than part of the constabulary.

"Bomb problems, John?"

"I think so, but I need verification."

"Shouldn't you be talking to MI5? I'd think they would be particularly interested in domestic bombs, especially one hidden in an ordinary looking ball-point pen. Sounds like the makings of a spy operation."

"I'd rather start with my friends first. If it is an incendiary device, I'll—you'll—have to bring them in, but for now I'd just like to find out what we're really dealing with," Braemhor responded.

"All right. But I will have to call in MI5 if it is a bomb, you understand. I'll ask my bomb boys to see what they can find. How do you think it's detonated?" Sinclair's conversation had gotten very serious.

"I don't think it's on a timer. Otherwise it would have gone off by now—it's been over two days since I've had it. My guess is that it will detonate when the ball-point is moved into writing position, by the button on the top. Can your boys find out?"

"Oh, I think so. I'll send a disposal van over to Daraichburn and have them pick it up.

****

After Sinclair's bomb squad picked up the pen, John and Mary drove Rita back to the Cottage over her protests.

"But I did so want to see the criminal captured. Can't I go with you?'

"No, Aunt Rita, it will be too dangerous," Mary explained.

"But I so love a mystery," Rita whined.

John then tried to convince Rita by also assuring her that it would not be safe for her. "We want as few people involved as possible," he intoned.

"Oh, like too many cops would spoil the capture?" Rita asked.

"Something like that," John muttered. Despite his irritation with her, it was somehow comforting to have a bit of the childlike levity that she exuded in the midst of the tension of the wrap-up.

"Well, you must promise to tell me all about it when you get back." Rita sparkled.

"That's a promise," Mary assured her as Rita went into the Cottage wearing a long face pout.

****

When John and Mary arrived in Edinburgh they went directly to Sinclair's office. He greeted them with a broad smile and a wiry handshake.

"Give us about an hour. There's a nice little tea room down the street if you and Mary would care for some refreshment while you wait."

"We know where it is. We'll be back in an hour."

****

The tea room was refreshingly bright and clean, with white linen gracing each table and a clear view of the street and the passing throngs of people. John and Mary sat quietly at the table, John staring down at his tea and scones. "Reading the tea leaves, are we?" Mary asked.

"Not really, just thinking about what might have been if either you or I had tried to use that pen. I must be slipping. I knew that there was something very peculiar about Montgomery from the outset. If I had been on top of my game, I would never have picked up the pen when I left the Golden Pheasant."

"Stop berating yourself, John. You couldn't have known that there was anything sinister about an apparently forgotten pen. Thankfully, not everything about us is sinister or evil. Besides we don't know for sure that the pen is anything other than what is appears to be. And if it is dangerous, you've saved some innocent person from possible injury."

"I suppose you're right, but still I need to be more suspicious when a case walks into our front door. Every step of the way there was something odd about him, his story and his actions....Well, let's get back and see if Sinclair can add to the mystery."

"Relax, John, we've only been here a half hour. Let's give James time to investigate your suspicions."

John smiled. "Right." But as he settled back from the edge of his chair, the door opened and in strode Sinclair. He sat across from John and Mary.

"You were right, John, a bomb it was."

"Yes?"

"The boys put it into a bomb box, remotely manipulated the button on the top to release the ball-point, and *bang*, it went off. Enough explosive, I'd say, at least to take off the hand of the user and most likely to kill him. Where do you find these stationers, John? I don't want to shop there myself. Time to call in the National boys, don't you think?"

"Not quite," Braemhor spoke in a conspiratorial tone. "If you will bear with me for another few hours, I think I can deliver the owner of the pen to you with a full confession. Then you can do what you want with him and with MI5. Here's what I'd like you to do."

****

On the way back to Daraichburn, the Braemhors stopped at a stationers and bought a gold pen exactly like the one Montgomery had left at the Golden Pheasant. Back at Daraichburn they drove to the Inn down the road from the Cottage. John parked and stood by the Vauxhall as Sinclair and two of his plainclothes officers parked nearby and walked into the Inn bar.

John and Mary took a table between Sinclair's and the one where his two officers had seated themselves. Mary was right, it was not long before an exceptionally tall, blond-headed, freckled-faced man in a light overcoat walked in. "What did I tell you, John?" She spoke in a whisper. "It's him."

"So it is," John said as he rose from his chair and called to Montgomery, "Mr. Montgomery. Over here. Please join us for a drink."

Montgomery's surprise could not be hidden. He hesitated at first and appeared to be contemplating making a move back out the door, but his suave calm reasserted itself and he moved cautiously to the Braemhor's table, all the while quickly looking over the other bar guests. Finding nothing amiss, he let a pinched smile cross his face and sat down between John and Mary.

"Good to see you again, Mr. Braemhor. I'm so sorry I had to run out on you at the Golden Pheasant, but Estinto and I had a great deal to discuss. I thought you'd understand, and I do want to thank you for finding him for me. Again, I'm sorry for not getting back to you sooner."

"Quite all right. I fully understand. When you have urgent business with a former colleague, it's easy to get caught up in the moment and forget other things." Braemhor was unusually gracious. "I'm just happy to see you again so that I can return the pen you forgot when you left the Golden Pheasant." Braemhor reached into his pocket and produced the gold pen he had just purchased on the way back from Edinburgh.

Montgomery blanched a flatter white than when he first came to Dunmoor Cottage. "The pen!" But he quickly recovered himself and held up his hand. "Oh, no. I didn't forget it. I...I left it there specifically for you. A small token of my appreciation for your finding Nick Estinto for me. No. No. It's my pleasure to make you a gift of the pen. Say it's payment for assisting me in my search." He tried to smile, but the best he could manage was a grimace.

"Like a fee for services?"

"Yes, yes. That's right. A fee for services." Montgomery was clearly rattled again. It was apparent that he wanted to leave the Braemhors as rapidly as he could.

"Then I should write you a receipt. You know, good business form and all that." With that Braemhor produced a slip of paper and held the pen aloft, his thumb poised on the ball-point release button.

"No! No! For God's sake don't push that button!!" Montgomery had lost all control. He stood up.

"Why not?" Braemhor asked, his eyes narrowed.

"Because...because...because it's a bomb, for God's sake. If you push that, we'll all be killed!" With that, he made a rush for the door, but Mary deftly put out her foot and tripped Montgomery, who fell splayed out on the barroom floor. Before he could recover himself, Sinclair and his officers were on him, pinning him to the ground and placing cuffs on his wrists.

"I think we've heard enough, Mr. Montgomery, or whoever you are," Sinclair said as he flashed his police identification, and his officers dragged Montgomery out of the bar to their waiting car.

"Well done, John...and you, too, Mary. Fancy footwork, I'd say." His eyes twinkled as he turned to Mary. Then to John, "We'll be taking your tall friend back to Edinburgh with us and booking him on attempted murder and possession of explosives, at least. Might even let the MI5 boys have a go at him. See what they can find about where he got the explosives and that sophisticated little device he gave you. I'll let you know the wrap-up as soon as I can. In the meantime, enjoy a good supper and rest easy. One more criminal out of the way, thanks to you." Sinclair waved good-bye as he went to join his officers and Mr. Montgomery in the car park.

"Fancy a pub meal before we go home?" John asked.

"So long as I can soak my foot as soon as we get home." Mary smiled. "But what about Aunt Rita?"

"I'll pop back to the Cottage and get her. The three of us can have a nice supper."

****

The train was hurdling down the track like a bullet. John looked up just in time to see it bearing down on him and Mary as they were crossing the tracks.

"Look out!! Look out!!" he shouted as he tried to push Mary out of the path of the oncoming locomotive.

The rumble of the approaching train shook him again and again.

"John! John!" Mary screamed. "Wake up! Wake up!" She had his shoulders in her hands and was shaking him vigorously.

"What?...What is it?" The fog of a nightmarishly deep sleep slowly parted and he realized he was in bed with Mary navigating a frighteningly realistic dream. He opened his eyes, looked at Mary, and mumbled, "It's OK. It's OK, but what is that noise?"

"I think Aunt Rita is vacuuming the hall carpet." Mary giggled.

"At four o'clock in the morning?" John was incredulous.

"Maybe she likes to get an early start." Mary smiled.

"Thank heavens we don't have any guests. Maybe you could tell her it's too early to clean the rugs," John suggested.

"Me? Why me?"

"She's your aunt, I believe." John observed as he gently pushed Mary out of the bed and rolled over to try to resume his slumber.

Mary fumbled on her robe and went out into the hallway where Rita, wearing a happy, smirky smile on her pursed lips, was busily vacuuming the carpet.

"What are you doing, Aunt Rita?" Mary tried not to show her displeasure.

"Vacuuming the carpet, can't you see?" Her smile broadened.

"But it's four o'clock in the morning!"

"Of course, dear. I like to get an early start. Early bird gets the worm, you know." Mary's now obvious irritation failed to mute Rita's delight.

Mary tried another tack, "Maybe it would be better if we waited until the sun is up and we can see better."

"Oh, you really think so?" Rita asked.

"I certainly do! Why don't we put away the vacuum and go back to bed until morning?"

"Well, if that's the way you feel about it. I can do this later, if you like. But it would be nice to get this done now."

"You can finish when we have all gotten up. After breakfast, maybe. That would be better." Mary suggested.

"All right, dear. If you say so." With that Rita turned off the vacuum and toddled back down the hall to her room.

Mary gave an audible sigh of relief and returned to the warmth of hers and John's bed.

****

Three days later, Sinclair called Dunmoor Cottage and told Braemhor what had transpired since Montgomery's arrest.

"I was right." John looked up as he hung up the receiver. "The name on his passport was Steinmutter, Jacob Steinmutter, younger brother of the late Wilhelm Steinmutter of New Boston. I *had* seen him at the inquest and he *had* taken a particular interest in me. Sinclair still doesn't know where his explosives and the pen originated, but he has turned Mont...Steinmutter over to MI5 for investigation into any international criminal connections he might have. I think Mr. Steinmutter will be spending a long, long time behind bars. So for now let's take Candide's advice and just 'cultivate our garden.'"

"Until the next case, you mean," Mary concluded.

Chapter 3

Life at Dunmoor Cottage once more settled into quiet retirement, the case of Montgomery was closed and Aunt Rita had gone back to Blanefield. As was his wont, John Braemhor found it increasingly frustrating not being on the chase. He did tend his apple trees and entertained traveling guests in the evenings, but neither were enough to quiet his adrenalin-driven nature.

This evening, as John and Mary were reading, Mary thought aloud, "John, I've been thinking about your sketches." John occasionally sketched people from his various criminal cases.

"Yes?"

"Have you ever thought of rendering them into oil or watercolor?" She was trying to suggest a new hobby that might allay the tensions he felt between cases.

"I tried watercolor once, you may remember. Kept running the colors together and making a mess." He smiled. "But oil might be interesting."

"Maybe we can go into Melrose tomorrow and get you some painting supplies. We can use the spare room where I write my poetry. You can paint. I can write. Together."

"It's certainly worth a try," John admitted.

Mary smiled and went back to her book.

****

John took to his new hobby with the same intensity with which he approached life in general, but it did not fully dispel his restlessness when there was no investigation to pursue. He had not quite reached the caged panther-like pacing that so often signaled to Mary the need for either another investigative adventure or a holiday away from the Cottage. Then, with a small peat fire cutting the January evening chill, the ring of the telephone interrupted Mary's quiet repose reading Emily Dickinson and John's attempted reading of Turgenev's *Smoke* amid his agitated restlessness.

"It's Stanley Howard, John." Mary handed the phone to her husband.

"The professor with the study group from the States that we met at the Manchester New Year's party?" John queried as he took the phone. Mary nodded her assent.

The Braemhors occasionally attended university functions with their friend and professor of criminal law, James Witherspoon. Just after Christmas they went to a party celebrating the beginning of the New Year and met, among others, Stanley and Jane Howard from America.

"Braemhor here."

"John, this is Stanley, Stanley Howard. We met at the New Year's party last week. I hope you remember me."

"Very well. How are you and Jane?"

"Fine, thanks. I have an awfully big favor to ask. We have just received some very bad news, and I wonder if Jane and I could drop by and talk with you about it? We have to make a brief trip to Melrose tomorrow, and I thought, if it were not too inconvenient, we might pop over to Daraichburn and see you and Mary."

"The Howards want to stop by tomorrow," Braemhor said to his wife, cupping the phone in his hand. Mary again nodded her assent.

"That would be fine," Braemhor said to Stanley. "Care to tell me what the problem is?"

"Of course. Briefly, a distant relative of Jane's has died under what we think are very strange circumstances, and since Jim Witherspoon mentioned that you have a reputation as a private investigator, I thought you might be interested. Maybe Jane and I have blown this all out of proportion, but I'd like to run it by you and see if you, too, think maybe there is something odd about his death."

"We'd be glad to have you stop by. Say about four? We can have some tea and scones and discuss the matter. Our B&B is on the Daraichburn to Melrose road just east of the village of Daraichburn. If you're coming from Melrose, look for the sign on your right—Dunmoor Cottage."

"Fine, we'll see you then. And thank you."

****

Jane and Stanley's odyssey had actually begun a week ago when Jane rang the Gentle Repose Rest Home on the outskirts of Manchester. She wanted to ascertain the calling hours for the Home. Her mother's uncle, Frank Neal Winslow, retired ship's captain, had been living there since his retirement two years ago. He was tall, almost six feet, six inches and large boned. The ravages of age seemed to have passed him over. Though he was in his mid-eighties, his vigor was more that of a spry 60 year old. The ruggedness of his countenance attested to 50 years at sea, first as a cabin boy at the age of 15, then working his way up to ship's captain, a position he had held for the last 30 years before his retirement. He had commanded freighters and tankers alike, and was considered one of the most able of seamen. His nose and heavy brow projected from his leathery, weathered face which was framed by a circle of close-cropped whiskers from his sideburns to the circumference of his mandible. His hands were equally weather worn and showed the years of assault by salt and wind, as did his face. Heavy wrinkles graced his cheeks and large deep crow's-feet spread from the corner of his dark brown, almost black, eyes, which were shadowed over by thick, black, bushy eyebrows that met just above his aquiline nose, to near reach of his temples. In short, his was a commanding presence, which made most people he encountered immediately defer to him.

Jane had always admired, from afar, her great-uncle Frank for the life he led and for the decisiveness he projected through his appearance and booming bass voice. He dominated any social setting in which he found himself. Though, as Jane well knew from her brief encounters with this legendary family patriarch, Frank Neal Winslow was a gentle giant. Winslow had amassed a notable fortune through his years of sea life, a life which afforded little opportunity for spending his considerable sea captain's salary. Jane thought that, since she and Stanley were near Uncle Frank's retirement home, a family visit was in order.

The Howards were living temporarily in Manchester, where Stanley was guiding a year-long foreign study group for Carter University in upstate New York. They were a unique couple. Jane, a large-boned woman in her mid-fifties with an oversized beehive hairdo that she had meticulously styled every week, was thought, even by her friends, to be more out of the 19th century than the 21st. Her attire was always just so with nothing out of place and all of its elements perfectly matched. She much enjoyed university soirees. In fact, she and Stanley often funded large gatherings of the "right people," even during this year of leave from his home university.

Stanley was the perfect mate. With his full head of white hair and a ruddy complexion he always appeared to be on the verge of an emotional outburst, though his demeanor was quite the opposite. A calm, quiet, studious professor of Medieval Studies, he shared Jane's love of a lifestyle of upper middle-class aristocratic pretension. His academic credentials had led Carter University to offer him the position of Dean of the Faculty, which he was to assume after they returned from this year abroad. Jane was already planning extravagant parties for the faculty where she could display her acumen as the perfect hostess in the Dean's residence.

****

Stanley and Jane arrived promptly at four the next day and were ushered to the deep leather settees in the Braemhor's cozy den where a small peat fire added to the warmth and the aroma of the room. Mary had already set out the tea cozy and fresh scones, one of her specialties, in anticipation of their guests, and the four of them settled down to hear Stanley's narrative of Jane's sea captain great-uncle.

"Frank Neal Winslow, Jane's great-uncle, was a seaman of long standing, who commanded ships all over the world and gained a reputation for competence, which was legendary, to the point that many a seaman through the years actually requested to be assigned to ships under his command. His reputation was not only based on his seamanship, but his honest, straightforward dealings with members of his crew. Few were the altercations he had had with seamen, longshoremen, or company agents.

"Since the last 60 years of his life were spent at sea, he literally amassed quite a fortune, hence his ability to afford the Gentle Repose Rest Home. As you may know—we didn't until we made inquiries—the Home is renowned for its accommodations and service and is very expensive. Uncle Frank was quite comfortable in his retirement.

"Jane corresponded with her great-uncle on a regular basis from home in the States, and continued her contact with him by phone once we moved over here for the year—until about a week ago when the

Home informed her that Uncle Frank was 'incapacitated and could not come to the phone.'"

"You can imagine my alarm upon hearing this, since I had spoken with Uncle Frank only a week before that," Jane interjected.

"When Jane inquired as to the nature of his 'incapacitation,' the manager of the Home, a Mr. Trever, brusquely told her that he was not authorized to reveal that information over the phone."

"Brusque! More like hostile, I'd say." Jane was in high dudgeon.

"True, true—I was on the extension. At any rate, we decided to go immediately to the Home and see what was the matter. We drove out that afternoon."

****

When the Howards arrived, they parked on the circular front drive and entered through two massive oak doors into an entry hall that was opulent. It was more like a great estate house than what is usually imagined as a retirement home. Sitting behind a large, polished desk, the receptionist surveyed them before finally asking, "May I help you?"

The receptionist, a Miss Forsyth, according to the plaque on her desk, was a prissy little woman with a bun of chestnut hair pulled tightly back from her temples. She certainly was not what the Howards expected. They thought the first person greeting visitors at such a fine retirement home would have been more warm and friendly. But, no, she was all business.

"We'd like to see Mr. Trever, please," Stanley spoke.

"Do you have an appointment?" was her response.

When they told her they did not, she informed them that Mr. Trever did not see anyone without a prior appointment.

"I just want to see him about my great-uncle, Frank Neal Winslow." Jane entered the dialogue.

"Oh, the sea captain," spoken with unveiled disdain.

"That's the one," Stanley affirmed. "We are concerned about his health."

"As well you might be," countered the receptionist. "I'll see if Mr. Trever can see you today." With that she rose and primly walked through the polished door to the left and behind her desk.

When she returned, the Howards were ushered into a large room furnished in Victorian decor and told to "wait here."

Since both Jane and Stanley were admirers of Victorian furnishings—their home in the States was so decorated— they walked around the room admiring the various velvet settees, chairs, tables, and wall decorations. Some of the latter, the portraits, appeared to be of individuals of landed gentry from the late 19th century. But surveying this palatial room could only consume so much time; fifteen minutes of admiring the room and its furnishings passed quickly and still no Mr. Trever. Finally, three-quarters of an hour later a side door between two regal portraits opened, and a small, balding man dressed in a light blue smock entered. He appeared to be in his mid-forties. His black eyes focused penetratingly on the Howards.

"You are the Howards, I presume?" he asked in precisely spoken words that hinted of a slight accent of Welsh origins.

"That's right. I'm Stanley and this is my wife, Jane." Stanley extended his hand which Harwell Trever ignored, keeping both of his hands firmly planted in the pockets of his smock. "We came to inquire into the health of my wife's great-uncle, Frank Neal Winslow."

"I told your wife that the gentleman was indisposed and could not talk with her." Trever's icy response pointedly ignored Jane.

"I understand that, but what is the nature of his incapacitation?" Stanley's frustration was beginning to melt his usual diplomatic approach to situations.

"Your wife's uncle died night before last," delivered with as much emotion and empathy as if he were reading the daily newspaper.

"Died!" Jane was dumbfounded. "How? Why?"

"Old people do that. He was, after all, 84. It's not unusual at that age." Trever would not give an emotional inch.

"But I spoke with him just a week ago. He sounded fine. Didn't convey any indication that he was feeling badly." Jane was still in disbelief.

Trever shrugged. "Now if you will excuse me, I have important matters to attend to." With that he turned to exit through the door by which he had entered.

"Wait!" Stanley arrested Trever's exit. "We need to talk about funeral arrangements. As direct family we should handle that, notify others of the family, and make sure he has a proper burial. Jane is, after all, the closest next-of-kin."

"It is not your concern. The Home has already taken care of that. It is part of the service. We are authorized." Again he reached for the doorknob.

"By whom? Who authorized you to attend to funeral arrangements?"

"Captain Winslow, of course. It is part of the contract the guests sign when they become part of our community. It is already taken care of. You do not have to bother yourselves."

"Bother ourselves!! But where is he buried?" Stanley pressed on.

"He has been cremated."

"What?" Jane and Stanley were in utter disbelief. "Then where are his ashes? We would like to take them and dispose of them properly." Stanley was thinking fast.

"His ashes have already been scattered. I do believe we still have some of his personal effects, although his clothes have been distributed to the poor. You can take what we have as you leave. I'll send an attendant with them in a few minutes. Now, I really must go." And with that Trever left the room leaving Stanley and Jane befuddled as they stood in the midst of Victorian splendor.

As the trauma-shocked couple left the building and walked dejectedly to their car, a girlish voice called to them. "Mr. and Mrs. Howard, I have the Captain's things here." She was carrying a small, brown leather valise that looked like a shipboard map box.

The staff member, Daisy Carson, was a wisp of a girl in her early twenties. Her blond hair cascaded over her shoulders from beneath the nursing cap she wore. Her complexion was very pale, attesting to her many, many hours of indoor work in the Home, where the sun seldom penetrated.

"I'm so sorry about the Captain. He was such a nice man. Always friendly and kind. It was a real pleasure to look after him. And so sudden. I could not believe it when they told me he had passed away in the night. I'm on the day schedule and I came in at seven. I just could not believe it. He seemed so healthy when I left after supper. He was arranging a game of chess with one of the other guests when I waved good-bye. So sad." She handed them the valise.

Stanley and Jane spent the next half hour talking with Daisy, trying to understand better what had happened to Captain Winslow. But they were able to gather little further information. They drove slowly back to their Manchester apartment deep in sadness and bewilderment.

****

"And then when we got back to the apartment," Stanley continued his narrative, "We had a letter from Captain Winslow, mailed, we think, just after Jane had talked with him. In with a brief note were three bank books of Uncle Frank's accounts in three different banks in and around Manchester. He had truly amassed quite a fortune over the years. His note said simply: 'Keep these safe for me. F. N. W.'"

"I see." Braemhor thought for a minute; then he looked at Stanley. "It's quite clear that the circumstances you describe are unusual. However, the fact—you do know for a fact that he was cremated?"

"All we know is what Mr. Trever told us. But, yes, he said papers duly signed by a Manchester physician certifying his death and noting his cremation were in hand, although we did not see them."

"Hmmmm. That's very unusual." Braemhor thought for a moment. "Well, if he was cremated, it will be very difficult to find out what exactly happened to him." Jane and Stanley immediately looked terribly crestfallen. Sensing their disappointment, Braemhor continued, "But why don't you give me a few days and let me see what I can uncover? You have a phone where you can be reached?"

"Of course." Stanley took out a small pad and pencil and handed Braemhor the scribbled number. "Here."

"We really appreciate your help," Jane said as Mary poured more tea and passed the scones again.

The Howards stayed for another half hour of small talk and then took their leave and headed back to Manchester much encouraged that John Braemhor also saw the strangeness in the circumstances of Uncle Frank's death.

****

"Well, what do you think?" Mary could see John's analytical thinking astir.

"I think they have presented me...us...with a very difficult puzzle. If he has been cremated, the chances are that we are already at a dead end."

"No puns please, John." Mary smiled.

"Right, but still we have a very difficult case. What bothers me is that cremation so soon after death makes the circumstances all the more ominous. It is not unheard of, but just not the usual procedure. I need to know who the physician was who certified the death and where Winslow's body, or rather his ashes, are buried or scattered. I'd best go down to Manchester tomorrow and see what I can find. Want to come?" As in almost all of his cases, Mary was an equal partner.

"I would love to, but we have more guests coming in the morning. You go and I'll play innkeeper."

****

Late the next evening Braemhor turned the Vauxhall into the lane, now covered with little rills of runoff from the afternoon's rain, leading to Dunmoor Cottage. He parked his car next to the guests' in the car park. The smell of the wet fields surrounding the cottage greeted his arrival.

"Any success?" Mary asked as John hung up his great coat.

"Yes and no. I found the registration of a death certificate for F. Winslow; says he died of *natural causes* on December 20th. Could be him; at least the date is about right and the F. could stand for Frank or Francis. Then I checked all of the crematories around Manchester and found no record of a cremation in the last two weeks."

"That's odd," Mary said.

"Quite. I then tried to locate the physician who had signed the death certificate. Do you know how many Singhs—that was his name—there are in and around Manchester? However, I finally found him or at least his clinic offices and his place of business. He runs a small Manchester medical company, Bioderm, from his offices. It supplies body parts to various hospitals for transplantation—dental implants, knee and hip replacements, that sort of thing."

"John, you don't suppose?" Mary's voice was filled with distress.

"Let's not jump to any conclusions yet. But odd. Very odd," John pondered as he spoke. "I left a message for McGinty before I came home."

"The DCI in Manchester?"

"The same. Maybe he'll know something. But for now, how about a bit of supper?" Mary and John retired to the kitchen so that their guests could have the sitting room to themselves for the rest of the evening.

****

McGinty's rough, gravelly voice thundered through the phone line so loudly that Mary could hear it across the room. "I got your message. What do you need?" She could easily imagine this large, gruff man with his great shock of salt and pepper hair and walrus-like moustache.

"I need some information, Owen."

"Still at it, John? Last I heard you were helping Killmart up at Hadrian's Wall. I guess you just can't retire, can you? What can I do?" His benevolent smile coursed through the wires.

After Braemhor finished telling McGinty the narrative Stanley and Jane Howard had brought him, he finished up with, "I need to know more about Bioderm and Dr. Singh."

"Funny you should mention that parts provider. We've just closed them down this morning."

"What's the charge?"

"Body stealing, grand larceny, forgery, you name it. Our Dr. Singh is going to be charged with it all. Seems he was stealing bodies from the morgue, from hospitals, all over. He even had a dummy funeral home set up to enhance his procurement. He'd hack up the bodies without permission and without screening for disease, and sell the parts for transplantation. When we got there, he still had several fairly fresh bodies in his cooler, partially harvested. Gruesome. He was in the middle of shredding his paper work. What are you looking for, John?"

"First, the body of one Frank Neal Winslow. Second, whatever paper work pertains to him. How far did he get with the shredding?" Braemhor was hoping Dr. Singh was shredding his files alphabetically.

"Let me check my preliminaries." McGinty left the phone.

While Braemhor waited, Mary looked at him quizzically. "Don't know yet," he answered her unspoken question.

"John, if you weren't a Scot, I'd say you have the luck of the Irish." McGinty was back. "All three of the partially harvested bodies were male. We're checking DNA now for identification."

"And the paper work?" Braemhor was on the edge of his kitchen chair.

"Are you sure you're not Irish? Singh only got halfway through the Ns. There may be something there, but I don't have time to look now."

"I'll be there this afternoon. Can I see what you've got left?"

Mary went into the bedroom and started packing a small valise.

"Glad to have you. We'd like to tie up as much of this case as we can, and if you can help us at all with the identification of any of the bodies, it would be much appreciated. I'll see you this afternoon." A click and the gruff voice was gone.

"I need to head to Manchester," Braemhor said to Mary.

"I packed an overnight for you," Mary smiled. "What did you learn?"

"I think we may have found something, but it's too early to tell. It may be what we suspected when I found Bioderm."

"Oh, John, how are we going to tell the Howards?"

"We're not going to tell them anything at the moment. We'll have to wait and see what else I can find in Dr. Singh's paper work in Manchester. But I'd best be on my way; I have to stop and get some petrol before I go." With that, Braemhor retrieved his great coat from the closet, picked up the valise and headed out the door, saying a brief hello and goodbye to the guests who were eating their breakfast in the sitting room.

Chapter 4

Braemhor arrived in the late afternoon at McGinty's offices and was ushered into a small room where on the small desk were piled four stacks of files and miscellaneous paper work marked "Bioderm."

"Dig away, John, I've got other cases to solve," McGinty smiled his way into the space, holding out his oversized and hairy hand to Braemhor.

And so John Braemhor "dug in" to what was the most tedious and, he felt, boring part of any investigation—sifting through paper work that might or might not provide the answers he sought. As he sat down, he thought, *How can they stand to work under such conditions?* The room was enveloped in the acrid, stale odor of cigarettes snuffed out in ashtrays, both dry and wet. *Well, the science of detection is not all thinking and deducing. It's equally a lot of searching through papers, trash and other people's garbage. Best get on with it. Hope my lungs won't mind too much.*

And so for the next two hours he skimmed what was left of Bioderm's records. Finally he found what he wanted, a paper noting the acquisition of a male body, "F. W." from "H. T." on December 20th. "Now we're getting somewhere," he muttered to himself as he made notes from the record. He quickly wrote McGinty a brief note, laid it beside the pile of files and left the office.

****

Braemhor returned about tea time the next day. From the look on her husband's face, Mary could tell that the news was not good. "Well?" she asked.

"It's possible we may have found Winslow's body, or what is left of it, among the three still at Bioderm, but we can't be certain until McGinty's crew finishes running the DNA," Braemhor said as he put his valise down on the kitchen floor beside the table. "I've asked McGinty to have an autopsy done to ascertain the specific cause of death. You remember Dr. Singh had said *natural causes*. But it was the paper work that was most interesting. Seems Singh bought one of the bodies, which his paper work identified as "F. W.", from a "H. T."

"Jane's uncle and Harwell Trever!" Mary interjected.

"Possibly...for £1500." Braemhor finished.

"Oh, John, that's dreadful!" Mary was in disbelief. "What will happen to him?"

"Nothing, for the time being."

"Nothing!" Mary was incredulous.

"Without the positive identification of one of the bodies in question as Frank Winslow, we're at a standstill. An autopsy report might help, but there is nothing in Singh's paper work to identify the seller other than 'H. T.' Of course it's illegal to sell bodies in the first place, but we're not in a position right now to pin even that crime on Trever. We have to wait," Braemhor concluded.

"How long?" Mary was displaying the impatience she usually saw in her husband at this point of an investigation.

"McGinty said he'd have the autopsy report day after tomorrow—the DNA, a little longer."

****

Two days later McGinty's gruff voice shook the Braemhor phone line again. "Got the autopsy report, John. One of the bodies died of COPD, another of cirrhosis of the liver, and the third of an overdose of Coumadin—bled to death internally."

"That's Warfarin, a common rat poison," Braemhor responded as he thought...*an old person's medication. I think we've found Frank Winslow.*

"Precisely, but we still need to identify the body for sure."

"DNA should help." Braemhor could not contain the anticipation in his voice.

"Right, John, if we can match it to any of our databases. But that will take awhile. I'll call you when I have the report. You sure you're not interested in the other two bodies?"

"No, our victim did not have COPD, as far as I know, and, surprisingly for a seafaring man, he was not a heavy drinker. I think body number three is our best bet. Call me as soon as you have the DNA." Braemhor hung up, turned to Mary and brought her up-to-date. "We have a body that could be what we're looking for, but it will take a positive DNA identification before we know."

"Oh, John, this is so terrible. What will you tell the Howards. We can't wait too long to contact them."

"I know and I've been thinking about that."

****

"John, Owen McGinty here," boomed the DCI from Manchester again. "The DNA won't help. It doesn't match anything in our databases. We need something to match it against. Any ideas?"

"Possibly, let me see what I can find." Braemhor hung up and turned to Mary. "I need something of Winslow's, something that would carry his DNA."

"Maybe the Howards would have something, a scarf, a handkerchief, something like that?" Mary asked.

"Worth a try." And with that Braemhor placed a call to Manchester.

"Have you found something, John?" Stanley's enthusiasm warmed the phone only to be crushed by Braemhor's negative response. He explained what he needed, carefully skirting the detail of what he had found and hoped to find.

"We may have something. Remember, I told you that the staff person at the Home gave us what of Uncle Frank's effects they still had? Well, we looked at them and there are several combs, his electric razor and some other toiletries. Do you think that would help?" Stanley asked.

"It just might. I'll be down later today and pick up what you have."

"John, there's something else. The last couple of days there has been a strange automobile parked near our apartment. I can't be absolutely sure, but I think the person sitting in it looks like Mr. Trever from the Home. I thought about going out and confronting him, but thought I'd wait until I talked with you."

That changes everything, Braemhor thought. "Stanley, now listen very carefully to what I am going to tell you. Stay inside. Do not go out, even to get the mail. I will call you when I get there this afternoon and give you further instructions. And, Stanley, how were Jane's uncle's effects given to you?"

"What do you mean? The staff member just handed them to us."

"In a bag? In a box? In a suitcase?"

"Oh. I see. They were in a smallish map box, like they might have aboard ship."

"All right. Take them out of that. Handle them carefully. Touch them as little as possible and put them into plastic bags in small enough packages that you can put them in the pockets of your overcoats. So when I pick you up later, it will not look as if you are going on a trip with a suitcase. Understood?"

"Yes, but why? You make it sound like a murder mystery?" Stanley was trying to lighten the conversation.

"I hope it's not. And another thing. You mentioned three bank passbooks that belonged to Jane's uncle."

"Yes?"

"Bring them with you, too. I'll call you again in a couple of hours." With that Braemhor rang off, put on his great coat, briefly told Mary what was happening and headed again to Manchester.

****

A little over two hours later, Braemhor parked his black Vauxhall behind The Sachet, a small tea room down the street from The Prince Charles Hotel, and rang the Howards on his mobile.

Stanley answered. "My, that was quick," he observed.

"I probably exceeded the speed limit," Braemhor smiled. "But I wanted to get here as early as possible. Have you done what I instructed with Winslow's effects?"

"Yes, but I still don't understand why." Stanley was mildly irritated.

"You will soon enough. Now, I want you and Jane to put Winslow's effects and his bank books into the pockets of your coats, get into your car and drive to the public car park just down the street from the Prince Charles Hotel. You know where that is?"

"Yes."

"Good. Park your car there and go across the street to The Sachet tea room. Have yourselves some tea and scones until I arrive. Look casual. Two Americans out for an afternoon tea, but sit in the back of the shop, not near a window. If Trever comes into the shop, do not—I repeat, do not—acknowledge me when I arrive, but continue having your repast. If that happens, I will leave and call you on your mobile. Give me the number now."

Stanley, more perplexed now than ever, gave Braemhor the number.

"Fine. I will see you within the half hour." Braemhor rang off.

****

Following Braemhor's instructions explicitly, the Howards took seats near the display counter at the back of the tea room and waited. Fortunately, the tea room was small, having only five tables, so it was not difficult to survey the entire premises for Mr. Trever. Also, fortunately, they were the only customers. Though the scones were exceptional, neither Jane nor Stanley had much appetite for appreciating the excellence of The Sachet's offerings.

Ten minutes later, Braemhor entered through the back door, quickly looked around and approached the Howard's table.

"Get your coats and follow me," he ordered as he continued to look outside of the shop for any approaching customers.

Once outside, Braemhor hurried the Howards into his Vauxhall, quickly drove down two back streets, entered the main road three blocks from The Sachet and then headed toward McGinty's offices.

"Where are we going?" Stanley finally managed while Jane sat in subdued silence in the back. Both were shaking in fright though they did not fully understand why. Perhaps it was Braemhor's sudden brusqueness and his commanding presence. They were not quite sure.

"First, to see a DCI friend of mine, then to your uncle's banks, and then to Daraichburn."

"Daraichburn! Why?"

"This man—Harwell Trever—may be very dangerous, and it would not be prudent for you to remain in Manchester tonight. I don't know what he'll do, but it is best to get the two of you out of the city for now." Braemhor snaked his way through the afternoon traffic.

"But we have no clothes!" Jane exclaimed.

"I'm sure we can do something for the short range," Braemhor tried to reassure her as he parked near the municipal building where McGinty had his offices.

"Give me your Uncle Frank's effects," he ordered. Jane and Stanley emptied their overcoat pockets into a small valise Braemhor held open. "You stay here. I'll be right back," he said and went inside where he gave Winslow's effects to McGinty.

"Now the banks," Braemhor said as he got back in the Vauxhall.

At each bank Braemhor took Jane to the manager to ascertain the up-to-date balances in the passbooks. At each, the story was the same. A man from the Rest Home had attempted to withdraw all the funds from the account, but was refused because he did not have the passbook to the account, although he did have papers which indicated that Captain Winslow had transferred the running of his affairs to the Home.

Fifteen minutes later the three were on the highway to Daraichburn, midst mild, but not very strenuous complaints from Jane about her inability to look her best for the next few days.

Two and a half hours later Braemhor pulled into the car park of Dunmoor Cottage. Mary was waiting in the sitting room.

****

Next morning as the Braemhors and Howards sat in the kitchen having soft-boileds, the phone rang. Mary answered and then handed it to her husband. "It's McGinty again."

"John, what's your gimmick? Every time you get involved in a case, things start to heat up and speed up."

"What's going on?"

"I got a call from university security. They apprehended a man in the apartment where your friends, the Howards, are living. Broke in. Was trashing the place at two a.m. Made so much noise the neighbors called. Thought maybe the Howards were having a domestic dustup. We're holding him now. Breaking and entering. And this you will like, he's a workman at the Gentle Repose Rest Home," McGinty thundered.

"Good news!" Braemhor smiled at the Howards and Mary. "How long will the DNA take, and can you hold him until we have those data?"

"We're holding him on breaking and entering and vandalism. I'll put a rush on the DNA. Should have the report in the next two days. And, John, where are the Howards? No one can locate them."

"It's all right. They're here in Daraichburn with Mary and me. Tell the university that they're on holiday and will return in a few days. And, Owen, let me know as soon as you have the DNA report."

"O.K., John, I'll talk with you in a few days." Click and he was gone.

Braemhor turned to the others and told them what had happened, the break-in, the apprehension of Trever's handyman, and why they were waiting for the results of the DNA tests.

"Do you really think he meant us harm?" Stanley asked.

"Most definitely. You see, if he did all the nasty things I think he did—we'll know for sure when we hear from McGinty—he would want to get rid of you two before you went to the police. He didn't realize that I had already alerted the police to what we thought was going on, so as far as he was concerned, you were the only possible danger to him on this side of the Atlantic. And so if he could silence your voices, he was free of any suspicion. Also, he probably figured out that you two had the bank books he needed to obtain your uncle's savings. That was why he sent one of his workers to search your apartment. Now we just have to wait and see if the findings justify our suspicions that Trever is a body seller and possibly a murderer of retirees."

"Oh, this is just terrible," Jane moaned. Stanley, John and Mary turned to her.

"I know," Mary commiserated, "but unfortunately there are evil people in the world."

"Oh, no, no, no, no, not Mr. Trever and what he did," Jane responded.

"What, then?" Mary was perplexed.

"Tomorrow is my appointment at the hairdresser, and I'll just be an utter mess if I can't go."

Braemhor couldn't suppress a chuckle. "Better alive and a mess than the alternative," he offered.

Jane, recognizing the gravity of the alternative to an undressed hairdo, managed a quiet smile and said, "I suppose, but I will look a fright without a change of clothes in the next few days."

Mary comforted her and suggested a shopping trip to Melrose the next day.

****

"John, you will never convince me you are not Irish," McGinty boomed again.

"You've got good news, then?"

"Better than you think. The DNA from the effects you brought me is a perfect match for the overdosed body. With Singh's paper work alone we could have prosecuted him on body selling at least. But...and here is the best part of it...the man from the Home confessed that he was instructed to find some bank passbooks Mr. Trever thought might be in the Howard's apartment. Then when we picked up Trever, he crumpled under interrogation and admitted all. He sold Winslow's body to Singh after he had him overdosed with Warfarin! We have enough evidence through the Winslow body—thanks to you—to wrap up the whole Bioderm operation, Singh, his associates, Harwell Trever and several of the Home's staff. The Home was the perfect conduit for body parts. No one thought much of older folks dying and the Home taking care of all of the 'funeral' arrangements. Trever had a constant stream of people to sell for the extra money the Home needed to keep up its palatial pretenses. The money in the banks was to be just icing on the cake. His operation was perfect until you and your friends came along. It's really too bad about the captain though. He sounded like a person well worth knowing. "

"I'm pleased I was able to help," Braemhor smiled.

"I'll bet you are. And, John, anytime you and Mary want to help out on any more of my cases, I'd be glad to have the two of you."

Braemhor smiled again, hung up the phone and turned to Mary and the Howards to tell them the end of the Frank Neal Winslow tale.

Chapter 5

The successful completion of the Winslow case placated, for a brief period, John's need for investigative stimulation. He actually seemed comfortable painting and looking after Dunmoor Cottage, for a while.

"You know, Mary, painting is one of the most relaxing things I do," John said as he leaned back from his easel and looked at her at her writing table. "What do you think of this?" He had rendered a small portrait of Francis Neal Winslow from a photograph Jane and Stanley Howard had given them.

"Very nice. It looks just like an old sea captain," Mary allowed. "Now sit back and listen to the poem I've just written about him. It's called 'The Third Year.'"

Mary had hardly finished reading when John said, "Let's think about putting your poems into book form."

"Oh, John."

"No, Mary, I'm serious. We should publish your work."

Mary smiled and said, "Only if you'll agree to illustrate them."

****

Two more weeks of the sedentary life and an article in the paper caught Braemhor's eye.

"I'm not so sure," John mused as he scanned the newspaper accounts of the Gorman suicide while seated before the peat fire having after-supper coffee.

"Not so sure of what, John?" Mary queried, looking up from her reading.

"Did you read the account of Lester Gorman's suicide? Look here."

"The American we met in Manchester last month?" Mary recalled.

"That's the one, and *was* is the correct form of the verb. Newspaper says he jumped from a hotel balcony last week while attending a convention of archeologists."

"Oh, my! He seemed so full of life, so happy. Why would he do such a thing?"

"I don't think he did."

"But, John, it says he left a suicide note to his wife." Mary was rapidly scanning the article.

"Look at his recreational pursuits, and you'll see what I mean." John had ignored Mary's remark.

"Avid fisherman and hunter," Mary read. "So what does that have to do with it?"

"Why would he come all the way to the U.K. to jump off of a balcony? That's point number one. Point number two is that when a man commits suicide he more than likely chooses a method that is irreversible. Women tend to choose methods that, should they change their minds in the process, can be reversed. Like taking an overdose of tablets. For a limited time after ingesting the pills there is the possibility of taking an antidote, or having her stomach pumped. Not so with men. Once the act is initiated there is no turning back. The scenario plays out to death, and Lester Gorman had a gun collection."

"But surely jumping from a height is irreversible, John," Mary argued.

"Maybe, but not always. He could have survived the fall, though he might have been severely injured. No, I don't think this was a suicide. Professor Gorman would have shot himself at home in America, if he were really intent on ending his life." At that moment the telephone rang.

"Who can that be? It's rather late for a rental, don't you think, John?" Mary lifted the receiver. "Dunmoor Cottage," she said. After a brief pause, "Yes, he's here. May I say who is calling?"

"John, it's a Richard Gorman." She handed the receiver to John.

Braemhor raised his eyebrows and, holding his hand over the speaker, whispered, "As in Professor Gorman?"

"Braemhor here."

"Mr. Braemhor, this is Richard Gorman. I'm calling from the States. I'm Lester Gorman's son. You met him last year, I believe?" The voice was young.

"Yes, we met him in Manchester. I was just reading about the tragedy. I'm very sorry," John replied. "Can I help you?"

"I hope so. I'm a student at Carter University, and Dean Howard said you might be able to help me and my brother and sister.

"We just don't think Dad would do something like that—suicide, I mean. And now we can't find our mother. She was with him at the convention, and nobody knows where she is." Gorman's voice faltered and he had to stop talking. "Is there anything you could do to help us?" This last was more of a plea than a question.

"First, I want you to tell me as much as you can about your father and the type of work he did."

For the next half hour Richard Gorman told Braemhor as much as he knew of Lester Gorman's work, both as a renowned archeologist and his efforts to engage the Palestinians and Israelis in meaningful dialogue toward rapprochement.

"I don't know if I can help or not, but let me see what I can find out. Is there some place I can reach you easily?"

Gorman gave Braemhor phone numbers and an email address where he could be reached, then profusely thanked him for being willing to try to help.

"I'll get in touch with you as soon as I have any information for you," Braemhor ended the conversation and turned to Mary. "I think I need to talk to Inspector McGinty in Manchester."

****

Newspaper accounts of tragedies are seldom as thorough or vivid and nuanced as the actual events. What had happened the previous afternoon at the Prince Charles Hotel sent shock waves through the international academic community.

The body hit the concrete in front of the Prince Charles with a sound resembling a minor explosion. So loud was the impact that the people in the lobby instinctively ran to the windows to see if there had been a car crash in the street outside. Some even thought it was the beginning of some sort of terrorist attack on downtown Manchester—until they saw what and who it was.

"My God! That looks like Lester!" shouted one of the convention attendees as he rushed outside. "Oh, good Lord, good Lord, it is!"

By then a crowd of onlookers were gathering, some pedestrians from outside the hotel and the rest from the assembled academicians inside. Two tried CPR, but their quest was hopeless; they could only sit dejectedly on the curb near the body awaiting professional assistance. A hotel employee thoughtfully brought out a blanket and covered the body.

Lester Gorman's academic career had been brilliant, and his public addresses were legendary; talks interlaced with insightful humor mixed with serious proposals for the future of whatever topic he was addressing.

In addition to being an academic leader, he also excelled in community projects, working tirelessly with both local Jewish and Palestinian groups to encourage rapprochement between the two. For his work he had achieved international renown and often made trips to the Middle East to confer with leaders of diverse groups there. His academic background was, after all, the archeology of Mesopotamia and few in the world rivaled his expertise. Despite the plaudits he received from the academic world for his extracurricular activities, official governmental agencies, in the United States as well as abroad, looked with disdain on his efforts. This was particularly true of the American CIA, who kept him on a close watch list.

Gorman was tall—and had a massive head of greying black hair and a close cropped, greying goatee. He was an imposing figure. And his career had just reached another pinnacle this year when he was awarded the prestigious Gold Medal for Academic Achievement, to be conferred at the Manchester meeting when tragedy struck. Lester Gorman, the leader, husband and father everyone thought had lived a past without comparison and looked to a future few could imagine much less aspire to, leaped to his death from his fifth floor hotel room balcony.

Both the academic world at large and the local community back home were stunned, and those on the scene in Manchester, were dumbstruck. "We will never understand it."

****

Next day Braemhor called Owen McGinty.

"McGinty here," said the familiar voice at the other end of the phone. Braemhor had helped him with the Bioderm case not long ago.

"John Braemhor here, Owen. I'd like to talk to you about the Gorman suicide."

"What got you interested in it?" McGinty was wary.

"His son called from the Colonies. Wants me to see if I can learn anything more about his father's death."

"You think there's something wrong?" McGinty did not sound surprised.

"Don't you?"

"Well, yes and no. We recorded it as a suicide—a note was left to his wife and the coroner determined it a suicide—and moved on to other, more pressing cases. Then I met Mrs. Gorman, Harriet Gorman, and I began to wonder. You see, she had attended the convention with him. Seems she's some sort of an archeologist, too."

"Nothing strange about that," John mused.

"No, but when I accompanied her to identify the body, she immediately wanted to arrange a hasty cremation—said, 'It'll be easier to carry a tin of ashes back to the States than an embalmed body.'"

"Doesn't sound very loving."

"Loving! She was as cold and hard as a week-old dead fish."

"Go on."

"Well, I did think it a bit odd for her to have him cremated so rapidly, but you know Americans, they're a strange lot. Besides I had Gorman's suicide note and the coroner's report. But then a strange thing happened. She told me she was going to the U.S. Embassy in London to arrange passage home for the ashes—when she disappeared! Just vanished! Nobody at the Embassy saw her or even heard of her, except what they read in the papers of her husband's suicide! Now I've got a can of ashes and a lot of doubts. What do you think?"

"It sounds to me like you have more on your hands than the ashes of an eminent world archeologist. I think I'll come down to Manchester and poke around a bit. I'll call when I get there. Oh, one other thing. What room were the Gormans staying in?"

"What kind of a question is that?"

"Humor me."

McGinty shuffled some papers on his desk. "505, why?"

"Just curious, that's all. I'll see you soon." And Braemhor hung up the receiver.

"How about a short trip to Manchester?" John turned to Mary. "I'll book a room at the same hotel Gorman died in," he continued without waiting for Mary's reply.

****

The Prince Charles, a five-star modern, six-story structure with more than enough meeting rooms for the convention archeologists, was in the center of the city. Braemhor parked on the street and went in to registration.

"May I help you, Sir?" was the greeting from behind the desk.

"I'd like to book Room 505, please." Braemhor smiled.

The clerk's jaw dropped as he looked at his computer screen. "Well, I...I..."

"Something wrong?" Braemhor asked.

"No, but I...I...I need to speak with the manager. Please excuse me." He disappeared into a back room, and soon emerged with a small, officious-looking man dressed in a three-piece suit and sporting a thin, pencil-line mustache.

"May I help you, Sir." Braemhor felt as if he had entered a time warp.

"Yes, I'd like Room 505, please," Braemhor repeated.

"I'm afraid that won't be possible."

"Why not?"

"Well...eh...eh...." Perplexity covered his face and then after a pause, "I'm sure you would not want *that* room. In fact, we have not even decided if we should rent that space. I have a number of nice rooms on the fourth or sixth floors, 405 or 605, perhaps?" He smiled, trying to defuse the tensions of the moment.

"No, I'd like Room 505." Braemhor emphasized the first five. Is there a problem?" Braemhor pressed the issue.

"Well, Sir," the manager was now literally squirming, "it's just that that is the room where the unfortunate occurrence happened, and we didn't think..."

"You mean the suicide?"

"Well, yes, the suicide." The word seemed to stick in the manager's throat.

"I'm not superstitious. Room 505 will be fine." Braemhor continued the pressure. The banter back and forth continued for a full five minutes, much to the consternation of the clerk, William, who observed the interchange with a combination of awe and embarrassment. Finally, the manager acquiesced.

"If you insist."

"I do."

The manager turned to the clerk, "Book Mr....ah...ah..."

"Braemhor"

"Yes...Mr. Braemhor into 505, William." Then turning to Braemhor, he said, "The car park is in the rear. I hope you have a pleasant stay," maintaining his demeanor, but making plain his displeasure with the booking and Braemhor's attitude in general.

"Thank you." Braemhor registered, received his key and returned to Mary outside.

Meanwhile, the manager quickly disappeared into his office, ruffled through his Rolex, dialed the number he found under Gorman, and spoke quietly, "This is Fairweather. I need to speak with Mr. Street right away."

****

"It's working out better than I hoped. We've got the room Gorman jumped from," Braemhor said to Mary. He was clearly delighted.

"John, really, sometimes I think your sense of the macabre overtakes your good sense." Mary frowned.

"What better place to start an investigation than at the scene of the crime?"

****

Room 505 was a large room with two double beds, an extensive sitting area, an oversized bath and, of course, the infamous balcony. The beds projected from the right hand wall towards the bathroom door, with the sitting alcove, complete with round writing table and three chairs, between the beds and the balcony. The ubiquitous telly graced the wall next to the bathroom door, facing the foot of both beds, for easy viewing.

"Nothing unusual here," John observed and quickly put his index finger to his lips as a signal to Mary.

Mary watched her husband as he took the hotel phone pad and pen and wrote a cryptic note: "Talk about the room, how good the beds are, etc." She launched into a soliloquy, perhaps a mite too loud, about the wonders of staying in a luxurious room in one of Manchester's finest.

While she talked and John occasionally grunted his assent, he searched the room and the bathroom with the deftness of an espionage agent looking for hidden cameras and/or microphones—which is exactly what he was searching for.

Shortly, he interrupted Mary's commentary with, "Let's take a walk and see what center city Manchester has to offer."

Outside, a block or so from the hotel, Mary broke the silence. "What's going on, John? Is the room bugged?"

"Yes." John spoke matter-of-factly.

Mary was incredulous. "Why?"

"That's one of the things we need to find out. You see, when I booked, the manager was adamant that I not have that particular room. At first, I thought he was protecting the reputation of the hotel and didn't want to rent the room out of some misplaced superstition. A lot of people are very reticent to sleep in a room or house where someone has died, particularly if the death was violent. I understand that in the state of California a house seller must reveal to prospective buyers if someone has died in the house so the buyer can pull out of the sale. Such are the superstitions of people.

"Now either the bugs were left over from the Gormans' occupancy—and we have to wonder why they were under surveillance—or the manager was screening whoever might ask for that room specifically. They—and I don't know who they are—wanted information on the Gormans or are expecting someone to rent that room in whom they would be particularly interested."

"John, you're not making sense."

"I know, but bear with me. I don't know where this is going myself right now. But I do know that you do not bug a hotel room unless you expect to gather information about someone or something."

"Do you think we're in danger, if we stay in the room?" Mary was clearly getting concerned.

"Not yet. Particularly if the bugs are left over from a week ago. But then we have to ask why the room has yet to be swept clean. Right now I think the object may be new information, but once they get what they want, the whole picture could change. Meanwhile, we need to know more about the Gormans, especially what happened to Mrs. Gorman after she left McGinty. So, we need to talk with McGinty again and, if possible, someone at the U.S. Embassy."

"What about Aunt Rita's friend, Ellen?"

"Ellen? She's a computer consultant, isn't she?"

"Yes, and she's occasionally consulted at the U.S. Embassy. If she can't help, maybe she'll know someone who can. I can give Aunt Rita a call."

"Fine. You work on the Embassy angle, and I'll start with McGinty. But none of this is to be done from the hotel. Use phone boxes. We can meet back at the hotel about seven for supper. OK?"

Mary headed to the nearest call box and John went in the opposite direction towards McGinty's office.

****

On the way to McGinty's office, Braemhor made a brief stop at the public library where he skimmed through last week's newspapers and, finding what he wanted, purchased a Xerox copy of the picture on the front page. He was but a block from McGinty's when he saw a familiar face. He crossed the street and confronted the young man.

"You're the clerk from the Prince Charles," he stated.

"Yes, Sir." A sheepish look spread over the clerk's face.

"If you have a minute, I'd like to talk with you about the suicide at the Prince Charles last week."

"I really don't think I have the time." The clerk started to walk away, highly agitated.

"Just a moment," Braemhor pressed on, "you were on duty when it happened, right?" Braemhor was gambling he was right.

"Ye...yes, Sir, but I didn't see nothin'," the young man stammered.

"But something happened just before Professor Gorman jumped to his death." Again Braemhor was guessing. "What was it?"

"Well...well, please, Sir, don't say nothin' to Mr. Fairweather, please, Sir. I'd lose my job, if he knew I was talkin' to ya."

"Trust me," Braemhor said as he handed the clerk a five pounder.

The clerk looked up and down the street, then said, "Well, Sir, a strange thing did happen about twenty minutes before poor Professor Gorman died."

"Yes?"

"Two men all dressed in black, wearing dark sunshades came in and asked me for the professor's room number. Well, I couldn't give them that information, it's against the hotel policy. But they started arguing with me and threatened me, if I didn't give them the number. They made so much of a ruckus that Mr. Fairweather came to the desk and took them into his office in the back. It was like he knew who they were. I was really scared; they looked like they were out of an American gangster movie."

"How long were they with Fairweather?"

"Not long. Couple of minutes. What's this all about? First them and now you; who are you anyway?"

"Just a friend of Professor Gorman," Braemhor elaborated the truth. "I thought you might help me understand what happened. Anything more you can tell me?"

"No, no. All I know is that after you registered, Mr. Fairweather was very upset and rushed back into his office, and...."

"Yes?"

"Well, I noticed his line lit up on the switchboard."

"He was placing a call?"

"Yes, I guess so."

"To whom?"

"I don't know. I couldn't tell from the switchboard. And I don't care. I don't want no trouble, I don't. I've got my family to think of. And me. Yes, Sir, like I said, first them and now you. I don't...I don't want no trouble. I'm just a poor hotel clerk. Please, please don't tell Mr. Fairweather I spoke to you. Please, Sir." The young man looked on the verge of tears and was shaking from head to toe.

"Don't worry. I won't say a word. You've been most helpful." Braemhor was more gentle than he had begun. "Let's keep this conversation just between you and me, shall we? No Mr. Fairweather, nobody but you and me? Can you do that?" Braemhor returned to his pressuring mode.

"Yes, Sir. Yes, Sir. I...I won't say a word. To nobody." With that he turned and walked rapidly down the street away from the Prince Charles, mumbling to himself that he ought to find another job.

Well, I'll give him until tomorrow before he confesses to Fairweather, Braemhor thought, *but that should be enough time.* And he hurried on to see McGinty.

****

McGinty was sitting in his office—a glass-enclosed "goldfish bowl" he called it—on the periphery of a large room housing the desks of his DI's and secretarial assistants. He waved Braemhor on through the crowd to his inner sanctum.

"Good to see you again, John." His outstretched hand welcomed Braemhor into the relative quiet of his office. "How can I help you this time?"

"It's the Gorman suicide." Braemhor continued to use what he thought was a misnomer. "I've gotten Mary and me booked into Room 505 at the Prince Charles, and I've already picked up some disturbing information from the desk clerk. Did you know the room is bugged?"

"Yes, and it's more complicated than you may think."

"Oh?"

"My boys found the microphones when we searched the room after Gorman jumped. I told them to disassemble them and to bring them in as evidence, when I got a call from a local MI6 operative—an MI6 operative, would you believe? I was dumbfounded. They ordered me—not told, but ordered me to leave the devices in place until they okayed their removal, and they told me to record the incident as a suicide!"

"So MI6 is involved. More and more it doesn't sound like a simple suicide."

"I agree, John, but there was nothing I could do—not and keep my job. So I recorded a suicide and closed our investigation. And, John, I'd be very careful if I were you. MI6 and the American CIA—if they're involved, and I don't know for sure that they are, but I suspect so—both play for keeps and won't tolerate any interference from local authorities much less from a private investigator."

"Warning taken," Braemhor spoke pensively, then brought McGinty up-to-date on his booking into the Prince Charles and his talk with the desk clerk fifteen minutes ago. After a brief pause, he continued, "Can you quietly trace a phone call the Prince Charles manager made about an hour ago?"

"You didn't hear me? The more involved you become, the more dangerous it becomes. Can't you just leave it at a suicide and go on back to Daraichburn and run your B&B?"

"You know me better than that, Owen. Will you trace the call for me, or not?"

McGinty grumbled but put in a brief call on his secure line to the telephone exchange. As he finished his inquiry and hung up the receiver, he turned to Braemhor and shook his head. "This may be even more trouble than either of us realized. The manager, a Mr. Fairweather, put in a call to the local MI6 office here in Manchester. John, you're getting in over both our heads, and I don't like it one bit. Take my advice and go back north and forget Gorman."

"Not yet. I need to know more. Now what can you tell me about Mrs. Gorman? Is this she?" He showed McGinty the picture he had obtained earlier.

"Yes, where did you get that?"

"From the newspaper. Now tell me again what happened after her husband's death?"

"Like I said yesterday, she identified him for us, then almost immediately requested the body be taken away and cremated. I've never met a colder, more calculating woman. It was like his death was an irritating inconvenience. No tears. No emotion. Almost like she expected it," McGinty continued.

"Expected it?"

"Yeah. Usually relatives—particularly a wife—are pretty broken up by a death of a loved one—especially a suicide. She wasn't. Took it all very matter-of-factly. Very businesslike. 'How soon can we get the body cremated?' she asked. *What's the rush?* I thought, but I had already received one call from MI6 and wasn't about to chance another.

"After we helped her arrange the cremation, she left saying she was going to the Embassy, like I told you. But she never got there. People at the Embassy said they never saw or heard of a Mrs. Gorman. I did check immigration—just curious—and they record *both* a Professor and a Mrs. Gorman arriving a few days ahead of the conference, but nothing about her leaving."

"So, as far as the record is concerned, she's still here. Has anyone reported her missing?" Braemhor asked.

"No, but without a complaint, there's not much I can do officially, and I leave the private sleuthing to folks like you, John." McGinty smiled.

"O.K. but if you get anything more, get in touch with me."

"At the Prince Charles?"

"No, here's the number of a small B&B, The Cat and the Kitten, run by one of Mary's friends. They're very discrete and will take messages for us. I'll check in with them a couple times a day. One last thing, Owen. What was the suicide note like?"

"You can look at it, if you'd like." McGinty rummaged in several file folders on his desk and handed a photocopy of the note to Braemhor:

"Harriet:
It's no good. We can't continue. Our views are too different. You on one side, me on the other. It's time for me to move on to a broader horizon. I'm going over to the other side. Don't try to stop me or follow me. This is the end.

                    Lester"

Braemhor looked up. "Sounds more like a marriage on the rocks than an impending suicide. Why is everyone considering this a suicide?"

McGinty looked uncomfortable. "It's better that way, John, believe me."

"Well, I'd better go. I have to meet Mary and see what she's uncovered."

"So both of you are involved? Take my advice, John. Drop it and go home. It'll be safer that way." McGinty's voice disclosed real, personal concern.

"Don't worry. I'll mind our backs and I'll let you know before we go back to Daraichburn." Braemhor shook his friend's hand and threaded his way through the haze of smoke outside of McGinty's office.

****

Mary was waiting for John on a park bench across from the Prince Charles. She smiled as he approached, "I talked with Ellen and we're to meet her and a friend of hers at half past four in the tea shop in the next block. The friend, Paula, works at the U.S. Embassy, Consular Section." Pride radiated over Mary's face.

"Excellent! We're a team." John sat down and told Mary what he had gleaned from the clerk and McGinty, including his warnings and the call from MI6. "I've changed my mind. We'll stay at Martha's B&B tonight—I called her from McGintys—after we have supper at the hotel pub. But we'll leave our bags at the Prince Charles. No sense taking any unnecessary chances." Mary had seldom seen John so cautious and assumed it was because she was with him. They got up and walked to The Sachet for their tea date.

Chapter 6

The Sachet was a tiny tea shop fronting on a busy Manchester street. Paula Greene, a stout, cheery-faced woman in her mid-fifties and Mary's aunt's friend, Ellen, were waiting for the Braemhors at a table in the back of the shop.

"We thought it best if we stayed away from the windows," Ellen was the first to speak as she and Paula rose to greet Mary and John.

After the scones and tea were ordered, the conversation drifted to the mundane—the good weather, the joy of living in a small-sized city, and the like.

It was Ellen who diverted from the small talk by saying, "I thought Paula might be of some help to you." She looked at Braemhor. "She's worked at the U. S. Embassy for almost... eighteen years, isn't it, Paula."

"That's a long time. You must really enjoy your work," Mary half stated and half asked.

"Well, yes and no." Paula became very serious and stirred her tea a bit longer than required.

Braemhor bored right in. "What do you do at the Embassy?"

"Oh, a little bit of everything. Mainly secretarial, filing, that sort. They won't let a non-American do anything that might be security-sensitive. Still you learn a lot just being there. I've been there so long I've served in almost every section." Paula relaxed a little and her face broke out in a smile that engulfed her entire face.

"So you know the workings of the Embassy very well?"

"More than most and certainly more than the new station manager." Paula's countenance turned again somber and she was obviously uncomfortable with Braemhor's questioning.

"Don't like the section manager, eh?"

"Well...well...no, frankly. He's a political appointee, and.. .well...he doesn't know his job. He's arrogant, he's petty, bosses people around for no reason, and he...he...he knows nothing about foreign affairs or even how to conduct himself in a foreign country. I'm not even sure he knows who our Prime Minister is. Yesterday he referred to him as 'Mr. Black.' I guess that's as close as he could get to Brown. He's making The Section a laughingstock. Oh, I'm sorry. I shouldn't have said that, but...but...it's true. I...I...."

"Paula's thinking of leaving her position," Ellen quickly jumped in when she saw that Paula was about to disintegrate into tears.

"I'm sorry." It was Mary's turn to comfort the distressed Paula.

"So the section manager is a bean counter," John interpreted.

"Worse than that. Everything has to be done to make him look good. If whatever happens at the Section doesn't pump up his image, he's against it. I think he's trying for a full ambassadorship...on our backs. Claims he's a personal friend of the American Vice-President! Ha!" Paula had now collected herself, and felt freer to unburden herself to these friends of a friend.

"That's really too bad," John continued. "Relying on political appointments can ruin any country's foreign policy. But, tell me, do you see much of the comings and goings at the Embassy?"

"Quite a lot, why?"

"Have you ever seen this woman?" Braemhor took out the picture of Mrs. Gorman and showed it to her.

"Oh, yes. Just last week. Came barging in like she was the Queen, showed some sort of identification, and was quickly taken back to a secure area. I was filling in for the receptionist's secretary on the front desk."

"How did she seem? Was she calm? Was she distraught?"

"Arrogant, like the section manager. Acted like she owned the place. Why?"

"You say she was taken back to a 'secure area?' What does that mean?"

"It usually means that you are very important. Other diplomats are handled that way. Agents, too. They all go to secure areas for initial vetting when they first arrive."

"Agents? What kind of agents?" Braemhor felt he was on to something.

"Oh, the usual. CIA. FBI. Occasionally, MI6. MI5. In fact, shortly before she arrived, two men came in and were taken to the same secure area. CIA people, I'll bet. You can kinda tell them. They have a particular look about them. All purpose, no nonsense types. Dark suits. Dark glasses. So much a stereotype. You'd think they'd learn and put on some disguise, a false beard or something." Paula had loosened up considerably now and seemed to be enjoying unburdening herself again.

"You say they came in just before Mrs. Gorman?"

"Mrs. Who? Did you say Gorman?"

"Yes, why?"

"That was a name on the next day's diplomatic courier flight manifest. I typed it, just before they left." Paula was intrigued.

"Those flights and their contents don't have to check through the usual filters, do they? So no one in the host country knows what's coming in or going out." Braemhor knew he had found very valuable information now.

"That's right. Is this some sort of spy story?" A frightened look crossed Paula's face.

"No, no, nothing of the sort," Braemhor quickly assured her and smiled, "we're just trying to find an old American friend who was attending a convention here a short while ago. We had hoped to see her before she went back, but I guess we missed her."

"Pretty important friend, I'd say," Paula observed.

"Not really, it's her husband that's the important one, but she often travels with him. You've been most helpful, Ms. Greene. You've saved us a lot of time. Now that we know that our friend has gone back to the United States, there's no need for us to keep searching for her." With that Braemhor let the conversation drift back to the sites of Manchester and the excellence of The Sachet's scones.

****

After supper in the Prince Charles pub, Mary and John took the lift to their room.

"I thought we were not staying here tonight," Mary mused.

"Quite so. I just want to arrange a few things before we slip out and go to Martha's," John responded. As they entered the room, he walked onto the balcony and looked over. He motioned Mary to come out on the balcony and spoke in low tones with his hand over his mouth. "Look at this Mary."

Mary, doing the same, looked down from the balcony. "There're two large awnings below. Looks like they shade two patios on the floor below."

"Yes, and notice that there is a small gap between them through which you can see the front car park below. Gorman fell through that narrow gap to the park five stories below. Now imagine a man, so distraught that he is going to jump to his death, aiming himself to miss the two awnings—which would break his fall one floor below. Doesn't that seem a bit extraordinary?"

"A bit unbelievable, I would think," Mary added.

"Yes, more likely a person intent on suicide would just run toward the balcony and leap at the railing, not carefully aim himself to miss the two impediments to the success of his action," John spoke his thought quietly aloud.

"But, John, he left a note to his wife."

"The note was, to say the least, ambiguous. Well, let's set the stage here and be on our way. Give me a couple of strands of your hair."

"My hair? Oh yes, of course," Mary responded when she realized what he was about.

Braemhor quickly laced one strand around the latch on their overnight bag and, as they left the room, another between the door handle and the door frame. He and Mary then quietly descended the stairs and slipped out the side exit of the Prince Charles.

****

"What's next, John?" Mary asked as they settled into their room at The Cat & the Kitten after John had checked with Martha for any messages from McGinty.

"I think we need to find out more about Professor Gorman's academic and international activities. I thought I might speak with Professor Richard Petticrew at the University about Gorman's work in and outside of academia."

"Why Petticrew?"

"He knew Gorman well and may be able to give us some insight into what Gorman was working on just before his death. Gorman's academic expertise was Mesopotamia and I wonder if his attempts to reach a rapprochement between the Palestinians and the Israelis got him into trouble with MI6 or its American counterpart."

"Oh, John, you don't suppose he was engaged in some sort of spy work, do you?"

"I don't know, but it's a possibility we can't afford to ignore. I'll call Petticrew and arrange a meeting tomorrow, if possible." Braemhor went down to the B&B's common sitting room to use the telephone. Ten minutes later he returned. "All set, first thing tomorrow morning."

****

Professor Petticrew was a tall, rangy man in his mid-fifties. His hair, coal black with a sprinkle of grey, was combed straight back and down over the back of his neck where it ended at the top of his collar. His countenance was ruddy, his cheeks a rosy hue, but his nose a slightly purple shade. He struck Braemhor as a man who spent much of his waking life in his cups, a Dylan Thomas character, who, even through the fog of a perpetual state of inebriation, projected a massive intellect, more than a match for the non-academic riff-raff he observed at the end of his aquiline nose. He met Braemhor with a combination of disdain and curiosity.

"So you want to know about my colleague, the late Lester Gorman. Why?" Petticrew threw the gauntlet at Braemhor's feet.

"Because I don't believe he committed suicide." Braemhor met Petticrew's arrogant posture with a direct and withering stare that took Petticrew momentarily aback, and made him consider that the man in front of him was no ordinary non-academic.

"I see," Petticrew played for time, "What makes you think that?"

Braemhor sketchily outlined his thinking so far, keeping his explanation vague and circumspect, but by now Braemhor had taken control of the encounter. "I need to know more about the Professor's work, in particular his attempts to reach rapprochement in the Middle East."

"Why should I reveal anything about Lester to you? Who are you and what business is it of yours to pry into my dead colleague's life?" Petticrew had momentarily regained his superior attitude, though he was clearly shaken by Braemhor's forcefulness and directness.

"Let's just say I am an interested party. I know of Professor Gorman by his reputation as a scholar and leader in the field of Middle Eastern archeology, and the public accounts of his death have left much unsaid. Do you think he committed suicide?"

"That's...that's what all of the newspapers said," Petticrew stuttered slightly.

"That's not what I asked." Braemhor's stare could have melted the polar cap.

"No...no...of course you didn't."

For the first time since the conversation began, Petticrew appeared to relax somewhat and act like a person concerned about a colleague rather than trying to impress a stranger asking thorny questions.

"Maybe we could start again, Mr. Braemhor. I'm sorry if I seemed somewhat aloof, but Lester's death came as such a shock to all of us. And the way it happened. It just does not seem real. Like it's a horrible nightmare and I'll awaken soon and have a few drinks with Lester at the local pub. You understand." His last sentence was a plea for more understanding from this cold, direct interrogator. "Are you from MI6?"

"No, why do you ask?" Braemhor relaxed his posture towards Petticrew slightly.

"Because they were the first people to seek me out the day after Lester's death. Burst into my office as if I were some sort of a criminal or...or spy."

"What did they want?"

"I'm not really sure. They seemed to want to find out how much I knew about Lester's work—not his academic work, you understand, but his work with the Israelis and Palestinians."

"And you told them?"

"There was nothing I could tell them. I know Lester's work in archeology, but he was always very tight-lipped about his efforts with the Middle Eastern peace process. He never discussed his non-academic work, though there were times I think he was truly worried about it."

"Oh?"

"Yes, I don't know if he was worried about how his efforts were progressing or something deeper and more...more sinister. There was one time at the beginning of this last convention when he seemed very distracted, very...jittery, I think would be the proper word. And he was always such a happy, carefree person. Always had time to talk to you, exchange a few jolly remarks. To me, he seemed—I can't quite put my finger on it—scared, maybe. But I could never get him to talk about it, even over cocktails. It just made me feel uncomfortable, like something was wrong that I could not fathom. It just wasn't like him."

"What about his wife?" Braemhor asked.

"Harriet? Harriet is one of the coldest, most aloof women I have ever met. Frankly, I don't know why he stayed with her. They were the opposite ends of the spectrum. Her—hard, deadly serious, always determined on her work—she is an archeologist, too, you know, Mesopotamia, like Lester—him, more relaxed, open, friendly. Both brilliant scholars, world leaders. Why do you ask about her?"

"No one seems to be able to find her."

"I'm not surprised. She's a loner. Goes her own way, does her own thing."

"Did they stay in the same room?" Braemhor thought Mrs. Gorman might hold the key to the mystery.

"That's an odd question?"

"Humor me," Braemhor instructed.

"Well, as far as I know....Yes, they did. Had a group of us up to their room for drinks before the convention's opening banquet. Yes, I'd say they shared the room."

"Is there anything...anything at all Professor Gorman might have said about his Middle Eastern work that you can recall? Who he talked with. What about. Any person or place he may have inadvertently mentioned?" Braemhor was hoping Petticrew could recall something of value.

"Well, let me think...no, I don't thi...yes, yes, there was once when I visited him in America. He mentioned, almost off-handedly, how difficult it was to get the Israeli government to stop expanding the settlements on the West Bank, but when I tried to draw him out, he laughed it off as if he said nothing more important than the lack of rain in Jerusalem this year. Though I thought it a bit odd at the time, I didn't pursue it and the matter was dropped."

"So you think Professor Gorman was working on the problem of the settlements?" Braemhor jumped ahead.

"Oh, I couldn't say, but he did mention them that one time. Oh, dear, you're not suggesting that he was more than an academic scholar?" Petticrew was visibly shaken.

"I wasn't suggesting anything specific. Right now I need all the information I can get about him. Anything else? Did he act strange, tense, like here at the meetings?"

"Well, there was one thing. Oh, it's nothing really."

"Let me decide that," Braemhor pressed.

"After a morning panel on which he and I served, he left immediately—I presume to go up to his room. At least he headed directly for the bank of elevators at the back of the banquet hall. Usually he would linger after a session to exchange small talk with other panel members, but not last week. He left so quickly that even those of us on the panel weren't able to talk to him. Very strange. As if he had another important engagement."

With death, Braemhor thought.

"Professor Petticrew, you've been most helpful. I do caution you not to mention our conversation to anyone for the time being. I may want to talk with you more later." With that Braemhor took his leave and went directly to McGinty's office, leaving Professor Petticrew in a state of perplexity and confusion.

****

"John, I'm very glad to see you. MI6 called this morning to see if I knew anything about a pushy man named Braemhor who checked into the Prince Charles and demanded Room 505—by now I suspect they've found you in their databases. When they told me they couldn't find you, I really started to worry. I told them nothing, as if I hadn't seen you yet, but I told you to leave this one alone, John. My guess is that MI6 is on the lookout for you, and it won't be pleasant when they find you." McGinty's worry pervaded his repeated warning.

Braemhor ignored McGinty's concern and asked, "Where are Gorman's effects? I need to see what you've got."

"In an evidence drawer. Come on." McGinty started out of the office, knowing he could not put Braemhor off. Down the hall and in a secure room he emptied the contents of a drawer marked 'Lester Gorman' on the table. There were the clothes Gorman had worn to his death, some lecture notes, pens, pencils and a small hotel note pad.

"We only found one shoe on the body; the other one was still in the room," McGinty offered.

"A bit odd, wouldn't you say? Why would a man intent on throwing himself off of a balcony take off one shoe before he jumps? Perhaps it was pulled off as he jumped," Braemhor added.

"You mean someone was trying to prevent him from jumping?"

"Or helping him."

McGinty shook his head slightly. "You still don't buy the suicide conclusion, do you?"

"Less and less, the more I learn. Now, what's this on the pad?" Braemhor examined the small notepad from Gorman's effects and jotted down what was on the first sheet: Ester, 9/5; Daniel, 12/5; Joel, 3/8; Ruth, 4/7; Amos, 5/12.

"Just a list of people's names and some dates. We figured they were fellow archeologists. I was going to look into them when I got word to drop the investigation and put it down as a suicide," McGinty explained.

"I think they are more than names of people. Lester Gorman was trying to tell us something. I've got to get back to the hotel. I'll let you know what I find, if I find anything." With that Braemhor exited the room and the building and walked directly to the Prince Charles.

He entered the same side entrance he and Mary had exited by the evening before, hastened up the steps to the fifth floor, and slipped into Room 505. Quickly, he ascertained that the room and their bag had been entered—Mary's hairs had been broken—put the Bible from the drawer of the night table in the bag, and descended to the second floor. From there he descended to the first floor on the other side of the building, dropped his room key in the return slot and exited just as he noted two men in black talking with William, the clerk. From there he walked a fast pace to The Cat & the Kitten where Mary anxiously awaited his return.

****

"Now we're getting somewhere," Braemhor announced as he put their bag on the bed. He rapidly told Mary of his meetings with Petticrew and McGinty and his purloining the hotel's Bible.

"Why the Bible?" Mary asked.

"Look at this list of names. Does anything strike you about them?"

"Of course, they're books of the Old Testament." Mary smiled.

"Precisely, they're not names and dates Gorman jotted down, as McGinty thought. Gorman was trying to tell us...somebody...something. This, I think, is the beginning of a message for anyone astute enough to listen. Now, let's look at the Bible—this is the Bible that was in Gorman's room—and see what it tells us." He sat down at the small desk in the room.

"Let's assume the numbers after the names are not dates, but chapters and verse in the books of the Bible. Ah ha," he exclaimed as he turned to Ester, Chapter nine, Verse five. "Gorman highlighted certain letters in the words, much as students highlight important passages in their texts. Look here!" Braemhor went through each of the chapters and verses Gorman had noted on the pad and extracted:

"MDETTEAHERTHCLESEILEARAST."

"Doesn't make any sense," Mary observed. "It doesn't even break up into words."

"No, what Gorman did was highlight five letters from each book, but strung together they don't make much sense. So let's suppose he wanted the reader to look at the letters in another way, not just letters strung left to right."

"Like in a cube?" Mary asked.

"Possibly, let's see where that gets us." Braemhor took each five letter segment and wrote them in a vertically developed cube:

"MDETT
EAHER
THCLE
SEILE
ARAST"

"Yes! Yes! That's it!"

"What do you mean, 'that's it'? It still looks like nonsense to me," Mary rejoined.

"But don't you see? Read it vertically, not horizontally. Look.

"METSADAHEREHCIATELLSTREET." Now we can find the words. Metsada here hcia tell street. Petticrew was right. Gorman was scared, and with good reason."

"Yes?" Mary had not yet gotten the full impact of Gorman's message.

"Metsada is an Israeli special unit made up of combatants that carry out actions abroad. And if he was trying to leave someone—anyone—a message of their presence here in Manchester, he clearly was concerned, and, I think, for his own personal safety."

"But why would they be interested in him?"

"Because if Petticrew was right, Gorman was working on bringing West bank settlements to a halt. There are many powerful people in both Israel and the United States who don't want that to happen. When the stakes are this high, violence is always an option," Braemhor summarized.

"You mean Gorman was caught in the middle of an international plot to keep the main stumbling block to Middle Eastern peace in place?"

"Very possibly. This note makes it pretty clear that Gorman thought that Mossad, the Israeli Central Intelligence, was involved. What we don't know is who in the U.S. might be involved. The CIA maybe, because Mossad has a Political Action and Liaison

Department that works with MI6 and the U.S. CIA. Harriet Gorman may be the key."

"Why?"

"Look at this. HCIA. Read, Harriet, CIA. No wonder Gorman was shaken. This could mean his own wife was working against his efforts. Remember the note he left? 'It's no good. We can't continue. Our views are too different. You on one side, me on the other. It's time for me to move on to a broader horizon. I'm going over to the other side. Don't try to stop me or follow me. This is the end.' At first I thought it could be a note announcing the breakup of his marriage, certainly not a suicide note. The marriage was breaking up, but the implications of why are even broader."

Then abruptly Braemhor said, "I've got to call McGinty."

****

"McGinty here." The voice was gruff and irritated.

"Braemhor here."

"What is it this time, John? Calling to tell me you're taking my advice and going back to Daraichburn?"

"Not yet, Owen. I need to know who Street is. Any ideas?"

"Could be Nigil Street, head of the local MI6 office. Why do you ask?"

"Remember the names on Gorman's pad? I broke the code and part of the message says, 'Tell Street.'"

"John, you just won't back off, will you? I'm telling you, if you get mixed up with MI6, you could be in big trouble. Why won't you take my friendly advice. Believe me, I know what I'm talking about. Don't mess with MI6. Go home. Tend your apple trees. " McGinty's voice conveyed genuine concern.

"Not when I'm this close to understanding Gorman's death. I do appreciate your concerns though. Don't worry. When I see Street, I won't mention your name. Thanks for the tip." Braemhor hung up and turned to Mary. "Time to see MI6, tomorrow morning."

****

Braemhor entered the large, stone, fortress-like building two blocks from the Prince Charles, and, after passing through a metal detector, was stopped by a security officer who took him to a receptionist's desk at the far end of the massive, marble-faced entry hall.

"I'd like to see Mr. Street, please," he instructed the middle-aged woman behind the desk.

"I'm sorry. Mr. Street doesn't see anyone. Perhaps someone else can help you. What is it about?" She smiled.

"Tell him John Braemhor is here to see him. I have some information he may find of interest."

The receptionist looked at Braemhor quizzically, picked up a blue phone and conveyed the message to someone at the other end. Her eyes widened as she listened to the response and before she could tell Braemhor that someone would be there shortly, four heavily armed men appeared and surrounded Braemhor.

"No need for all that." Braemhor smiled at his new escorts. "Just take me to Mr. Street," he ordered.

With two men holding his arms on either side and one in front and one in back, he was walked briskly out of the reception area and onto a private lift next to the public lifts. Inside the lift they searched him thoroughly, but found nothing more than his personal identification and a small pad and pencil. By the time they had reached the second floor, the four had relaxed somewhat and quietly accompanied Braemhor down the hall and through a series of locked doors to a small office where Nigil Street stood behind his desk.

"Mr. Braemhor, you're a hard man to find. You've made my job much easier." Street's smile was a cross between a genuine greeting and a sardonic leer. "Excuse me a moment, won't you?" He pressed a button on his desk intercom and spoke in a low—but not so low that Braemhor could not hear him—voice. "Call off the Braemhor search." Street then turned to Braemhor, motioned to a chair in front of the desk, and took his seat behind the desk.

"How can I help you?" Street asked.

"I think it might be the other way around." Braemhor's hard face showed he was not about to be intimidated by the likes of a local MI6 district chief.

"Mr. Braemhor, let me be very clear. You have already cost the Queen's government quite a bit of money. Not only have we been searching for you in the city of Manchester, but I have had Dunmoor Cottage under surveillance for the past few days. My agents have more important things to do than chase after a nosy private citizen. Now why are you here? I've already done a background check on you. I know your past history doing police work in Rhodesia and that now you dabble in private criminal investigation—quite successfully, I understand. But that does not excuse your snooping around Manchester in something that is none of your business. I could have you incarcerated under any number of statutes." It was clear that Street was irritated that his turf was being trespassed upon.

"Had I known that Lester Gorman's so-called suicide was of national concern, I would have come to you first, but I am here at the request of Gorman's children, who do not believe their father would have committed suicide. And, frankly, when I first read the news accounts of the incident, I didn't think he had either." Braemhor then told Street of the events of the past two days, his discovery of the surveillance microphones in Room 505, the rather clumsy search of Room 505 while he and Mary were out of the room, his observation that Gorman could not have aimed himself between two large awnings in the free fall of his suicide jump, and that Mrs. Gorman had been whisked out of the country on a privileged embassy flight. He concluded with, "I think I've got some information that might be of value to you and the government."

"What makes you think MI6 would be interested in the suicide of an American archeologist?" Street played his cards close to the vest, as they say.

"Because immediately after his death, MI6 was interviewing his colleagues. MI6 wouldn't be interested in just any American suicide. No, Gorman was special, and I think I've found out why."

"Oh?" Street leaned back and put his fingertips together as if pondering how much he could share with this meddlesome—yet seemingly quite skilled—private investigator and not overstep the bounds of the National Secrecy Acts.

Braemhor related his discovery of Gorman's coded message and its contents, which indicated to him that the Israeli and possibly American governments were involved in Gorman's death.

"Mr. Braemhor, let me be clear. I can neither confirm nor deny your surmises. You understand that. But the message from Gorman that you've decoded will fit into the picture quite nicely. In fact, it may just be the information the Queen's government needs to take action. I must, however, caution you not to reveal any of this information to anyone, including your good friend, Inspector McGinty. For now and forever, you must view Lester Gorman's death as a suicide and drop the matter. You must trust me that we will take appropriate action regarding what we think really happened in Room 505 in due time. I know that that is not as clean and neat as some of you working in the private sector like it, but that is the way it must be. I could, you understand, bring charges of interfering in government business and policy, but I am sure that will not be necessary, will it?" Street rose and extended his hand to let Braemhor know that the interview was at an end.

Braemhor rose, grasped Street's hand and nodded slightly, knowing that this was one case he would not be able to see through to its final conclusion.

"By the way," Street said as they walked down the hallway, "one piece of your information was wrong. Mrs. Gorman did not leave by courier plane. We picked her off on the Heathrow tarmac."

****

"What will you tell Gorman's children, John?" Mary asked as they drove back to Daraichburn.

"I don't have any choice but to let them think their father did commit suicide. As for their mother, the story isn't yet finished. Maybe someday they'll find out what her role was in this sordid matter." Braemhor was not happy, but resolved to the inevitable.

As they entered the Cottage the phone was ringing.

"Dunmoor Cottage," Mary answered. "Oh, Aunt Rita. It's so good to hear from you. Yes, yes, your friend, Ellen was a big help."

Rita talked on for the next twenty minutes, while John went into the kitchen and started preparing dinner. Mary tried to motion to him that she would do that.

"Oh, really? That is interesting. I'll tell John. Now, I really must run, Aunt Rita. Say hello to the family for us." Mary was finally able to bring an end to the conversation.

Mary chuckled as she hung up the receiver. "You'll never believe this, John."

"Oh?"

"Aunt Rita says that Ellen thinks you a handsome fellow who reminds her of her husband."

"That's nice," John absently remarked as he set the table.

"Yes, except that her husband died three years ago!" Mary laughed.

****

A few weeks later the peat fire was once again warming Dunmoor Cottage as John Braemhor read the evening newspaper over coffee.

"Look at this, Mary." He handed the paper to Mary and pointed to a short article on the back page headlined, 'Government Files Official Complaints to Israel and the United States.' The article told of the United Kingdom filing an official complaint with both foreign governments, accusing both of allowing their agents to operate within the UK without official sanction. The complaint grew out of an incident that happened during the recent meeting of archeologists held in Manchester. An unnamed CIA agent was being prosecuted under an official espionage act and would be brought to trial within the month.

Chapter 7

Mary felt summer would be a good time to visit family in New Boston in the States—the "Colonies," as John liked to refer to the United States. Aunt Rita had offered to come down and look after the Cottage in their absence, and Mary thought the visit would placate John's investigative restlessness for a while.

James, their youngest, and his wife, Jennifer and the two grandchildren, Daniel and Donna, lived in New Boston. James had gone to the States for college and while there met Jennifer. An American, she was born and grew up in New Boston where she now practiced law with a small law firm.

"Who's running the Cottage while you're away?" James asked at the dinner table.

"Aunt Rita agreed to come and look after things," Mary answered, as she noticed James roll his eyes skyward. "Do you think that is a problem?"

"I just hope she doesn't feed your guests green potatoes!"

"Green potatoes?"

Hesitantly, James continued, "Well, you remember when she flew to Rhodesia to look after the three of us while you and Dad traveled to South Africa? I think you..." James turned his eyes to John, "were going to look at a new position."

"I remember that," John allowed.

"We kids thought she was a very funny lady. Always had a wine or a beer in her hand and she fed us green potatoes."

"Green potatoes?" Mary asked again.

"She found some potatoes deep in a storage bin and thought, in fact insisted, that they be used up. 'We mustn't waste food' she said. So she peeled and mashed them, but they were green."

"Of course, I remember. I was going to throw them away before we left, but I forgot. And when we got back they were gone," Mary recalled.

"She fed them to us, for almost a week. The day after you left, I was making myself a salad sandwich, about to take my first bite when she stopped me and said, 'Here, this is good for you.' And she put a dollop of green potatoes on top of my tomato. And I was so looking forward to my salad sandwich," James remembered. "Then, as I said, almost all we ate for a week was green mashed potatoes. We thought it was amusing and finally got to like them pretty well. They were a little sweet."

"Amusing, my foot," John huffed. "Of course they tasted a little sweet. Did she not know that the potato is of the deadly nightshade family? The green is the toxic part—atropa belladonna. I'm surprised you're all still here. Well, at least now you have some natural immunity to belladonna."

"In very low dosage, it's also used as a medication, reduces intestinal activity and as a muscle relaxant," Mary added. "I do remember that Aunt Rita did say you three children were awfully quiet while we were gone."

"I guess," James said, and the whole family had a hardy laugh over another of Aunt Rita's eccentric activities.

Though the family spent some humorous times together over "Aunt Rita stories," it soon became apparent to Mary and to the rest of the family that the lack of a case to engage his deductive skills increased John's general agitation. He did not pace, but it was clear that he needed more focused activity.

Searching for a way to calm John's ardor, Mary suggested a side holiday to pursue John's new interest. Of late, he had been studying the American Civil War in his spare time, and the Confederate raid into Vermont from Canada in 1864 caught his fancy, since the raid was a criminal act—the Confederates had robbed several St. Albans banks of over $200,000. Each year the people of this northern village on Lake Champlain relive the event by reenacting the raid and the bank robberies.

"It might be fun to see a bit of living history," John concurred with Mary's suggestion. And so they travelled north to see this strange ritual of reenacting the past, through which Americans remember, and relive part of their history.

****

"From Manchester, you say?"

"Manchester, New Hampshire, that is," Elinus J. Morrison answered.

"Oh." John Braemhor thought he had found a kindred spirit from Manchester, England. Braemhor briefly told Morrison where he and Mary lived, of his interest in the American Civil War, and of their holiday trip to St. Albans to see the reenactment of the Confederate raid of 1864.

"Oh, yes, I come over from New Hampshire every year for the reenactment," Morrison explained to the Braemhors.

"And you participate?" Mary asked.

"Just briefly. My role is very small, but reliving the past seems to be my fate. I've been doing it for years and years. It seems like centuries." E. J. smiled a smile that was more of a grimace. Morrison was a square man with a worn, tired look. He spoke slowly and, it seemed to John, in a very deliberate, measured way as if picking his words with great care. Though his general appearance and his reenactment clothing indicated a man of an outdoor trade, his skin had a pallor expected more from a person who spends his hours inside, in darkness rather than light. His movements were labored and hesitant. "I really have to be off. Got to get to my post. Maybe we can talk later, after it's all over. Your best place to see will be at the corner of Bank and Main, near Kingman."

"Thanks. We'd like to see you afterwards," John called after him. He and Mary then went to the vantage point E. J. had suggested where they could best view the coming bank robberies.

Soon the Confederate reenactors arrived, entered the three banks—the Franklin County, the First National, and the St. Albans—and proceeded to "rob the banks and terrify the citizenry." The raiders collected some "citizens" as prisoners on the green in front of the old American Hotel site. Reenacting the historical event, some of the townspeople fought back, one trying to strangle one of the Confederates on the steps of the First National Bank. Soon, aroused citizens arrived with arms and started chasing the raiders out of town, but not before one of the citizens was gunned down while trying to escape into Miss Beattie's Millinery Store near the City Hall. The entire reenactment did not take more than thirty minutes, but was well worth the viewing both John and Mary felt.

"Interesting pastime," John mused, "reliving the violent past of a nation on an annual basis."

"Certainly seems to be a big tourist attraction," Mary added, looking around at the several hundred onlookers lining the streets in the center of St. Albans. "Oh, there's Mr. Morrison, John." She pointed towards the man in nineteenth century garb approaching them from the Millinery Store.

"Educational?" Morrison asked.

"Quite. And you were right, your part was small."

"But pivotal," E. J. stated flatly. "Here, I want you to have something." He handed a folded yellowed paper to Braemhor. "One of the Confederates dropped it. Considering your detective work, you will find it a challenge. And it can be a memento of your trip, too. I must plod on now to repeat the whole thing again next year. Good to make your acquaintance, finally." He turned quickly and strode down Bank Street.

Mary and John looked at one another in bewilderment. "What did he mean by that, John?" Mary asked, "to make our acquaintance finally? As if he knew us before?"

"I don't know, and how did he know I did detective work?" John stared down at the weather-worn scrap of paper in his hand and wondered.

****

Back in their hotel room John studied the paper Morrison had given him. The paper was yellowed and old and tended to crumble around the edges. He handled it with some care. On one side was a string of what looked like random letters: BU NTYMNBRX BE HTYOH GQTSJKSN FOGTSPSBP WMUD YG ULEJ YA MROWLDL FYZ; the other side contained a faded image of the Confederate battle flag and the words, *come retribution*. It could have been a facsimile, yet it looked authentically period. John puzzled over it.

"What do you make of it, John?" Mary asked.

"I'm not sure, but it looks like a coded message. Part of the reenactment maybe; yet it could be something more real. A real message to persons unknown."

"Really, John, aren't you leaping to conclusions. Everything isn't some nefarious plot with secret messages passing back and forth among evil villains. I bet they give those scraps of paper to all the tourists. Makes the reenactment seem more real. Added excitement for the onlookers."

"Maybe. Maybe. Yet it would be interesting to decode the letters."

"How would you do that?"

"Well, if it is a real coded message, we could start with a frequency analysis."

"Frequency analysis?"

"Yes, the most often used letter in English is 'e,' so you replace the most frequent letter in the encrypted message with 'e.' The next most frequent is 's,' so you replace the next most frequent message letter with an 's' and so forth. Let's try that."

It quickly became apparent that a simple frequency analysis would not decipher the letters on Braemhor's paper.

"No good, there must be a more complex key. If I can find the key, I can apply it to the message to see if it makes any sense....Wait! You remember the book I was reading at the children's house just before we came up here?"

"Yes, *The Telegraph Goes to War,* wasn't it?" Mary recalled.

"That's the one. In the appendix the author discusses Civil War ciphers, in particular the Confederate Vicksburg Square system. Curiously enough the Confederates only used three key phrases for encoding messages through the Vicksburg Square. Now, let me see, one of them was 'come retribution.' Another was...oh, yes, 'complete victory,' but what was the third?"

"Maybe you should start with 'come retribution,' since it's on the paper Mr. Morrison gave us." Mary was intrigued enough to go along with the idea of decoding the message.

John went to the desk in the room and took out a sheet of hotel stationery on which he drew a twenty-seven by twenty-seven matrix and put the letters of the alphabet across the top row and down the first column, starting with the second row. Then he filled in each row across with a complete alphabet, beginning with the letter in column one.

John took the message and made a table. He wrote the key phrase letters under the message letters, repeating the phrase as required, and applied each pair to the Square to find the decoded letter for that pair.

After a half hour John muttered in frustration, "Neither 'come retribution' nor 'complete victory' is the key. I just get more gibberish when I try to decode using them."

"Maybe it's not a coded message." Mary was trying to dissuade him from developing another mystery where, in fact, none may have existed.

Undeterred, John thought aloud, "I need that other Confederate code. Now what was it?...Wait!...I've got it! It was 'manchester bluff.' Of course! I should have remembered."

"Why?"

"Because Morrison said he was from Manchester. That should have prompted me to remember. Ah, Mary, the old brain isn't as sharp as it once was. Let me try 'manchester bluff.'" He set to work once again with his Vicksburg Square.

Fifteen minutes later. "That's it! Look at this, Mary! The deciphered message is: 'Pu arriving at notch tomorrow edmondson pick up take to memphis bhy.' I told you there was something there!"

Mary began believing. "Maybe Mr. Morrison was trying to tell you something after all. He seemed to know that you've done detective work. But who is 'pu,' what does 'notch' mean, who is 'edmondson,' and what is 'bhy'?'"

"First, 'Pu' is not a 'who'; it is a 'what.' Pu is the chemical symbol for plutonium. You don't suppose our work in Nova Scotia a few years back was incomplete? Maybe MacLaine and I were able to shut down a main conduit but not the whole operation. Someone may yet be trying to bring more radioactive contraband into the Colonies. But who? And, if this message is any clue, by what route? We need to know the meaning of 'notch.' We can worry about 'edmondson' later. I think the letters 'bhy' are the initials of the leader of the original raid—Bennett H. Young. I'll be right back." With that, Braemhor left a startled Mary in their room and descended the stairs to the hotel desk.

****

Ten minutes later, John entered the room and said, "Pack the bags, we're leaving."

"Where are we going, John?" Mary was perplexed.

"To a small village near Smuggler's Notch, the 'notch' of the coded message, I believe. I'll tell you what the hotel clerk told me on the way."

Fifteen minutes later the Braemhors were driving southeast "on the wrong side of the road," as John characterized American driving. "The hotel clerk told me that twenty miles or so along this road is a place known as Smuggler's Notch, famous for smuggling activities since the eighteenth century. In fact, there is a trail, the Long Trail, that courses some 270 miles through Vermont from Canada to the state of Massachusetts. At the notch—an actual notch through the Green Mountains—there are innumerable caves where smugglers through the years used to hide their contraband. If the message we've deciphered is real and not, as you suggested, just something to amuse the tourists, it could be that smuggling is still active in the Green Mountains. At any rate, I thought we could extend our holiday and see more of the Vermont scenery. All right?"

"Fine, but where will we stay?"

"There's an Inn near the notch. I've booked a couple of nights there." John smiled, trying to control his enthusiasm for being once again on the chase.

Thirty minutes later he turned the car into the Inn parking lot and went in to register. Advertised as a restored 1790 structure, the Inn retained its narrow staircase to the sleeping rooms and the pitched floors, which told the traveler that the whole building had settled considerably over the last couple of centuries.

"I feel like I'm on the deck of one of Francis Winslow's ships in a storm," Mary remarked as they made their way down the narrow hall to their room, "and it's so quiet. Is anyone else here?"

"Summer's the off-season, I suppose—this is a skiing area—but it does seem inordinately quiet. We'll ask at the desk later, but for now I want to drive up to the notch proper. There's a small state park there."

After a brief stop at the local general store for the purchase of a torch and extra batteries, they drove toward the notch.

****

The road to the notch wound its way through some of the most beautiful mountain scenery the Braemhors had ever seen. Mostly enclosed by woods, the road occasionally coursed out of the wooded areas to take the traveler into open, extended vistas of Mt. Mansfield, a favorite subject of numerous Vermont artists in the early part of the twentieth century. A few miles before the park, the road narrowed slightly and melded into a series of tight turns and curves. A road sign indicated that weather conditions disallowed travel through the notch in winter. Hikers only were allowed and they were warned not to undertake the notch road without proper preparation and equipment.

"Good thing we came in midsummer," John remarked as he downshifted to begin the assent to the notch. Shortly, a small car park came into view off the side of the road with two small sheds at either end. "This is it," John noted as he parked the car. "Let's explore."

The wooded area surrounding the car park was thick with birch trees, both golden and paper. Though the lush greenery appeared seasonal, the brisk breeze let the Braemhors know that winter winds were not far off. No more than fifty yards from the park they found a series of caves, some not much more than a niche among the plethora of rocks and boulders interspersed with the trees, others quite large, one the size of a full room. John switched on the torch and entered the largest. Though dank and damp, the cave did provide some haven from the wind with its foreboding chill. Inside were several smaller boulders set around a larger, flat stone.

"Almost looks like a conference table and chairs," Mary observed.

"At one time it probably was. It certainly affords easy access and not far off of the road," John answered as he rummaged in the back of the cave, behind the conference setup. "Look at this. There are several hidden pockets here in the back. Could easily hold small packages and not be seen unless you knew what to look for. Perfect, just perfect. I think tomorrow we will spend the day hiding near this and some of the smaller caves and see what transpires. What about some supper back at the Inn for now?"

"John, you really do think there is something to the message you decoded, don't you?" Mary asked as they descended from the park down the road to the Inn.

"Too early to tell, but a day in the Vermont woods wouldn't be that bad, would it?"

****

Dinner at the Inn was typical Vermont fare, not gourmet, but a satisfying menu of poached fish and vegetables. While Mary arranged for a packed lunch for the next day, John placed a call to Charlie MacLaine in New Boston. MacLaine, a grey-haired and mustached, athletic-looking man in his mid-forties, was the FBI agent with whom Braemhor had partnered in breaking up a plutonium smuggling ring at Point Dread, Nova Scotia, a few years back. They had also coordinated on another smuggling case in New Boston last year.

Braemhor wanted to let MacLaine know what he had found so far in this sleepy backwoods country of Vermont. After he had related his and Mary's holiday so far, MacLaine broke out laughing. "You're up to it again, aren't you, John?" MacLaine said through his chuckles. "Let me see if I got this right. You're given an old scrap of paper by a Civil War reenactor with a string of unintelligible letters on it. You think it's a real coded message and not a tourist gimmick. Then you translated it using a code key used almost 150 years ago, disclosing a message of smuggling plutonium through the Vermont mountains. And you want me to believe that the baddies are at it again and trying to get ready to build a nuclear device here in the U.S.? You're stretching again, John."

Though irritated, Braemhor chose to ignore MacLaine's cynicism. "Maybe. Maybe, but you see what I'm driving at, don't you? Plutonium is no laughing matter. If I'm wrong, fine, we can all go to bed and sleep contented. But, if I'm right in my assumptions so far, it could be far more ominous than Nova Scotia. Right? And how many times in the past have I been wrong, even when you thought I was leaping to unwarranted conclusions?"

"Point taken, John. Point taken. But what do you want me to do?"

"If I'm right, I'll need backup. I don't have any official status here, and I'm sure the local authorities would be hesitant to help."

"Probably think you're just another nutty tourist," Charlie concluded.

"Something of the sort, yes. So what do you suggest?"

There was a brief pause at the other end of the phone. "Tell you what, John, I can be there day after tomorrow. Would that help?" MacLaine had been impressed in past cases with the way that Braemhor's conclusions, even when based on scant evidence, more often than not proved correct. He admired the accuracy of Braemhor's intuitions, though he claimed to be a man of data and hard facts. Despite his appearance of disdain, MacLaine felt—intuitively—that his friend might just be on to something.

"Leave your bicycle home this time and make it tomorrow night, so we can plan the surveillance of the pickup." MacLaine was an avid biker and was on a biking vacation around Nova Scotia when he and the Braemhors had first met. "I'll book a room for you here at the Inn. And, Charlie, thanks." MacLaine rang off, all the while marveling at Braemhor's confidence in his own deductive ability.

As Braemhor booked MacLaine's room, he casually remarked, "Not many other guests."

"No," the clerk admitted, "off-season, winter's really our tourist season. Skiers, you know. No, you and the missus are the only ones tonight."

"Strange, I thought my wife and I saw a woman upstairs earlier."

"No, not unless it was our resident ghost." The clerk chuckled, then responded to Braemhor's raised eyebrows, "Spy for the South during the Civil War, so the story goes. Met her comeuppance when she was caught up at the Notch by some Union Green Mountain boys. They hung her up near the big cave. Happened right after the St. Albans raid in 1864. Name was Rose Edmondson."

****

"What's so funny?" Mary asked, responding to the twinkle in John's eye as he entered the room.

"I found out who Edmondson is, or was," he chuckled.

"Who?"

"She's the Inn's resident ghost."

"John, be serious. What did you find out?"

"I am serious. The desk clerk tells me, first, that we are the only ones booked in the Inn...."

"But we saw that woman," Mary interrupted.

"...and the Inn has a resident ghost, named—are you ready?—Rose Edmondson!"

"You're kidding me, John!"

"Not at all. But there's more. She was a spy for the Confederacy and was hung at the Notch near the big cave in 1864."

"Maybe the message Morrison gave us *is* a tourist hoax, then? And we're running around chasing...ghosts?"

"And maybe the ghost story is just a tourist fable, and the Inn is part of it. Just to play holiday tricks on the tourists," John countered.

As he spoke, both of the Braemhors heard the sounds of footsteps in the passageway outside the room. Quickly, John opened the door only to see a wisp of a dark, patterned hooped skirt turn the corner at the end of the passage. He strode after the figure, making a quick left, then a quick right, up two stairs and another left to a long passage leading to five other rooms. But to no avail. The figure was gone and all he saw was another fleeting movement at the dead end of the hall where there were no doors or windows. Braemhor searched the end of the corridor for possible exits, but there were none. He returned to his and Mary's room.

"Well?" Mary asked.

"Nothing. Nothing at all."

****

Next morning the Braemhors got to the Notch before dawn and threaded their way carefully through the birch trees near the large cave they had explored the day before. The undergrowth was dense, and there was little difficulty finding a suitable hiding place from which they could observe both the large cave and three other smaller caves. Well hidden, they settled in for a daylong vigil of watching.

The morning passed quietly. Early on, a small group of boy scouts with their leader arrived on a school bus. Once off the bus and organized, they marched into the woods on the opposite side of the car park, the scout master leading them with an animated talk about the history of Smugglers Notch.

Through the morning a number of tourist couples drove into the park, then wandered around the area, exploring the caves. One couple even stumbled on the Braemhor's hiding place so John and Mary pretended to be studying some of the flora, smiling a greeting as the couple walked on by. The Braemhors then moved to a more secretive location where they could still observe the large cave and other smaller ones and unpacked their lunch, eating while observing.

Most of the afternoon was the same. More tourists in cars, a few hikers probably walking the Long Trail, judging from their equipment. About five in the afternoon, John was contemplating going back to the Inn and chalking the day and the whole mystery of the coded message up to a tourist hoax. He had about concluded that his intuition had failed him this time, and he was having growing regrets about calling MacLaine.

Then it happened.

"Mary," he whispered and pointed to the three figures approaching the car park from the South, obviously hiking the Long Trail. All three were dressed in grey pants and hiking jackets and wore large knapsacks to which were attached sleeping rolls and ground covers.

The three came to within ten yards of the Braemhors, but fortunately did not see them huddled down in the dense foliage. They looked around as if searching for something or someone. Then one of them spotted the large cave opening ahead, pointed in that direction and led the others to the cave. John and Mary watched intently as the three disappeared.

Ten minutes later the three emerged and proceeded along the trail in the woods near the car park. As they disappeared into the foliage, John pointed out to Mary that a critical change had occurred. "Look at their rucksacks."

"One's missing," Mary observed.

"Precisely, they left one rucksack inside the cave." John's confidence in his intuitions returned. "Give them five or ten minutes, and then we'll see what the cave offers us."

The waiting was nerve-racking for both of the Braemhors, but, at last, they determined it was safe to go. Just to hide their intent, however, they returned to the car park and approached the cave from that direction—just two foreign tourists exploring the attractions of Smugglers Notch.

"You stay out here and look out for the three couriers, in case they return," John instructed Mary, then entered the cave and turned on his torch.

As before the interior of the cave, except for near the opening, was black. Only Braemhor's torch allowed him to see anything. But a quick sweep of the cave revealed no rucksack. He went to the very back of the cave and moved aside a number of small boulders and stones. Still no knapsack. *Strange,* thought Braemhor, *it's got to be here somewhere. Three went in, but only two came out. Must be an opening or cave within the cave where they could have put it.*

Again he surveyed the back, darkest parts of the cave with his torch. Nothing but rocks and stones on the cave floor. He looked up, swept the ceiling with his torch. Still nothing. Then he carefully examined the large, flat, table-like boulder he and Mary had noted before. *Hmmm. Nothing amiss here... but wait, it looks like one of these seat-like stones has been moved.* There were clear scrapings on the cave floor near one of the seats.

With effort Braemhor pulled the stone outward in the path of the scrapings. Sure enough behind the stone and under the table was a rather large cavity. "Ah ha," he said aloud, for there in the hollow space was the greenish-grey rucksack. Quickly he dragged the bag towards him and opened it. Inside were three smallish wooden boxes. He lifted one out, *About five kilo, I'd say.* He quickly placed some stones into the sack to match the weight he had removed and put it back in its hiding place, carefully sliding the stone back to its position in front of the opening under the table. Putting the box under his long raincoat, he returned to Mary outside.

"What did you find?" she asked.

"Three boxes. I've purloined one for the time being," he said.

"What are we going to do with it?" Mary asked.

"Put it in the boot and go back to the Inn. When MacLaine gets here, we can verify the contents and make plans accordingly," John answered as he pulled his long coat further around his stolen evidence. Mary scouted the area between the cave and the car park, and when it was clear of people, they took the box to their car and deposited it in the boot.

****

At the Inn the Braemhors awaited their friend's arrival in front of the smoldering fire in the fireplace of the lobby. Even in midsummer a crackling fire was welcome in the northern reaches of Vermont. About half past six MacLaine bounced in through the side door, small travel bag in hand and a broad smile animating his face.

"We meet again, John...Mary," was the cheery greeting from behind his outstretched hand. "What have you got for us this time?"

"Let's talk it over over supper after you've registered," John suggested.

Later in the white table-clothed dining room, Braemhor told MacLaine how he and Mary had spent their day—watching boy scouts, many tourists, and three suspects in the case that had developed since receiving the message from Morrison at St. Albans.

"So you've got a box of you-don't-know-what in the trunk of your car. Maybe we should verify its contents. Maybe they're just boxes of candy for the boy scouts when they return from their hike." MacLaine smiled.

"Rock candy by the weight." John entered into MacLaine's levity. "But you're right, let's take it to our room and open it—carefully."

In the room Braemhor slit the wax sealant around the top lid of the box and was about to open it when Charlie waved him off.

"Let's see how hot it is." MacLaine opened his own bag and took out a small Geiger counter. Sweeping the area around the box the counter emitted a few, random clicks, but then, when Charlie opened the lid slightly and placed the sensor under it, the needle on the dial jumped instantaneously to the redline, maximum reading. The clicking mimicked the dial reading with the emission of a continuous rat-a-tat-tat.

"Bingo," MacLaine muttered. He turned to John. "I don't know if its plutonium or not, but it sure is radioactive hot. Let's reseal it before we all start to glow." He quickly removed the Geiger counter sensor and closed the box. The counter returned to its occasional click, click and the dial faded back into the green, or safe, zone.

"Box is probably lead-lined," observed Braemhor, "no wonder it was so heavy."

"I'd vote for uranium-lined; it's even heavier and a better barrier," MacLaine said.

Braemhor looked at MacLaine. "I don't think we should go retrieve the other two, do you?"

"I agree. I think not. We need to know where and to whom this shipment was intended. I'll arrange for immediate additional surveillance of the cave and a group of followers, who can stay with the other two boxes when they're removed. With luck, we can wrap up the whole operation. It'll take me about half an hour to make arrangements."

"We should keep this box," John stated.

"Right," Charlie concurred, "we'll keep it as initial evidence. Besides we might be able to create internal divisions among the smugglers when they find out that one is missing. A family feud among the baddies always works to our advantage. I'll be back after I make my arrangements." MacLaine slipped out of the room taking the prize box with him.

Thirty minutes later MacLaine tapped on the Braemhor's door.

"We're all set. My watchers are headed to the Notch as we speak. They'll do night duty, then another crew will take their place at sunrise. John, you and Mary and I can join them in the morning and, hopefully, observe the pickup first hand. But for now, I've had a long day and I think some sleep is in order. Oh, by the way, I thought you said we were the only ones booked here."

"We are, as far as we know," Mary offered.

"Well, who was that woman I saw in the upper corridor?"

"What did she look like?" John joined the conversation.

"I don't know. I only caught a fleeting glance of her, but it seemed like she was dressed in a long, hooped skirt."

John and Mary smiled. "Oh, that's the Inn's resident ghost," Mary said with a twinkle in her eyes.

"She has the same name as the person Mr. Morrison's message said would pick up the boxes."

"Yah. Sure. And you probably have a bridge in Brooklyn you want to sell me. I think I'll call it a night," MacLaine said as he left the Braemhor's room.

****

The next morning arrived bright and brisk—sunny and forty-two degrees.

The Braemhors and MacLaine were at the car park at the Notch by half five and well-hidden in the foliage by the time of the changing of MacLaine's guard—five well disguised agents taking over the day shift of watching, some dressed as tourists, some as hikers. They did not have long to wait.

About half past six a dilapidated green Ford pickup truck with Tennessee license plates pulled cautiously into the car park and parked between the Braemhor's rental and a new SUV belonging to two early morning tourists. Two men and a woman got out, looked warily around, and walked toward the big cave. Curiously, the woman was dressed as if in a Civil War reenactment—long dress, frilly blouse, a bonnet, and dainty gloves. They stopped short of the entry, turned and watched the tourists get into their SUV and pull out of the park. Then they went in.

Ten minutes later muffled sounds like gunfire were heard from the cave. MacLaine arose and was about to approach the cave when Braemhor stopped him. "Let it play out, Charlie. I think our keeping one of the boxes is already paying off." MacLaine waved off the other agents, and all of the watchers—the Braemhors included—settled back to see what had transpired in the cave. Shortly, the woman appeared with the knapsack from the cave on her back. She quickly looked around, ran to the truck, threw the knapsack into the cab and started the engine. With a squeal of the wheels, she exited the car park and headed south from Smugglers Notch. Two agents' cars and a motorcyclist fell into line behind her at a safe distance.

Charlie pulled out his radio. "The red hots are headed south," he barked quickly, then turned to the Braemhors. "More of my agents will move into the road in front of her so we can keep track of her from the front and rear. They should be able to stick with her for the rest of her trip, wherever it ends. Hopefully, she'll lead us to bigger fish." Charlie smiled.

"You think she's just a courier?" John queried.

"Would a CEO deliver the mail?"

"Right. Let's check out the cave, shall we?" John concluded.

Inside the cave the two men lay in pools of their own blood having been shot a number of times at close range.

"I recognize them," Mary was the first to speak. "They were part of the re-enactment at St. Albans—Confederate raiders."

"Perhaps an interview with the remaining raiding party is in order." John looked at Charlie.

Charlie, who had been on his mobile calling for medical and local police assistance, turned back to John, "I'll take care of that as soon as I instruct the locals here. Meantime, I'm in your debt again, John. And I apologize for doubting your intuition yesterday. I should know better. What will you two be doing now?"

"I think we'll spend a day or two sight-seeing here at the Notch, then I'd like to go back to St. Albans and find Mr. Morrison and thank him for his help. Do you need a ride back to the Inn?"

"No, thanks. The locals will take me back. I'll call you as soon as I have any information on the whereabouts of our lady with the two hot boxes."

MacLaine then strode to meet the local authorities who had just arrived.

****

Later the next day MacLaine called the Inn from New Boston and asked for Braemhor.

"What do you have?" John asked.

"She took the stuff all the way to Memphis, Tennessee. When she tried to unload it to a group of well-known business men, we moved in. Strange, I didn't think she'd go directly to the big fish. Acted like she had no concept of modern-day surveillance techniques. Didn't seem at all aware that we were on to her. You remember how she was dressed? Like something out of the middle of the nineteenth century. Well, her smuggling skills were just about as dated. As if she were still living in the mid-1800's. I guess I will never understand the criminal mind, John."

"Nor I, Charlie," Braemhor concurred. "So you think you've wrapped up the whole operation, then?"

"We're still investigating the rest of the Confederate raid reenactors to make sure we haven't missed anything, but, yes, I think we've wrapped it up for now. I'm sure there are dozens of other baddies out there just waiting to try their luck against us. It's a never ending battle, as you know, John.... Well, got to run for now; if you have any more wild intuitions of a national nature, let me know and I'll see if I can help." Charlie's smile radiated through the telephone. "I guess you're off to find Mr. Morrison?"

"Right. Mary and I are heading to St. Albans in the morning."

"Oh, by the way, our lady smuggler was named Sharon Edmondson, same last name as in Morrison's coded message. She's a descendent of the famous Civil War Confederate spy with the same last name. Odd, don't you think?"

"Very little surprises me anymore, Charlie," John admitted.

****

In St. Albans the Braemhors headed straight to the mayor's office on the second floor of the City Hall. The oil soaked floors smelled as if they were from another era, which, of course, they were. One of the town clerks was sitting at a small table laboriously sorting through a tall stack of three by five file cards, looking carefully at each and then placing them slowly and deliberately on one of three smaller stacks, by some—unknown to the onlooker—criterion. The other clerk sat at a central desk reading the local newspaper. He looked up slowly, stared for a moment at the Braemhors and finally said, "Help ya?"

"I hope so." John smiled. "We are trying to find one of the actors from the reenactment last week."

"You, too? We've had a bunch of Feds in here asking questions about our reenactment. What do you want?" This was not a warm, welcoming question.

"Nothing sinister." John again smiled. "One of the men gave us a memento of the event but he left before we could thank him. We just want to tell him how much we appreciate what he did for us."

"Oh, okay. Who was it?" the clerk's attitude softened a bit.

"Elinus J. Morrison."

"Nope."

"What do you mean, 'nope'?" Braemhor was becoming a little irritated at the clerk's abruptness.

"Ain't got no reenactor by that name. Sorry." And he went back to his newspaper.

"What was the name again?" The raspy voice came from an elderly, withered codger sitting in the shadows in a corner behind the sorting clerk. He was dressed in work pants, held up by bright red braces that clashed horribly with his pink and white checkered shirt.

"Morrison. Elinus J. Morrison."

"Morrison, you say? Hmmmm." The old man scratched the back of his head as in deep thought. "Oh, yeah. I knowed that was familiar."

"Yes?" John was pleased that at least someone knew Morrison's name.

"Yeah. Elinus J. Morrison was the feller what was killed in the real raid back in 1864. He's been dead for nigh on ta 150 years."

John and Mary looked at one another in disbelief. Mary broke the silence first, "Maybe it's best if we go back to New Boston."

"Maybe. Maybe. At least there the real and the unreal don't intermingle."

And so the Braemhors returned to New Boston to continue their visit that they had interrupted with the side trip to St. Albans.

Chapter 8

However, they had hardly settled in again in New Boston when, while having a leisurely midweek dinner, the telephone rang.

"It's for you, Dad." James Braemhor handed the receiver to his father.

"For me? That's strange. Who knew we were here except Charlie and Aunt Rita?" John turned to Mary.

"Braemhor here," John spoke into the phone.

"Mr. Braemhor, this is Stanley, Stanley Howard. I hate to be calling you again after all the help you gave us in Manchester last New Year. We can never repay you, of course."

"Yes, Stanley. How are you and how is Jane?"

"We're fine. I'm almost embarrassed to call you, especially at dinner time and while you're on vacation with your family, but we have a continuing crisis here in Carterville. "

"Yes?"

"Over the past few years we've had a series of unexplained deaths among our faculty. I think I mentioned them to you briefly in Manchester, but we were so involved in finding Jane's uncle that I never got to talk with you at length at that time. Oddly, each one died of anoxia, a lack of oxygen to the brain and heart, but the local police and the state police are at a loss to explain how or why, and have now written all of them off as unsolved cases.

"No one on our faculty has paid particular attention to these deaths except to mourn them as lost colleagues. Most thought them just the normal course of events in an aging faculty. In fact, in order to hide the mystery of these deaths, the University has conveyed to the faculty and the general public that each did die of natural causes. No one except myself, as Dean of the Faculty, the President and a few other high-level administrators even knew of the odd circumstances of the deaths, and I certainly was not going to raise a general alarm. But as Dean I feel a particular responsibility to discover what has been happening and not let these events just drift into forgotten oblivion. Then I remembered that you had mentioned something similar from your days in Rhodesia and thought I would call you." Howard's voice trailed off.

"So you called us at our Dunmoor Cottage in Daraichburn, and Mary's aunt told you we were visiting our son in New Boston."

"Yes."

"So now that we have established how you found us, what do you propose?"

A hesitant pause on the other end. Then, "Well, I...I... would it be too much of an imposition to ask you to come up here to Carterville for a few days and see if you can help us? I have some funds available and could pay expenses for both you and Mary, and a per diem. We have a small apartment for visiting dignitaries that I'm sure would be quite comfortable for the two of you."

"How long have these mysterious deaths been going on?" John's curiosity was clearly aroused. "And why call me now?"

"The first one occurred eight years ago, long before I became Dean. The Dean at that time started hiding the circumstances of the deaths from the college population, and my predecessor and I just carried on the ruse. Each of the next two years someone died under the same circumstances. Then there was a gap of a year, then two more deaths in successive years and then another gap. Now, just yesterday, one of our colleagues in the English Department—a novelist of national repute—was found in his office, dead. So I called you in the hope that you might help."

"Give me your phone number and I'll call you back within the hour. Satisfactory?" Braemhor asked.

"That will be fine. I hope you can see your way to coming," Howard concluded and gave Braemhor his private office number.

"Well, John, another holiday interrupted?" Mary asked.

"What was that all about?" James asked his father.

Braemhor outlined to the family what Stanley Howard had just conveyed to him and looked at Mary. "It's very much like what I encountered in Rhodesia." Then turning back to the family, "Your mother will remember. Years ago, when we lived in Rhodesia and you, James, were just an infant, I worked on a series of mysterious deaths. Each of the victims was found asphyxiated, but there was no apparent method—no bruising on the throat, no fractured larynx, no signs of a major struggle, no rope or wire, not even a pillow nearby that could have been used. Yet each of the autopsies pointed to death by a lack of oxygen to the brain and heart. The only clue we had was a faint pungently sweet odor near each of the bodies, but we were never able to make anything substantive out of that. Turned out to be one of my unsuccessful cases."

"His only one," Mary interjected, and recognizing the enthusiasm written on her husband's face, added, "I think we ought to go. We've never seen the northern reaches of New York State, and it sounds like it will be an expense-free trip."

Turning to James and Jennifer, John Braemhor said, "We can come back and visit more in a week or so if that will fit your schedules."

"That'll be fine, Dad," Jennifer agreed. "That way we'll get to hear the details of another one of your cases."

"That's it then. I'll call Stanley back and let him know we'll be there tomorrow," Braemhor concluded. The faint flicker of a smile illuminated the corners of his mouth, betraying the rush of enthusiasm that brought more spring to his step and more animation to his countenance.

Mary, in the meantime, barely hid her own smiling display of pleasure at seeing her husband once again strain in the slip to launch their lives into another adventure. And, besides, she welcomed the opportunity to visit a small college town in rural New York—certainly far removed from the hustle and bustle of city life that encompassed the lives of their son and his family.

"Why don't I pack while you check the train schedules?" she said, as John concluded his brief conversation with Stanley Howard.

****

Except for the crush of people in New York City's Penn Station where the Braemhor's had to change trains, the trip to Carterville was a pleasant excursion through the Hudson and Mohawk Valleys. From New York northward they enjoyed the scenic Hudson River with its occasional barge traffic and many small islands, some graced with small castle-like structures, and the fortress-like architecture of West Point. The scenery along the Mohawk was more rural and dotted with old factory towns.

"What do you think of Stanley's call?" Mary asked as the train slowed for its first stop at Croton-on-Hudson and the engine emitted its mournful moose-like call.

"Not much to go on yet. The only clue we have now is the odd pattern of when the deaths occurred. One death eight years ago, followed by one in each of the succeeding two years, then none the following year. Then two years in a row, followed by another gap. And now, just two days ago, another similar death. Three, zero, two, zero, one. Mean anything to you?"

"If it's based on diminishing returns, there should be another gap and no more." Mary smiled.

"So, if you're right, we're going to have to solve the current death quickly." John looked pensive. "Well, we'll just have to see what other information Stanley can supply when we get there."

****

Stanley Howard, unable to meet the Braemhor's train, sent a University van for them at the railroad station nearest Carterville. Both of the Braemhors admired the train station, a building spread over more than a city block and, since its restoration a few years ago, displaying the opulence that once was the hallmark of American train travel in the early twentieth century. Massive marble columns lifted the ceiling untold stories above the lobby floor and supported a skylight admitting more than enough light for the entire area.

Near the ticket office was a bouncy, vivacious redheaded student wearing a sport jacket prominently emblazoned with "Carter University." "You must be the Braemhors. I'm Becky. Professor Howard sent me to pick you up." She smiled. "You look sort of British."

"Scottish, actually," Mary said.

"Oh, sorry. The van's just outside." And she bounced her way out into the brisk autumn air.

All the way to Carterville, Becky gave the Braemhors a nonstop, running account of the excellence of her university as one of the better-known private colleges in the Northeast, catering to sons and daughters of the wealthy. As they drove through the center of the village, the Ambrose Inn, a large white, 1920s vintage, three-story clapboard structure, stood overlooking a lush village green with a small business section—a number of boutiques and small town shops on one side and two churches and a nineteenth century village office building on the other.

She drove on through the village to the campus. As they entered the campus and ascended the hill on which the University stood, Becky guided the van even farther up through a dense wood. As the trees parted, there emerged a low building nestled among the trees they had just passed through.

"This is The Retreat, a special haven for visiting dignitaries. It should be quiet. I think the only other guests are two Vietnamese monks here visiting our Philosophy Department and the hostess, Mrs. Parker. She manages The Retreat and prepares and serves the meals, except for tonight. Professor Howard said he would get you about six-thirty and take you to dinner at his house," Becky concluded as she parked the van.

****

"It certainly is quiet," Mary noted as she surveyed the wooded area directly outside the small living room of the apartment on the lower floor, "and it is austere." The furnishings were sparse, but adequate, certainly more than the Braemhors needed for their short stay.

Promptly at six-thirty Stanley tapped on their door. "All ready?" he queried.

"Quite," John responded.

****

The Howard's home was opulent, a mixture of Indian and nineteenth century European art surrounding a plethora of outstandingly fine furniture and bric-a-brac. All the polished hardwood floors were covered in the most expensive oriental rugs. The dining room alone contained a twelve by fifteen Isfahan.

Jane was her usual gracious hostess self, making the Braemhor's feel at home in her house. "It is so nice to see you again," she gushed, "I will never forget your taking care of us during that horrible affair in Manchester. You could not have been more helpful and caring. I am so glad to be able to return your kindnesses in a small way. We owe you two so much."

"You really don't owe us anything. We were only too glad to help," Mary said as the four seated themselves at the immense teakwood dining table.

After dinner they retired to a small sitting room for demitasse and a light dessert. Braemhor opened the discussion, "Well, what more can you tell me about the strange deaths here at Carter University?" He looked at Stanley.

"Perhaps Mary and I should excuse ourselves while the men discuss that horrible business. I can show you the picture album from our year abroad," Jane suggested.

"I'd really rather stay, if you don't mind. John and I share many of his investigations, and this one sounds especially intriguing," Mary replied, hoping she had not offended Jane.

Seeing Jane was somewhat flustered at this breach of the roles she normally assigned to men and women in her world, John smiled and said, "We often find two investigators are better than one lone 'private eye.' You see, Jane, criminal investigation is not what you read in the tabloids. You often need all the help you can get, including from the criminal himself."

Jane was neither pleased with nor fully understood John's remark, but sat back with a curt, "Well, if that's what you prefer." She sat quietly although she was clearly miffed at this turn of events.

Stanley cleared his throat and began, "As I told you on the phone yesterday, we have had a series of unexplained deaths among our faculty over the last eight years. In each case the autopsies concluded anoxia to be the cause, but the police could never fix a precise method."

"And was there a particular pattern to the deaths?" John asked.

"Yes, three years in a row then a gap of a year, followed by two deaths in the succeeding two years, then another gap. And now another one this week. And another thing, they all belonged to the same clique. Do you think that's important?"

"Could be. We'll see. But right now I'm more interested in why the gaps in what started out as an annual event," John was thinking aloud.

Stanley went on, "Well, to continue, the first was eight years ago. A fairly young member of our Classics Department faculty, Willard Cook. As a child he had had several severe bouts with pneumonia. Almost died several times, I understand. I assumed his lungs been weakened by his childhood experiences. Yet he was one of our high risk takers—always going off and doing things no sane faculty member—in my estimation—would do. I thought maybe it was compensation for his years of confinement as a child."

"Like what?"

"Willard was an avid auto racer. He liked fast cars."

"And fast women too," Jane added sarcastically.

"He took up racing at a nearby NASCAR track. Did rather well. Won several silver dishes. But then he went into motorcycle racing. We—except for a few of his close friends—thought it was just insane, and when he broke his leg in his third race, we almost felt it served him right."

"He was quite an adventurer," Mary noted.

"And so when he was found dead of anoxia, the police and the faculty—and I assume the coroner also—thought whatever happened was due to his weakened lungs from childhood pneumonia," John interjected.

"Yes, but how did you...oh, of course, an obvious deduction."

"What about the others?" Braemhor asked.

"The next to go was James Westcott from our Economics Department. Jim was a roughhewn sort of fellow...."

"Roughhewn!" interjected Jane. "He was downright boorish, had no social manners and a very foul mouth. Every other word that crossed his lips was four-lettered and despicable!"

"It is true, he spoke his mind regardless of the time, place or company. Some—particularly his group of friends—thought it endearing and egged him on, especially when he was in mixed company. I think they just liked to watch others, who did not take kindly to his manner, squirm. And squirm they did. Some just quietly left the room when he entered, while a few others engaged him with repartee intended to put him in his place. He was certainly not the most liked of our faculty," Stanley understated. "Then one morning a student coming for his weekly thesis appointment found him slumped over his desk, an unlit pipe on the desk near his hand."

"And the next death?" John found Stanley's recitation interesting, but not yielding much in the way of crucial information.

"That would be John Bodner from Mathematics. He was the *bon vivant* of the campus. Amazingly handsome, with long raven hair he combed down over his forehead and swept back above his ears like the flow of a wave of lava and a trimmed and waxed mustache. I think he was really trying to hide a receding hairline and his cleft lip. There were few faculty wives he did not attempt to compromise at one time or another. Most were flattered by his attentions—particularly his friends, but others found him repulsive...."

"Repulsive, to say the least! He only approached me once and I told him what I thought of him and his whole covey of friends!" Jane still exuded outrage.

"...and some of their husbands took noteworthy offense. He had many a shouting match with some of the spouses and was threatened innumerable times, which of course led the police to interview the offended spouses after he was found in the Mathematics Department's faculty lounge, dead like the others. They were never able to connect any of them to John's death."

"And the fourth?" John quickly interjected.

"Let me see, following a year's hiatus Bruce Martin was found dead in his History Department office. Tall, suave always with a disdainful smirk on his face and an air of pretentiousness about him."

"Constantly looking down on everybody, except his group of friends. Made you feel as if you were unnecessarily taking up his valuable time and that you were not worth dirt in his presence!" Jane interjected.

"You certainly didn't like these people, Jane," Mary observed.

"*Not like* is an understatement. That whole group should have been purged from the faculty, but they all had tenure."

Stanley continued, "Bruce was much like John Bodner in his attitudes and dealings with the women on campus. In fact, when John arrived, the rivalry was palpable, and Bruce felt challenged, like an alpha male who has just had a new alpha invade his territory. But, after a short time, John was taken into Bruce's group of friends, their animosities faded, and nobody thought much more about their initial relationship. But it seemed to me that there was always an undercurrent of bad blood between the two of them, particularly on Bruce's part. John, on the other hand, seemed to carry forward no lasting grudge. He had a lightheartedness about him that seemed to me, artificial, not real, given the circumstances of their first encounters."

"You've mentioned that they all belonged to the same clique?" John asked.

"Oh, yes, they formed the core of a rather well-known group on campus," Stanley responded.

"'Rather well-known,'" Jane sniffed. "Notorious, if you ask me! They were known for their wild, uncontrolled parties with heavy drinking and sexual orgies. Why, do you know they even exchanged wives every week or so! Used to throw their house keys into a pile, then each husband took back a set of keys. Whoever's they got, that's where they spent the night. Disgraceful."

"Now, Jane, you know that those stories were just rumors. I'm sure there was some hanky-panky going on, but that sort of thing happens from time to time on any faculty, in society at large even." Stanley tried to soften Jane's vitriol. "Besides, their life-style and their politics—they are a decidedly radical leftist group—are not that important so long as their teaching duties are not compromised and they don't include students in their way of life."

"They were still setting a very, very poor example for our young people," Jane rejoined.

"Jane forgets that they were among our most outstanding teachers. Several had won national acclaim for their work in the classroom, particularly Paul Wheelwright, brilliant geographer, author of several prizewinning books and shortly before his death two years ago, nationally recognized for his teaching with the Holder Award. He was found in his laboratory.

"As I said, all of them were from the same social clique. They used to call themselves The Che. I think it was a reference back to the early Castro Cuban era," Stanley continued. "In fact, the last one, Rodney Elliot, four days ago, was also part of The Che. Found in his office in the English Department. The police are still working on Rodney's death—our local chief, Harry Phillips, is heading up the investigation. So far they have no more answers than before. It's most depressing," Stanley's voice trailed off as if defeated. "Now there are only three of the group left."

"Was this group exclusive, or did they welcome anyone who wanted to join?" John queried.

"Oh, no. There were several incoming faculty, who also envisioned themselves as unconventional that wanted to join, but, as far as we know, were not welcomed. I think only one member of the current faculty approached the group, but he was turned away."

"But his wife wasn't!" Jane interjected.

"Now, Jane, that was just another rumor. We don't really know whether she socialized with the group or not." Stanley tried once again to placate Jane's indignation.

"Well, rumor or not, Heidi Hess certainly played up to the men of that clique. It was disgraceful! Throwing herself at them at every faculty function, even the Friday afternoon gatherings." Jane continued.

"Gatherings?" John asked.

"Yes, an end of the week wine and cheese get together of the faculty. A weekly unwinding ceremony," Stanley clarified, and then continued, "The group dates back about ten or twelve years. Now, as I said, only three couples are left. I think they're quite scared now and very suspicious of each other."

"But the police have been unable to connect any one of them to these events?" John asked.

"That's right, for one thing they were either on campus during the years there were no mysterious deaths or were away when one occurred."

"The former isn't a conclusive observation but the latter might be important, although they could have returned to campus surreptitiously to commit the crime," John noted and made knowing eye contact with Mary.

Catching her husband's message, Mary rose and said, "John and I have overstayed our welcome, and we did have a long trip today."

"Yes, perhaps it is time we went back to our apartment for now and carry on tomorrow," John suggested.

"Of course, then tomorrow you can let me know how you would like to proceed with your investigation." Stanley smiled.

With that the Braemhors thanked Jane and Stanley for their hospitality and got into Stanley's car for the ride back up the hill to The Retreat.

****

"Well, John, what do you think of Stanley's concerns?" Mary asked as they entered their austere apartment.

"Certainly they appear well-founded, though taken individually each of the deaths may not seem so suspicious. It's the number and the similarity of the manner of death among the six that makes this case more interesting. Also the fact that all of the dead faculty were members of the same social group, and apparently quite a notorious group, adds to the mystery. You could almost make a case for some sort of a vendetta either within the group or from without. Stanley did mention at least one jealousy within the group. One question is whether we are dealing with one or multiple murderers.

"More than one?"

"Yes. Stanley said there was bad feeling between Bruce Martin and John Bodner. Martin could have done away with Bodner and then someone else taken care of Martin. Maybe there were other jealousies within the group Stanley didn't mention or didn't know of. Yet it's not likely that multiple murderers would all choose the same method, whatever it is. On the other hand, if there was only one culprit within the group, he would have to be one of the three survivors."

"But didn't Stanley say the police established that the three men's presence on campus did not coincide with the time of the deaths—that they were either not here one year that a death occurred or were here when a death did not occur?" Mary added.

"Yes, as I said to him, the former instance—not being here when a murder occurred— is important, but the latter—being here when a death did not occur— tells us nothing. Perhaps the murderer was very clever and decided to take a year off to throw off any investigation by changing the pattern."

"But you said yourself that the murderer could have been off campus and returned briefly to commit another crime," Mary interjected.

"True. True. So neither their presence nor their absence may add to our understanding, but it is a starting point—finding out who was here and who was not when the crimes occurred," John rejoined.

He paused, reflecting briefly on how much he enjoyed his wife's active participation in the investigative process, and then continued thinking aloud. "To me it's the pattern of the deaths that is most fascinating. Obviously we have to assume that the pattern—three, zero, two, zero, one—depends on the presence of the murderer, not on his—or her— deciding to take a holiday from the pattern. Since the three remaining members of the—what did Stanley call them, The Che?—have been exonerated we must look for disgruntled outsiders."

"Disgruntled outsiders? Like Jane?" Mary was fascinated by her husband's analysis of the situation but could not resist poking some fun at his investigative assumptions.

"Good point. I don't think so, but we can't eliminate her at this point."

"Really, John, do you think she's some sort of an 'avenging angel'?" Mary was taken aback that he would consider their hostess as a potential murderer.

"Jane is disgruntled by the group's behavior, not disgruntled because she can't be a part of the group, but yes, we must consider her as a disgruntled outsider. She has made her feelings about the group very plain. You see, human beings are social, group animals regardless of the façade they might present to the world about them. They like to belong. The Che was—is—a very exclusive club. I will bet that there were faculty members who longed to belong, but for one reason or another were denied entry. In fact, Stanley said there was at least one still on campus. Could they have harbored such resentment at being 'left out' that they exacted vengeance on the group members? And how and why would they do that?"

"Really, John, murder six people because they would not let you into their exclusive club?" Mary was a bit incredulous.

"It's been known to happen." John smiled. "But I think for the present we should get some sleep and let our slumbering brains work on what we have thus far assumed."

****

Next morning Braemhor paid a visit to the local chief-of-police, Harry Phillips.

"Professor Howard says he's asked you to look into the faculty deaths at Carter," said Phillips, a short round officer with a smile as large as his stomach. He put his pudgy hands into his belt, leaned back in his swivel chair and observed Braemhor. "You know I can't share much with you since you're not a police officer."

"Perhaps these will help." Braemhor handed Phillips his UK ID and the temporary FBI ID Charlie MacLaine had provided him in New Boston when he helped with the case of the hidden dentures. He hoped that the fact that both of these cards were temporary, given him for specific investigations in the past, would not be a problem.

Phillips scrutinized both cards with the importance he felt appropriate to establish his authority over his visitor. "That's fine. They look in order. What would you like to know?" he said as he handed the IDs back, trying not to show how impressed he was with the credentials offered by this foreign investigator.

"Where do you stand on the latest death, the one three days ago?"

"Not much further along than with the previous five. I just got the coroner's report this morning. Same cause of death—anoxia, but no signs of a struggle, no signs of strangulation. Found in his office, like the others—either their office or their laboratory—early in the morning. Had been dead since sometime late the night before." Phillips said.

"Any evidence showing who might have been with him?"

"We dusted everything. Not much there, except...."

"Except?"

"Just like the others, there was evidence of a drinking bout, two glasses, partly used up bottle of booze. And in every case there was one set of prints and DNA we couldn't identify. All the rest were accounted for—the victim, two of his students—who we questioned and I'm satisfied can be eliminated from suspicion—and the building janitor, who only works days. Professor Elliot phoned a colleague sometime after the janitor went home. We sent the unknown prints to the Feds, and they came up dry."

"So they probably belong to someone who was not in military service, held any other kind of government position or was in the FBI's criminal data bases?" Braemhor was eliminating possibilities.

"Right."

"Were the prints and DNA from the same person in every case?"

"Yes," Phillips responded, "as far as we could determine."

"Then we're dealing with just one murderer," Braemhor opined aloud.

"It would seem so," Phillips concurred.

"How big were the prints?"

"How big?!" Phillips was a bit incredulous.

"Yes, could they have belonged to a woman? Women do have smaller hands than most men."

"Oh, I see what you mean. Yes, they could have belonged to a woman, but there's another thing."

"Yes?" Braemhor asked.

"Elliot, like all of the rest, was dead drunk. Had a blood alcohol level almost two times the DWI limit."

"But the coroner didn't list that as cause of death—alcohol poisoning?"

"No, in each of the cases she listed anoxia as the cause. But I'm willing to bet that they might have been unconscious from the drink before the anoxia got them," Phillips offered.

"Hmmm," Braemhor thought for a minute, "no indication of any other drugs?"

"Nope, just the alcohol."

"I understand you've interviewed the three remaining faculty members of this social group. I think they call themselves The Che."

Phillips broke out in a loud laugh. "Yes, they call themselves The Che, some sort of in-group joke, I think. None of them are under suspicion. They were all away from campus when at least one of the deaths occurred and all on campus when one didn't."

"Why?"

"Why?" Phillips did not understand.

"Yes, why were they away from campus?"

"Oh, I see. They were on sabbatical leaves. Every seven years the professors can take a year off from their teaching duties. Pretty cushy, I think. Wish I could get a year off just to vacation every seven years. Harrumph! I'd settle for every ten years."

"So would I," Braemhor added to solidify his camaraderie with this slightly pompous repository of information. "So they leave campus every seventh year?"

"Or thereabouts. At any rate, they're OK. But they're plenty scared, I can tell you that. They're the only three left of The Che, and they're 'bout scared out of their britches. I told them not to worry until next year this time, but it didn't seem to help." Phillips guffawed at his own macabre humor. "I think they probably spend a lot of time watching each other. Some of the camaraderie of the group is pretty tarnished now."

"I can understand that." It was Braemhor's turn to smile a response. "Have you considered non-faculty? Towns people, for instance?"

"Yes, but we keep pretty close tabs on our local population. We know which ones might try a burglary or some local shoplifting, that sort of thing. We don't have any potential murderers among the locals, but we're still keeping our ear to the ground. It's a small town and I have a good group of informants. I would have heard something on that score if a local were involved. No, I still think the most likely criminal is among the Carter faculty."

"You're probably right. So what's next?"

"I really don't know. We're up a river without a paddle."

Braemhor was not sure he followed Phillips's colloquialism, but went on, "No suspects?"

"Nope, but if you have any ideas, we can use all we can get."

"I may have, I may have. I'll certainly let you know if I come up with anything. And many thanks for talking with me. I'd better get back to the campus for now."

Phillips paused for a minute like he did not want Braemhor to leave, "There was one other thing. In each case there was a faint but very sweet aroma in the room. Not the booze, almost like a perfume, but not what any woman would wear. Too sweet. Almost turn your stomach, if it had been stronger. I was first on the scene in every case and I sure smelled it. It faded pretty quickly though, so by the time the coroner got there it was gone. I talked to her about it, but she had no idea what it might have been."

"Let me think about it." Braemhor then took his leave.

Just like Rhodesia, he thought as he headed up the hill to The Retreat and his and Mary's apartment.

****

Mary was in The Retreat library looking over some manuscripts of ancient religions. She looked up. "Well, what have you discovered?" she asked.

"Not much yet, but I've got some ideas I want to discuss with Stanley."

"He called and wants us to meet him at the Faculty Club for lunch. Says he can quietly introduce us to some of the faculty without arousing anyone's suspicions. Also said he'll introduce us as old friends from Manchester."

"Let me wash up and we'll go. I take it you have a campus map, so we can find our way around?" John asked.

"Oh, yes. Mrs. Parker gave me one and I've already done a little exploring on my own. You know, John, this is really a beautiful campus, up here on this hill with all the wooded area."

"Maybe that's why they call it higher education," John chuckled.

"Really, John! Let's go meet Stanley."

Chapter 9

The Faculty Club was in a three story wood-shingled house with a massive fireplace in the living room and a unique set of bronze busts of former presidents of Carter University gracing the walls of the dining room. All of the first floor rooms—the living room, dining room and library—were now used for serving meals at noontime and the early evening. Rooms on the second and third floors, which were reached by a majestic staircase, were also available for visiting lecturers. On the landing at the top of the staircase was a large window seat from which visitors could enjoy the sweeping vista of the front of the campus which sloped down to flat terrain traversed by a trout creek that fed into a large lake surrounded by student housing units. Mary was right, the campus was extraordinarily beautiful.

Stanley Howard met them at the door and guided them to a table for three, nestled in a round alcove in what had been the library. "We'll be out of the way here. I want to know what you learned from Chief Phillips this morning."

"Not much, really. He has eliminated the three remaining Che members as suspects, but he's no closer to any other suspects or to the method used. He did say that all of the deceased were overdosed on alcohol, but the coroner did not put that down as the cause of death. He's rather jealous of your sabbatical leave program."

Stanley smiled. "Oh, yes, sabbatical leave is little understood outside of academia. It comes from the word, Sabbath or day of rest, you know. It's a major benefit to the university, because the faculty member returns to on-campus duties rejuvenated and more up-to-date in his or her field. Unfortunately the general public sees these leaves of absence as unwarranted and unnecessary vacations. It's almost as difficult to explain sabbaticals to the general public as it is to explain academic tenure.

"Even worse to explain, we have a quadrennial leave program also. You see, if a faculty member were to teach an extra course in each of three years, he or she can have a semester's leave."

"So it's possible for an individual to have two leaves in a seven year period, one based on the quadrennial program and one based on the sabbatical program," Braemhor summarized.

"Does that help?"

"It just might because, you see, the pattern of the crimes doesn't fit a simple seven year sabbatical program. Do you have records of such leaves of absence of your faculty members?" Braemhor asked.

"Oh, yes, would you like to look at them?"

"Yes, would after lunch be all right?"

"Sure. Oh, see the three who just sat down over there in the dining room? That is what is left of The Che. The tall one with the large, black mustache is Hollenbeck from Physics; the shortest one, bald with a slight goatee is Abbott from Geology; and the other one, missing an arm, is Spento from Chemistry. Lost his arm in a laboratory accident when he was a graduate student. They usually eat lunch together."

"I see they drink their lunch also," Mary observed.

"They don't all belong to the same academic department, " Braemhor noted.

"Not at all."

"What about the murdered members?"

"Let me see...they were from Classics, Economics, History, Mathematics, Geography, and English," Stanley counted.

"No commonality there," Braemhor was thinking aloud. "You mentioned that there was one member of your faculty who wanted to be a part of The Che but was denied membership. Could I meet him?"

"Yes, that would be Karl Hess, Biology.... Ah! There he is now. Karl!" he called, waving to the short, very slender person who had just entered the library, "join us, won't you? These are the Braemhors, visiting from Scotland. John is a professor there."

Hess put his tray down on the table and graciously greeted Mary, taking her hand and pulling himself up to a rigid posture as he nodded his head and brought his heels together in an audible click. "So pleased," he said in a deep guttural accent. Then he turned to John, shook his hand and grasped him with his eyes. "Professor Braemhor," he said darkly.

"Stanley tells us you're a biologist," Braemhor opened.

"Yes, actually, I'm a zoologist. My specialty is the animal brain and its functions." Hess then launched into an extensive and protracted dissertation of his teaching and research and ended with, "I have a lab in brain surgery—on rats, of course—this afternoon. Care to stop in and watch us explore the mysteries of the nervous system?"

"I'd like that very much." Braemhor jumped at the opportunity to get to know Hess better. "I have to stop by Stanley's office first, then I'll find my way to your lab." Braemhor surprised Mary as he displayed how well-versed he was in the anatomy of the brain and peripheral nervous system as he kept Hess engaged in a detailed conversation about his research and his teaching.

But then the conversation started to drift to things more prosaic: the weather in upstate, the beauty of the campus, the lovely antique home in which they were now having lunch. At that, Braemhor became restless and tried in vain to bring the conversation back to Hess's specialty. But the social moment had passed, and he felt now that there was a lack of substantive information to the conversation. Then Hess abruptly excused himself to go prepare the laboratory exercise for his students. He looked at Braemhor. "I'll see you later. The lab's in Morris Hall 102."

John, Mary and Stanley also left and walked up the hill to Stanley's office to look over the records on faculty leaves during the past eight years.

****

"Joan, show the Braemhors where the faculty leave records are. They want to peruse them for awhile." Joan, Stanley's secretary, nodded and led John and Mary to a small room filled with filing cabinets. She stopped at one, pulled open a drawer and said, "Here they are. You can use the table over there," and she left them to their search.

"Now we need to find individuals who have had leaves matching the staggered nature of the past six deaths."

An hour later they had almost finished going through all of the records for the past ten years when both Mary and John said simultaneously, "I found one!"

"Make a note and finish looking. There could still be more than two," John cautioned.

Half an hour later, John and Mary looked at one another. John spoke first, "This may be more difficult than I had anticipated. It looks like your 'avenging angel' is still in the running." A look of horror spread across Mary's face. "But for now I think I'll take Professor Hess up on his invitation to observe his lab. You want to come?" John continued.

"I think not. I don't find vivisection awfully interesting. I think I'll spend some time in the main library. Why don't you look for me there when you're finished?" Mary answered.

"Fine, I'll see you in an hour or so." Off they went, John up the hill and Mary down.

****

Braemhor found Morris 102 easily where Hess was holding forth with a combination lecture/laboratory demonstration surrounded by eight students eagerly observing their professor's surgical skills. Hess stopped abruptly what he was doing and said, "Ah! Welcome." Then he turned to the students. "This is Professor Braemhor from Scotland. He's going to sit in on part of today's exercise." John nodded to the class and then Hess continued, "Come join our intimate group. I'm just about to close up, then my friends here will practice the same surgery."

Braemhor squeezed into the circle and looked down at Hess's "patient," a black and white rat about 350 grams, mounted rigidly in a U-bar stereotaxic.

"It holds the animal's head in a rigid position so that we can precisely locate areas deep within the brain," Hess responded to Braemhor's obvious interest in the instrument.

The incision in the scalp had been cleanly effected so that there were no ragged edges, just a precise straight line cut. Hess had removed part of the skull and suctioned out part of the right hemisphere of the brain. When Braemhor approached, Hess was inserting a dissolvable sponge to fill the void and was about to close up the incision. To Braemhor's surprise, Hess did not suture the wound, but applied a thin line of clear fluid from what looked like a tube of glue and pressed the two edges together with a small hemostat.

Hess looked up at the students and said, "All right, to your stations and do what I just did." The students dispersed themselves around the laboratory and proceeded to anesthetize their own "patients."

"A hemispherectomy seems to be a pretty drastic surgery," Braemhor noted.

"Oh, you'd be surprised how few behavioral changes we'll see when the animals recover. That's why I start with this surgery. In a small way it shows the students how flexible and resilient brain tissue actually is," Hess explained.

"One thing did puzzle me," Braemhor continued. "I thought you would have sutured the wound; instead it looked like you glued it shut."

"Latest technology. Oh, I teach the students suture techniques. Also teach them to use wound clips—you know, metal clips you squeeze the wound together with—and surgical tape. That way they learn several skills. But with sutures, clips, and tape you have to remove them later, more time, more work."

"Unless you use dissolvables," Braemhor suggested.

Hess looked at him quizzically. "Are you sure you're not a physician or a vet? You seem to have a lot of technical information at your fingertips."

"No," Braemhor laughed, "I had some courses in anatomy and physiology many years ago; that's all. But tell me more about this glue you use."

Hess smiled. "Like I said, latest technology. Only been around about twenty years. Just now starting to be applied consistently in animal and human surgery. You've got to be careful with it though. You can easily seal your fingers together."

"Isn't there a solvent?"

"Oh, yes. We keep a can on hand in all of our labs. Students aren't always too careful no matter how often you warn them." He showed Braemhor a pint can of solvent from one of the lab drawers.

"Certainly has a pungent odor," Braemhor remarked, "one might also say like a super sweet perfume."

"Oh, yes," Hess laughed, "but I doubt any self-respecting woman would want to wear it to a party."

"Well, I've taken enough of your time. I'll let you get back to your students. Maybe we'll see one another again before Mary and I return to Scotland."

"I'd like that," Hess's remark was quite genuine. "Maybe Stanley will bring you to the faculty gathering this evening. It's at the Faculty Club. Heidi—that's my wife—will be there too." He turned and went back to help the students as they struggled to anesthetize their rats, and Braemhor left the building and walked to the main library where he found Mary.

She noticed the renewed bounce in his step immediately. "Found something?"

"Just maybe. Just maybe. Let's stop at Stanley's office before we go back to the apartment. I'll bring you up-to-date as we walk."

"First let me share something with you I found in the *New York Standard*. It'll only take a minute. Here read this." Mary handed John the paper and pointed to an article on the back page.

Though John was more interested in getting to Stanley's office, he read what Mary pointed out, and the more he read the broader became his smile, until by the time he had finished the article he was laughing so loud that a nearby librarian was shushing him.

"That's wonderful!" he whispered to Mary. It was the story of a criminal in New York City who had attempted to hold up a fast food shop. When the attendant was slow to give him the money from the register, he aimed his gun at the frightened young man and pulled the trigger. But the gun did not fire. So the would-be thief looked perplexed, turned the gun around, looked down the barrel and pulled the trigger again. This time the gun fired and the criminal became his own executioner.

Through his stifled laughter John again whispered to Mary, "Maybe we could reduce crime in the U.K.

by supplying all the criminals with defective weapons that only fired on the second pull of the trigger."

"I thought you would enjoy the macabre humor." Then she added, "Now we can go see Stanley."

At Stanley's, John and Mary made a commitment to return to the Faculty Club at four-thirty for the end-of-the-week gathering Hess had mentioned. Stanley said, "Of course, both of you are most welcome. Interesting that Hess would invite you. As you'll see, his wife is quite forward with new men in the area—to Karl's embarrassment at times. I would think he would be a little more protective of his bruised ego."

"Oh?" Braemhor prompted.

"Yes, he met her in Germany when he was in the service near Erlangen. Her parents escaped Hitler's regime in the early 1930's, and she was born here in the U.S. The family had lived in Erlangen before they left, and were back visiting old friends when he met her. When they first came to Carter, the campus was abuzz with rumors about her behavior. Well, you'll see this afternoon."

****

Before walking back down the hill from their apartment, Braemhor gave Mary some brief instructions concerning what he wanted her to do at the social gathering so that he could obtain information he thought might be critical to Chief Phillips's investigation.

They joined Stanley again at his office and together walked to the Faculty Club where Jane met them just inside the main entrance. Unlike lunchtime, the living room, dining room and library had all been cleared of tables and chairs, and serving tables were set in each room. These tables offered a variety of wines, non-alcoholic beverages and hors d'oeuvres. The steamed shrimp were the favorite, and a number of the faculty either stood by the shrimp constantly gorging themselves or piling small serving plates high with shrimp to be devoured elsewhere in the house.

Shortly after their arrival, the Braemhors were approached by Karl Hess. "Glad you could make it!" he greeted them, then turning to the tall, willowy woman beside him, he said, "This is my wife, Heidi. Heidi, this is John and..."

"Mary," John filled in.

"Mary Braemhor. They're visiting from Scotland. John is a retired professor of..."

"Criminology." This time it was Stanley who completed Hess's sentence.

Mary looked a bit surprised, but John took it in stride and added, "Yes, but my academic days are long behind me."

"Not so long ago, I'd guess," Heidi fixed her eyes on Braemhor and searched his face for some sign of more than just a casual greeting. Stanley and especially Mary became noticeably uncomfortable until Heidi broke the silence. "I'm so pleased to meet you," she oozed, only adding to the tension until Stanley interrupted with "Wine, anyone?"

"Excuse me, won't you?" Karl Hess drifted off to chat with two members of the Che who had just entered.

Heidi Hess was a tall, slender woman in her mid-forties. Her platinum tresses were cropped short and form-fitted her face. Her flowing, gossamer green dress served to accentuate her lithe form and blond coloration. *Reminds me of a praying mantis*, Braemhor thought, as she approached to take his arm. Her eyes sparkled as she was obviously—all too obviously to Mary's way of thinking—taken by Braemhor and intended to try to make more of the evening than a few casual glasses of wine. "Oh, you're not drinking," she mewed as she noticed John's tumbler.

"No, I prefer the non-alcoholic," John said and smiled an "I know what you're about" grin.

"Pity," she mewed again and took his arm and directed him to the shrimp compote.

John leaned over to Mary as he was led away and whispered, "Change of plans. You take my part; I'll take yours." He hoped Mary understood his meaning, though the jealous look on her face made him worry that her emotions were getting in the way of the plan he had outlined to her before they left their apartment.

Mary, who at this point was by no means happy, took Stanley's arm and directed him to the other side of the compote from where her hijacked husband and Heidi Hess stood. "She certainly is forward," Mary observed.

"Oh, I think she's just trying to be friendly to a visiting dignitary," was Stanley's weak reply. Even he did not believe his own surmise.

"You Americans indeed have a strange definition of friendly," Mary rejoined, and was then immediately afraid that she might have offended their host. "Oh, I'm sorry; I shouldn't have said that."

"Not at all. You are quite right, of course. We do tend to be a bit coarse at times."

"Some of us are coarser than others!" That was Jane who had just joined the group. "Particularly that one!" She stared directly at Heidi, who by now had drawn herself up close to John's sleeve and was pressing her hip against his thigh. "She is not only direct, she is downright whorish! I'll put a stop to this!" Jane began to stride toward Heidi and John.

"No, wait," interjected Mary quickly and took hold of Jane's arm, restraining her. "Excuse me," Mary said and went to the other side of the compote table where Heidi and John stood with their backs to a silver tray of shrimp. She dropped her napkin over the empty wine glass at the edge of the table and deftly picked up both the napkin and the wine glass beneath and put them into the rather large handbag she was carrying. Only Jane actually saw what had happened, but for reasons even she did not understand she refrained from saying anything about the strange purloining of a wine glass.

At that moment Heidi turned back to retrieve her glass only to discover it was gone. "Where's my glass? I thought sure I had left it here." She looked around bewildered.

John quickly said, "I'll get you another," and walked past Mary, Jane and Stanley to the wine table. As he passed he flashed a quick smile at Mary and whispered a second message, "I think it's time to go."

He gave Heidi, who had now returned to where Mary and Jane stood, the glass of wine and said to the two women and Stanley, "Mary and I have really got to be heading back to The Retreat. Mrs. Parker said she would have our supper ready promptly at five-thirty and we don't want to be ungracious guests."

"Oh dear," pouted Heidi, "we were just getting to know one another."

"Sometimes short friendships are best," John offered.

"Oh well, maybe another time," Heidi said as she looked around the room. "Oh, there's Bill Hollenbeck. Oh, Bill!" she called and glided over to her next conquest.

It was Jane who then intervened trying to deflect attention from Heidi, "Maybe you and Mary can come to our house for dinner tomorrow evening. Say about six?"

"We'd be delighted." The Braemhors exited the Faculty Club and climbed the hill to The Retreat.

****

On the way up the hill, John and Mary reviewed the evening's events.

"I was certainly pleased you understood my whispered message about changing roles," John stated.

"Well, you were certainly keeping the praying mantis occupied," Mary feigned jealousy.

"Oh, you noticed," John grinned. "She was definitely possessive and not very subtle. And interesting you should mention the mantis metaphor. I thought the exact same thing." John was always startled by the concordance between his and Mary's thought patterns.

"Jane was so incensed. If I hadn't stopped her when I did, she would have gone up to Heidi and scratched her eyes out...and thwarted all our plans."

"As always, you did the right thing. I don't think I could have taken Mrs. Hess's glass without making everything very obvious, but I did get the one Jane was using." John wrapped his arm around Mary's shoulder and gave a hug. He then proceeded to bring Mary up-to-date on his investigation.

"Now that we've gotten the glasses, what's next?" Mary asked.

"First, let's see if Mrs. Parker can give us plastic bags for our wine glasses, then I want to call Chief Phillips. I think he'll be pleased with what we have."

As they entered The Retreat, Mrs. Parker greeted them with, "Dinner is ready. I was afraid you were going to be too late. Come into the dining room and sit down."

Before he ate, John slipped out to the main reception area and used the telephone to call Phillips—there were no phones in the separate apartments. "I think I've got some things you'll be interested in. I can't talk now, but can you come up to The Retreat?" Phillips said he would be there within the hour.

At dinner John transferred the wine glasses into the plastic bags provided by Mrs. Parker and handed the napkins to Mary. "Here, we can take these back to Stanley tomorrow night."

Phillips arrived as they were finishing their coffee. "What have you got?"

"Let's go downstairs to our apartment," John answered as he led Phillips and Mary down the stairs to the guest room area. Once in the privacy of their apartment, John told Phillips what he and Mary had done at the wine party and how he thought it would fit into his investigation. Phillips was grinning from ear to ear. "I had a good feeling when I talked with you this morning that something was going to break. And like I said, I need all the help I can get." He took the plastic bags with the glasses and put them into one of his evidence bags. "I'll get these to the lab at the county seat tonight and we should have their preliminary report by noon tomorrow. I'll call you as soon as I know." Phillips left and headed to the lab twenty miles away.

"How about a quiet evening of reading and relaxation," John suggested. "We've had enough sleuthing for one day, don't you think?"

"I agree, particularly when we have to deal with the likes of Heidi Hess."

"Jealous?" A twinkle danced across John's eyes.

"Hardly, John, but I can understand why people like Mrs. Hess upset some wives."

****

Following breakfast, what Braemhor considered the worst part of any investigation began, the waiting for something to happen or someone else to do something. Mary was only too familiar with his agitation and his pacing and suggested they take a long walk around the campus to try to defuse his tension. Feelings of self-doubt always attacked Braemhor at this point in an investigation. Had he pieced together the bits of evidence and hunches correctly? Had he overlooked something? Could there be an entirely different understanding of what he had before him? Had he deduced too quickly? Jumped to too many conclusions, too soon? *Well*, he tried to comfort himself, *we'll know by noon.*

He interrupted his cogitation and pacing, realizing Mary had suggested something, what he wasn't quite sure—he hadn't been listening, really. "Yes, that sounds fine," he said absentmindedly, not fully knowing what he was agreeing to.

The walk helped or at least distracted Braemhor from his self-absorption. By the time they had seen all of the beauty of the campus, they were ready for lunch.

With a light knock on their apartment door, Mrs. Parker announced, "Call for Professor Braemhor." Braemhor leapt to the door and ran up the stairs to the telephone.

Phillips's voice grinned through the receiver. "Professor, we've got a match! The prints on one of the glasses match those at the scene of Elliot's death. I think the DNA probably will, too, but that'll take a few days." Phillips was bubbling. "I can't thank you enough, Professor. You've solved a lot of our problems!"

"Your findings should let the remaining three Che members breathe a little easier, too," Braemhor added, trying not to let his own delight at the news show too much.

Phillips continued, "That, too. I'm sure they will rest easier when the news breaks. But I can't talk any more right now. I and the state boys are going to pick up the Hesses and advise them of their rights. I'll call you later this afternoon. Bye."

****

That evening Stanley Howard greeted the Braemhors at the door with, "John, Mary they've arrested the Hesses! Come in! Come in! Tell me what has happened. Oh, this is terrible, terrible, a member of my faculty arrested and carted off to the county jail!!"

"I'm afraid I'm to blame. I was particularly interested in Mrs. Hess as a suspect," John said, as Jane appeared behind Stanley.

"Good riddance to bad rubbish, if you ask me," Jane summarized her feelings with one breath and with the next recaptured her role as the gracious hostess, saying, "Why don't we sit down to some cheese, crackers and libations."

Seated in the cozy, Indian-decorated den off of the dining room, the four reviewed the events of the last two days. Stanley continued, "How are you to blame, John?"

"Simply because I—we," he looked at Mary, "supplied Phillips with the evidence he needed to close the case of Professor Elliot's death...and the recent deaths of the other members of The Che. You see, as you know, I was fascinated by the pattern of the deaths, three then a gap of a year, followed by two more, then another gap and this year another. I tried to tie the pattern into your leave programs, looking at both your sabbatical and quadrennial leaves.

"Also, at first I, like Phillips, centered on the three remaining Che members, assuming there were some sort of internal conflicts going on within the group, but none of their leave patterns matched the pattern of the deaths either.

"The next obvious place to look was for someone outside the group who might have resentments toward the group as a whole or some of the individual members. You yourself had mentioned that there were faculty members who were rejected by the group and resented being left out. The question was, then, was there anybody whose combined sabbatical and quadrennial leaves coincided with the timing of the six deaths. There were two, Professor Hess and you." Braemhor looked at Stanley.

"Me?... Oh, good Lord, you're right. I hadn't even thought about it. Are you saying that I was under suspicion?" Stanley interrupted.

"Of course, both you and Jane." John turned his glance to Jane who sat rigidly in a fog of indignation and disbelief. "I couldn't eliminate anyone until all of the evidence was in. I'm sorry, but your leave pattern fit what we were looking for, and Jane had certainly expressed her extreme dislike of the Che members. I had to keep the two of you in the mix until we could conclusively tie the fingerprints at the last crime scene to one of our suspects."

"But why did you center on Heidi Hess instead of Karl?" Jane asked after she had recovered her composure.

"Mainly a hunch. Phillips told me that at each of the death scenes over the last eight years there was a clear indication that heavy drinking had taken place. Two glasses and a bottle of Schlehenfeuer—that's what the Germans call your sloe gin—almost empty. At each scene one of the glasses contained a set of prints and DNA that he was never able to match to anyone, and they were the same at each of the crimes. All he could do was list each case as 'unsolved' and put the 'natural causes' story out to the public for propriety's sake and to protect Carter University from unwanted press.

"You told me yourself, Stanley, that the Hesses had a strong connection to Germany, in fact, that her parents are German nationals."

"But why did Mary steal Heidi's glass and not Karl's?" Jane asked, revealing that she had noticed Mary's surreptitious maneuver at the gathering.

"I asked Phillips about the size of the prints."

"Size?" Stanley asked.

"Yes, we often make the mistake in murder cases of assuming the perpetrator is male, but women can be equally guilty of capital crimes. Women generally do have smaller hands than men, and he allowed that the prints could have come from a woman. Also, had the prints been from Professor Hess, your FBI would have identified them from his military records. So I decided to concentrate on female suspects. But I still did not have a good idea of the method used.

"It was not until I visited Hess's lab yesterday afternoon that the method became apparent. He uses a surgical glue to close up the incision he makes in animals. It seals tissue very quickly, in some cases almost instantaneously. And he keeps a solvent for the glue in each of his labs. In addition, it has a pungently sweet odor, and Phillips told me that upon arrival at each scene he thought he noticed a sweet odor like a very strong perfume. In fact, that is what first led me to think of a woman murderer. It wasn't until I learned of Hess's glue solvent that I realized what the method used might have been. You see, she first got her victim so drunk that he became unconscious, sealed his nostrils and mouth with surgical glue, waited while he struggled for breath and finally expired, then wiped his face clean with solvent."

"What a horrible way to die!" Jane shuddered.

"Yes, but that is exactly the scenario she confessed to under police interrogation this afternoon," Braemhor added.

"So she was a sort of a praying mantis," Mary concluded.

"Yes, and my thought and your remark after meeting Heidi only further convinced me that the pursuit of the female was the right course. The praying mantis often ends the mating ritual by decapitating her mate."

"But what about Karl? They arrested him, too." Stanley asked.

"Probably as an accessory for supplying the glue and solvent, but I think he will be exonerated when the investigation is complete. I don't believe he knew anything about what she was doing. Oh, yes, he was disappointed when he was rejected by The Che, but not to the point of murder. Strange as it may sound, I think Heidi Hess is intensely dedicated to her husband. My guess is that she was satisfying her inordinate sexual appetite and taking revenge on The Che members who rejected Karl." Braemhor sat back, having concluded his summary.

"Well, John, as messy as this is going to be for the University, I'm certainly glad I called you. Again—I, Carter University and what is left of The Che owe you a debt of gratitude," Stanley concluded.

"Not at all. Mary and I were happy to help and to get a chance to see the beauty of upstate New York and Carter University. But answer me one question." John responded.

"Of course."

"Why did you introduce me as Professor Braemhor?"

"I just thought my faculty would be less guarded if they thought they were speaking with a fellow academic. And I thought it was a particularly nice touch to say that your field was criminology." Stanley beamed as the four moved into the dining room for another of Jane's sumptuous meals.

Chapter 10

Leaving the beautiful campus of Carter University, John and Mary returned to New Boston to complete their stay with their son and his family. Several evenings were spent with James prying from his father the details of the faculty deaths at Carter. John had always been reluctant to discuss his investigations, but in the case of family, he made an exception.

The phone rang the afternoon of their third day back. It was for John, Thomas Sweeney, a DI from Melrose, inquiring about a certain Rita Erskine.

"Yes," John said. "That's my wife's aunt. She is looking after Dunmoor Cottage in Daraichburn while we are away."

"That's what she said, Sir, but I just wanted to verify what she's told us."

"Why, Inspector, is anything wrong?" John was concerned.

"No Sir, it's just that she had a dustup with a purse snatcher this morning. She's a feisty pensioner, Sir."

"Is she all right, Inspector?" John kept his voice down.

"She's fine, Sir, but it looks like the snatcher has a broken wrist."

"What happened?" John stayed calm in order not to concern Mary and the family.

"Well, Sir, a young thug, in his twenties, made a grab for her purse in the center of Melrose. As he tried to run away with it, she hung on and tugged back. A pretty strong tug, I'd say. Anyway, she pulled so hard that he was pulled to the ground, striking his head on the way down. Must've dazed him, because she stepped up to him and sat on him. Put all her weight in the middle of his back, and proceeded to pound him about the head with her shoe. It must have been a funny scene, Sir. Here she was sitting on this bloke hitting him with her shoe, yelling at the top of her voice 'Help! Help!' At the same time he was yelling and cursing and trying to squirm out from under her and keep her from hitting his head. Fortunately, some nearby store customers came to her aid, separated them, and held them both until one of our constables could get there.

"Our constable brought them both here to the station where we've been sorting it out. I just wanted to make sure she's caring for your cottage before I let her go back to Daraichburn.

"Like I said, she's a feisty one. I certainly wouldn't want to meet her in a dark lane," DI Sweeney smiled through the wire. "We'll be booking the snatcher and I'll see that she gets back to your cottage this evening."

"Tell Miss Erskine we will call her tonight. And thanks for taking care of her." John hung up, smiled, and turned to Mary and the family, who were waiting in anticipation, having heard just enough to be concerned. "Just another Aunt Rita story," he shook his head and said. "Rita is attacking the purse snatchers of Melrose and winning." After he told them Sweeney's tale the whole family had a good laugh.

That evening Mary called Dunmoor Cottage and got Aunt Rita's side of the story. She said she did not even have a bruise, but that her right arm was a little tired from beating the "young man" about the head with her shoe. "No purse snatcher's going to get my purse! The idea that he would even try!!"

****

After two weeks of enjoying the grandchildren, the Braemhors reluctantly flew back to Daraichburn, the warmth of their B&B, and "feisty" Aunt Rita. Two days later she was on a train back to Blanefield.

Early next evening, Mary opened the Dunmoor Cottage door to the knocking of a young American couple.

"Hi, do you have a room?" the American asked.

"Yes, we do and you're just in time for tea, if you would like."

"That would be very nice. I'll get my wife and our bag. Park in the front?"

"Yes, that will be fine."

After the two had deposited their bag in the room Mary had shown them, they came into the sitting room where Mary had put out a setting of tea and her specialty, freshly baked scones.

"Boy, the fire feels nice. It's colder than we expected. The dampness, I guess, makes the temperature seem so much lower than it really is. Do you always have this much rain? We've been traveling for almost two weeks and haven't seen the sun but one day."

"Welcome to Scotland," that was John Braemhor who had just come in from the garden. "Traveling through the lowlands?"

"Headed for the highlands. We're hikers and Bidean nam Bian near Glencoe sounds like it could be a challenge." The young wife shook Braemhor's hand after her husband introduced the couple as Bob and Jean MacIain.

"It's a beautiful area but can be a treacherous hike, depending on the weather and where among the Sisters you go. The Hidden Valley is where your ancestral namesakes used to hide their stolen cattle," John continued.

"Oh, yes. Part of our vacation is exploring my husband's ancestors," added Jean MacIain.

"Glencoe is the place to go then," Mary said as she poured the tea and offered the scones.

"Is it far?" Jean asked.

"Should be an easy drive in the morning," was John's reply. "The MacDonalds were part of a very bloody history, you know."

"Oh, yes. We know. That's part of the fascination with our search," Bob offered. "I'm descended from Alastair MacIain, 'Old MacIain' as he was known, the leader of the MacDonalds when many of them were murdered by Robert Campbell and his men over three centuries ago. Campbell and his men were welcomed into MacIain's castle, but before they left they murdered thirty some MacDonalds, including Old MacIain. We want to see if the ghosts of MacIain and his two sons, who escaped the 1692 massacre, are still hiding out in the Valley."

"Did you say 'ghosts'?" Braemhor's voice announced his incredulity.

"Of course. Don't you believe in ghosts?" MacIain met incredulity with incredulity.

"I can't say that I do. The real world holds enough mysteries for me." John tried to maintain the politeness he felt he owed the guests. "And what will you do if you find these...ghosts?"

"Engage him or them, of course," Bob continued, "see if anything can be done to secure proper retribution for the past." His eyes flashed with anger, so much so that all in the cozy room felt the tension.

"We can't really know the past unless we can cross the boundaries and discuss events with those who lived them, can we?" It was Jean who took up the conversation trying to defuse her husband's ardor.

"I suppose not," Mary added as she gave a warning look to John not to let his true feelings about such ideas show to their guests.

"Quite so," John said quietly and excused himself from the repast to attend to other work.

"How did you happen to pick Dunmoor Cottage?" Mary continued to engage the MacIains.

"Oh, it was in our tour book." Robert MacIain said, then, after a pause, "Is it true your husband is a private investigator?"

Mary hesitated, then, "Well, John does occasionally do some private work. Why do you ask?"

"The man at the gas station down the road mentioned it when we stopped to fill our tank. It seems like you husband has quite a local reputation."

"I suppose," Mary demurred.

There was a short, awkward pause in the conversation. "Where can we get a supper?" Jean changed the subject.

"The Inn down the road is very nice, and they start serving pub meals about five." Mary smiled and started to clear up the tea service.

"We'll head there, then. What time's breakfast?"

"Eight to ten, in the coffee room."

"Well, then we'll be on our way." And the young couple left the Cottage for a meal at the Inn.

****

"What did you think of our guests?" Mary asked later as she and John sat down to their own supper.

"Not much. I can't say that ghost chasers hold much interest for me. There are enough real things to people my world."

"Even after Professor Estinto and Mr. Morrison?" Mary enjoyed occasionally reminding her husband that for all his reality-based experiences a number of his investigatory escapades projected a hint of the supernatural, or at least of natural events not too easily explained by adherence to real world reality.

"True. True. Those two cases did hint of the supernatural, but I can't help but believe that there are natural explanations for all that happens. Yet I suppose that one man's superstition is another's reality. But I will be surprised if our young friends find any real ghosts up at Glencoe."

****

Two weeks later Braemhor's attention was arrested by an article in *The Daily Record*.

"Look at this, Mary."

The headline read: "Sir Robert Campbell Found Dead," and the story told of Sir Robert being found in his bed by his dresser, Burt, with his throat slit. The evening before, Sir Robert had been entertaining, and nothing seemed amiss when he and his guests retired for the evening. One of the guests was a descendent of the MacDonald clan, which prompted the writer of the article to opine that the crime appeared to be a replica of the famous massacre of the MacDonalds led by the then head of the Campbell clan in 1692, though the roles of assassin and victim were reversed. The local police did not put any credence in that interpretation, since the MacDonald—actually MacIain—descendent was an American tourist searching for ancestral records.

"John, do you suppose it was the couple that was just here, the MacIains?" Mary spoke as she read the article.

"I'll call Donald Livingstone. He's one of the DCIs in Glasgow. Maybe he will know."

Ten minutes later John came into the cozy sitting room warmed again by the peat fire.

"It was our MacIains, wasn't it?" Mary offered. *How does she do it?* John thought. *She reads me like a.... It's uncanny.* He smiled.

Just then the telephone rang. "Dunmoor Cottage," Mary answered the phone, listened a moment, then handed the receiver to her husband. "It's Robert MacIain."

"Braemhor here. Sounds like your holiday has taken a bad turn.... That's too bad....You need what?...Yes, I think we can do that....We can be there later tomorrow. Will that be all right?...Of course, we'll come to the Sleat Inn....Bye." John hung up the receiver, and turned to Mary.

"Fancy a trip to Glencoe? It seems our ghost chasers need our help."

"Yes, a little holiday would be nice. I'll pack our bags, and we can go in the morning."

****

Next day the trip past Loch Lomond was uneventful, and the Braemhors arrived at the Sleat Inn just before twilight. The MacIains were in the small lobby to greet them.

Jean MacIain was particularly distraught at being caught up in a murder investigation in a foreign country. Her husband, though concerned, appeared disdainful of the local authorities and their ability to bring an investigation to a reasonable conclusion. The more they told the Braemhors of their activities in Glencoe in the past few days, the more Braemhor became convinced that underneath Robert MacIain's thinly veiled hostility towards the Campbell clan was an even less controlled temper. However, Braemhor agreed to help as much as he could by exploring the circumstances of Sir Robert's death. He even suggested that the two young people go about their holiday in the vicinity of Glencoe as they had planned—they had already been told by the local authorities not to leave the immediate area until the investigation had been concluded.

However, he did suggest that their planned hiking trip to Hidden Valley might be deferred until better weather returned to the area—it had begun to rain heavily as John and Mary entered Glencoe. It was clear to John that, although Robert MacIain had called for help, he was not inclined to moderate his bull-headedness regarding the mess in which he now found himself. John concluded that it was his wife who was really the one behind yesterday's call to Dunmoor Cottage.

Following a less than satisfactory discussion of the situation, both couples retired for the night.

****

The next morning the weather continued its grey misting of the Scottish landscape. John inquired about the MacIains at the desk. The clerk, red-faced and round, responded, "Oh, yes, the Americans. Nice young couple. Here looking for ancestors, until that horrible thing at the Campbells.

"They left at sunrise. Not that they had anything to do with Sir Robert's death, you understand. Local police questioned them right here in our lobby, but nothing ever came of it. The MacIains said they'd go hiking for a few days. Went up to the Three Sisters. Said they wanted to see the Hidden Valley. You know, where the MacDonalds hid their stolen cattle long time ago. Said they might even climb Bidean nam Bian. Quite a challenge in this weather, I'd say. They were young, but they didn't look like hikers to me. And, you know, the weather's caught many an experienced hiker unawares."

"So they've gone?"

"Sort of. They asked us to store a couple of their cases, but we don't have a lot of storage space so I hope they'll be back sometime soon."

"Where is your storage?" Braemhor asked casually.

"Shed out in the back, behind the car park. How do you know the MacIains?"

"They stayed with us in Daraichburn a few weeks back." Mary smiled as she and John went up the steps to their room.

"What next?" Mary asked John later as they were finishing their pub meal.

"I'd like to see the content of their cases, if I can persuade the local constabulary. Remember how passionate Robert MacIain got when talking about contacting ghosts from the past to obtain *retribution?* I'll check in the morning. Livingstone said an Ian MacDonell is the officer in charge of Sir Robert's murder investigation."

"As in *MacDonald?*" Mary startled.

"A common variation. If you're thinking the same thing I am, blood may be thicker than municipal duty, but let's not jump too far ahead. First we talk to DI MacDonell, then we start to draw some conclusions."

****

Braemhor slipped out before breakfast to look up DI MacDonell near the center of the village. When he returned, he found Mary just starting her wild boar bacon with eggs at The Haversack Bar. The Bar, a cozy anteroom and extension of the lobby, was wood paneled with small windows within the paneling, allowing a minimum of light to illuminate the cluster of tables and booths opposite the bar. Mary sat in one of the booths beneath a high, leaded glass window.

"You have to try the boar bacon. Delicious. What did you discover?" Mary asked as she took another bite of her breakfast.

"First, it is quite clear that our inspector MacDonell wants no outside interference in *his* investigation. Very possessive of his local turf. Also, like Robert MacIain, MacDonell lives in the past. He seems to hold a grudge against the Campbells. Though he's investigating the murder, it is obvious that he thinks that Campbell deserved what he got. Seems he was not a very likable fellow. Ruled the area politically with an iron hand. For anyone not seeing the world as he did he made a point of destroying them economically, or so MacDonell tells me. No, certainly no love lost between the present day MacDonells and the present day Campbells. Just reliving the past of over 300 years ago. Mary, it always amazes me the way the past has a way of spoiling the present. Why can't people grow up and deal with one another as mature adults?" John shook his head in disbelief. "Well, I'll get some breakfast, and then we'll go see what the Campbells can tell us."

****

The trip to Glenlyon Estates, where Sir Robert met his gruesome end, was but a ten minute ride. The structure was modern as castles go in Scotland, built in the late 1800's of red sandstone with grey slate on its varied roof lines and turrets. Surrounding it were several outbuildings, an old keep and a private chapel of sixteenth century vintage, in addition to the stables and greenhouses. The stone drive brought the Braemhors to the entry tower and its massive oak and iron door. John rang the bell.

"Can I help you, Sir?" The voice belonged to a tall, thin man about fifty years of age. His curly grey locks tumbled about his weather-lined face as a cluster of snowdrops, making his red face all the more prominent.

Braemhor briefly explained his mission, "I'm a private investigator from the lowlands looking into Sir Robert's recent death. I'm here at the request of Mr. MacIain." He flashed his temporary ID that DCI Peter Killmart had furnished him. "Is there someone with whom I could speak? You, perhaps?"

"That would be fine, Sir." The man looked questioningly at Mary.

"This is my wife and assistant." Braemhor responded to his look.

"Oh, I see. Come in, won't you? I'm Burt, Sir Robert's manservant. I found Sir Robert that dreadful morning. No one else is here now, I'm afraid. They've all retired to their own estates until the investigation is over." He led John and Mary to a semicircular staircase which raised them to the library, a paneled room lined with bookshelves. One wall housed a small writing alcove with a bay window overlooking the family chapel, another a large open fireplace in which a wood fire blazed its heat into the room, making it seem almost cozy.

"The police have already questioned everybody, myself included. I hope the ongoing investigation will be concluded soon. How can I help you?"

"First, what was your relationship to Sir Robert?"

"I'm his general handy man. Been with him eighteen years. I do the cooking. I do some of his bookkeeping, and in the morning and evening I assist him with his toilet. That's how I happened to find him, when I came in to help with his morning dressing. I live in a small apartment in the East Turret, so I am readily accessible, day or night."

"Are there other servants?"

"Just the one lady who keeps the house tidy. She lives in the village and usually arrives about half past eight in the morning and leaves after supper has been cleared. There are just the two of us full-time. Hard times have taken their toll, and the Campbells along with others have had to reduce their staff. They do hire a few temps if they are having a large party," Burt responded.

"Were there more than you and...?"

"Mrs. Hawkins," Burt filled in.

"Mrs. Hawkins in the house the evening of the dinner?"

"No, it was just a small gathering."

"Tell me what happened on February second," Braemhor proceeded.

"Sir Robert gave a small dinner party for some of his political friends the night before. Even invited an American couple who were visiting the area researching their ancestry. During dinner—I prepared and served the food, you understand—the conversation drifted to the famous 1692 massacre that occurred in Glencoe. Mr. MacIain became quite emotionally upset during the discussion. His wife took him away from the table for a brief time, but they returned shortly and apologized to Sir Robert and the other guests. Things seemed to go better after that, but I can tell you, Mr. Braemhor, I was quite worried at the time."

"Worried? Why so?" Mary asked.

"Because Mr. MacIain seemed so angry, particularly with Sir Robert, as if he held him personally responsible for what happened three hundred years ago. But, as I said, his apology was accepted and the rest of the evening went well. Most of the guests left about midnight, except the MacIains."

"When did they leave?" Braemhor interjected.

"I don't rightly know. I went to my quarters about one and they were still having brandy in the library, this very room."

"So you don't really know if the MacIains left at all, then?"

"No, now that you mention it, I don't. I just assumed they went back to the Inn at some time. Sir Robert had not invited them as houseguests, only for dinner." Burt became a little uncomfortable under Braemhor's questioning. "Do you think the MacIains are involved in Sir Robert's death? Except for his angry outburst, they seemed like such a nice couple. Oh, dear."

"I don't know yet who is involved. Did Sir Robert have any enemies you were aware of?"

"Oh, quite a few, I'm afraid. You see Sir Robert was heavily involved in local and regional politics. And he was a strong-willed man. If anyone crossed him, he did not hesitate to see that that person suffered."

"Suffered?"

"Economically, usually."

"Give me an example."

"Well," Burt thought for a moment, "there was a local petrol dealer who had a terrible row with Sir Robert—I don't know what about—and Sir Robert put political pressure on his suppliers until he drove the man out of business. That sort of thing." Burt was becoming increasingly uncomfortable with the line of questioning.

"Were there others Sir Robert offended?" Braemhor felt he was on to broadening the suspect list.

"Only four or five that I knew of."

"I'd like a list, if I might, before we leave."

"Of course. Oh, here is Mrs. Hawkins, Mr. Braemhor." Burt had turned as a small white-haired woman in her fifties entered the library, feather duster in hand. She smiled and gave a slight curtsy as Burt introduced her.

"I wonder if we might have a brief word?" Braemhor asked as he nodded in return. He looked at Burt. "Alone."

Burt immediately detected the intent of Braemhor's look, and excused himself saying that he would make up the list he wanted.

Braemhor introduced himself, then, "Mrs. Hawkins, I understand you were here on February first?"

"Yes, Sir, but only 'til the dinner was cleared. I helped Burt in the kitchen then went home." She looked down as if studying the parquet floor in front of her, holding the tip of her apron in her hand.

"About?"

"Must've been 'bout ten or eleven. Most of the guests had left. Only the MacIains were still here, sitting in the library having drinks with Sir Robert."

"No one else around, then?"

"No, Sir." Mrs. Hawkins looked up at Braemhor. "'Cept Burt. He was still tidying up. Why?"

"I'm just interested in finding out who might have been here to do harm to Sir Robert."

"I don't know, Sir. At one point during the dinner I thought Mr. MacIain was awfully angry with Sir Robert, but later they seemed to get on very well." She hesitated, looked furtively around toward the dining room where Burt was drawing up his list of individuals Sir Robert might have offended. "I'd worry about Burt, if I was you, Sir," she said quietly.

"Burt? Why Burt?"

"'Cause Sir Robert always told him that he'd come into quite a sum when he passed away. It's not fair, you know."

"Not fair?"

"No, it ain't. I work just as hard as Burt, but I ain't gonna get nothin'." Her eyes flashed through the tears that were welling up. "Burt always was his favorite, even when we had a big staff."

"Didn't Sir Robert have family who would inherit his estate?"

"Oh, yes. He has two sons, but they didn't get on well with Sir Robert. Both of 'em said they didn't want nothin' to do with the estate. They are both in business in Manchester and doing very well for themselves, you see."

"So you think Burt will inherit part of the estate?"

"Yes, Sir. Burt seems very nice and kind and quiet, but he's got a temper, he has. I seen it when he used to order the other staff around. He's...he's mean sometimes. And sometimes he scares me. His eyes just look full of hate and anger, sometimes." Then she quickly stopped talking as Burt reentered the room. "Is that all, Sir?" It was clear she wanted to leave.

"Yes, yes, thank you very much." Braemhor smiled at her then turned to Burt. "The list?" He held out his hand.

"Yes, Sir. These are all I know about, but like I said there might have been others." Burt gave the list to Braemhor. "Do you have any more questions, Mr. Braemhor?"

"No, Burt, I think that will be all for now. You'll be staying here for now?"

"Oh, yes, Sir. I'll look after the place until Sir Robert's sons get here and the will is read."

"And then?"

"Don't rightly know. It depends. I've got a sister in Stirling. I might visit her for a while. Then...we'll see."

"Yes, well, thank you very much for your help. My wife and I can show ourselves out."

"I'll do that, Sir. I certainly hope you and Inspector MacDonell can get to the bottom of this. It's upset the whole community," Burt said as he led the Braemhors down the stairs to the entry.

"I hope so too, Burt. And, Burt, it would probably be better if you did not mention to Inspector MacDonell that I've been here. If you don't mind?"

"Not at all, Sir," Burt said as he closed the heavy door behind the Braemhors.

No sooner had the Braemhors driven off than Burt picked up the telephone and dialed Inspector's MacDonell' office. "Inspector MacDonell, this is Burt here at Glenlyon."

Chapter 11

"Well, you were certainly quiet during the interview. What do you think?" John looked at Mary as he drove back to the Sleat Inn.

"I agree with Mrs. Hawkins. I'd look out for Burt," Mary said thoughtfully.

"Because he had the opportunity—after the MacIains left—and he has a motive, the inheritance, right?" Braemhor smiled at Mary.

"The foundations of criminal activity, didn't you always say—motive and opportunity."

"Yes, but...."

"But?"

"Why now? Burt has a comfortable position, his needs taken care of, and I suspect he receives a healthy remuneration. If he is to inherit part of the estate, all he has to do is wait. Sir Robert was some twenty years his senior. Burt's been with him for—what did he say?—eighteen years. Surely a few more would be worth the wait. What's the rush, and as I said, why now? Yet...."

"Maybe Sir Robert was about to rewrite his will. Isn't that the way it is in murder fiction?" Mary always enjoyed deductive sparring with her husband.

"Except that this is real. It's not an Agatha Christie tale. But I can probably check with Sir Robert's solicitor and ascertain if anything of that sort was in the offing. For the time being I think it best we go back to the Inn where I can make some telephone inquiries."

****

Following another hearty meal at the Haversack Bar, Braemhor spent the rest of the afternoon on the phone making inquiries of the individuals on Burt's list as well as Sir Robert's solicitor. At tea time he and Mary again sat down in the Bar.

John responded to Mary's inquiring look. "We can eliminate the five on Burt's list. One moved out of the country last year. Two have been living in the Colonies for over three years. One was attending a corporate party at the time of Sir Robert's death, and the last one died three months ago. But..." he paused for dramatic effect, "there was a planned change in Sir Robert's will."

"So Burt is still a suspect?" Mary summarized.

At that moment a short, burly man in his early forties strode up to the Braemhors' booth. His large stomach preceded him to the table where the Braemhors sat. His jacket and shirt were about a half size too small, the buttons of both struggling to carry out their intended task. The man's bulbous nose was as misshapen as it was scarlet, exaggerating the pores that lined its circumference. He had an air of officialdom about him and a blustering, take-no-prisoners attitude.

"Braemhor!" He looked at John.

"This is Inspector MacDonell, Mary."

Braemhor turned to MacDonell, "Yes?" John tried to keep it light, but he could see he was in for a confrontation.

"I want to know what you were doing at Glenlyon this morning. I thought I made it clear you were to stay out of my investigation." MacDonell threw down the gauntlet.

"I was trying to help you." Braemhor smiled.

"Oh you were, were you? How do you figure that?" MacDonell continued his attack.

"You know, Inspector, I sometimes find that more than one investigator can enhance the possibility of bringing a criminal to justice. Don't you think so?" Braemhor met MacDonell's hostile stare with benign neglect of the hostility.

The question left the Inspector a bit off balance. As soon as he righted himself, he continued, "I don't need any help, and I certainly don't need your interference. This is my investigation, and I don't need some amateur sleuth poking around upsetting the Campbell household."

Though "amateur sleuth" stung a bit, Braemhor controlled his own irritation and calmly said that he was sorry if he had caused any upset for the Campbell staff. "Maybe we could share data and help you solve the case sooner."

This latter suggestion seemed only to enrage MacDonell further, and his nose and cheeks flushed even more so with his rising blood pressure. "Look, Braemhor, just stay out of this, you hear? I'm perfectly capable of solving this one on my own. And if you don't stay clear, I'll bring you up on charges!"

"Like?" Braemhor stayed calm because he knew now that he had won the confrontation. MacDonell had lost what little composure he began with and was reduced to idle threats and petty official demagoguery.

Braemhor's challenge only made matters worse. "Like...like...like trespassing on Glenlyon Estates!" MacDonell fumed.

"Really now, Inspector, did Burt or Mrs. Hawkins complain?" Braemhor was beginning to enjoy the repartee, but realized that, though an amusing pastime, it was getting his investigation nowhere (or was it?). He switched tactics and said, "All right, Inspector, I will stay away from Glenlyon. If anything occurs to me that might be helpful, shall I call you?"

MacDonell ignored the question. "If I were you, Mr. Braemhor, I'd take myself back to the lowlands and stop interfering in my investigation. We don't need your kind up here." With that he turned abruptly and strode towards the door.

"Not a very nice man," Mary observed.

"To say the least. But did you notice he seemed very intent on protecting his turf. Several times he spoke of '*my* investigation.' I wonder why he's so protective of *his* investigation? 'He doth protest too much, me thinks.' Maybe he has more at stake than his reputation as a member of the local constabulary. People often hide their self-perceived shortcomings behind a cloak of bluster." He looked at Mary. "Shall we get a meal and then get some sleep?"

"And let sleep, the great reservoir of inspiration, solve the mystery of Sir Robert's death for us?" Mary intoned philosophically, reiterating one of her husband's oft stated observations.

"Precisely."

****

"Did sleep solve the riddle of Sir Robert?" Mary asked as John was doing his morning push-ups beside the bed.

"Partially, but as I said, I'd like to get a look at the MacIains' cases. Maybe you could stand lookout while I see if I can get into the Inn's storage shed."

"You mean break in?"

"Let's say, *surreptitiously explore*. The shed is behind some arborvitae, pretty well-hidden from observation from the car park and the Inn. Let's see what we can find after breakfast."

"And investigate your own client?"

"No one is above suspicion at this point."

****

Shortly after finishing breakfast at the Haversack Bar, John approached the shed behind the Inn. The lock was a simple padlock, and it easily yielded to Braemhor's pick. He quickly went through the contents of the two cases, while Mary stood outside the arborvitae and pretended to take pictures of the backside of the Inn. At one point one of the kitchen staff emerged from the back door, but was only delivering a bag of garbage to the bin near the door. He reentered the Inn without taking special notice of Mary and her digital camera. John exited the shed and the bushes within ten minutes, took Mary's arm and walked the two of them across the car park and toward the village.

"Well, what did you find?" Mary asked.

"The usual—clothes, toiletries, personal items," he smiled, "except for this." He partially withdrew a plastic bag from his greatcoat pocket just enough that Mary could see a bloody knife in the bag.

She did a quick inhale, then said, "Then the MacIains *are* involved in Sir Robert's murder. Oh dear, and they seemed such a nice couple. Shouldn't you report this to Inspector MacDonell? And shouldn't you give the bag to him, as evidence?"

"Maybe. Maybe. But first I want to have the knife analyzed, find out whose prints, whose DNA are on it. I'm going to pop down to Glasgow and see if Livingstone can help before I talk to MacDonell."

"Isn't that tampering with evidence, John? MacDonell already warned us about interfering with *his* investigation, didn't he?"

"True, but what he doesn't know won't hurt him— yet. Care for some Glasgow shopping? We should easily be back by evening."

While Mary stopped back at their room briefly, John called Donald Livingstone to apprise him of what he needed. Then, while he booked an extension at the Inn, he casually asked the desk clerk, "Who has access to your storage shed?"

"Oh, nobody, Sir, unless we let them in. We keep it locked especially when we are storing guests' items." The clerk smiled.

"So no one has been in there since you stored Mr. MacIain's cases?"

"No, Sir, no one except Inspector MacDonell. Part of his investigation, you see. Why are you so interested, Sir."

"Oh, it's just that the MacIains are friends of ours, and since they are not around I thought I'd make sure their cases are secure. That's all."

"Oh, quite secure, I can assure you. Now how many additional nights did you wish to book?"

"Two or three will do. I hope by that time our friends, the MacIains, will be back from their hiking." Braemhor then thanked the clerk, got Mary and then the two of them drove on to Glasgow.

****

Once in Glasgow, Braemhor dropped Mary at the Highlander Arcade and went to Livingstone's offices.

"I thought you had given up police work and retired, John." DCI Livingstone exited his office and greeted Braemhor in the large office which housed several of Glasgow's DIs. He was a small, wiry man in his late fifties. Only his bald head gave away his age, for his body was hard, that of an athletic man in his mid-thirties. His grip announced his daily morning workouts in the police facilities upstairs.

"I tried that, Don, but fascinating puzzles keep presenting themselves, and I find it hard to pass up an opportunity to see that justice is served." Braemhor smiled as he returned Livingstone's iron grip with a steel one of his own.

"Just can't quit, eh? Well, come into my glass fishbowl and tell me what you're working on now."

Inside the office, Braemhor outlined his concerns with the murder of Sir Robert Campbell, explaining who he thought might be involved. Then he produced the bag he had purloined from MacIain's case. "I need this dusted for prints, and I need a DNA analysis of the blood as soon as possible."

"The prints we can do right now." Livingstone pressed a button on his intercom. "But, John, you're walking a thin line. If this knife is what I think it is, tampering with Inspector MacDonell's evidence will not go down well. Why didn't you take it to him?"

"Let's just say MacDonell and I do not see eye to eye, and I need the knife evaluated before I return it. MacDonell doesn't know it's missing yet and with any luck, he won't."

Livingstone shook his head in mock disbelief. He knew Braemhor's techniques were not always legitimate and knew also that more often than not his unorthodox methods produced amazingly accurate conclusions. He was about to send the lab technician, who had entered the office, back to the lab to perform the analyses when Braemhor interjected, "Compare the prints to FBI records in the States and any databases you have on Scottish war veterans." Livingstone look momentarily puzzled. "If MacIain was in military service, his prints will be in the FBI records, and who knows, maybe Sir Robert's Burt has served Her Majesty in the past."

Livingstone nodded assent to the technician who took the bag of evidence with him. "Coffee, John, while we wait?" Over coffee the two men reminisced over the cases they had both shared in the past and brought each other up-to-date on their respective families. It was not too long before Starkly, the technician, returned, a smile of satisfaction written across his face. "You were right." He looked at Braemhor. "MacIain did serve in the military in the States and his prints were in the FBI data base. But none of the prints on the knife were his. However, there were three other sets on the knife."

"Belonging to?" Braemhor quickly asked.

"Well, Sir Robert Campbell, for one. He served in India years ago."

"Not too surprising, since I suspect the knife came from his kitchen." Braemhor's mind was clicking off possibilities. "And the others?"

"Sir Robert's man, Burt Marsh, and...." Starkly looked questioningly at Livingstone, who nodded his okay. "Detective Inspector MacDonell."

"You probably discovered sloppy police work; MacDonell was never known for his carefulness handling evidence," Livingstone added.

"So if this knife is the murder weapon—and the DNA should ascertain that..." Starkly quickly added, "that will take a couple of days, provided we have something of Sir Robert's for comparison."

"Then we have three suspects." Braemhor looked at Livingstone, who in turn looked at Starkly.

"Have you taken what you need from the knife, Starkly?"

"Yes, Sir," and he handed the bag to Livingstone who gave it to Braemhor and said, "I think you had better return this before it's found to be missing."

"Right," said Braemhor as he took the bag, returned it to the plain paper wrapping he had had it in and put it into his greatcoat pocket. "The funeral home in Glencoe should be able to get you some comparison material for identifying the blood, shouldn't they?"

Livingstone ordered Starkly, who was heading out the office door, "Call the home in Glencoe and see if they can supply our need. If so, go up there today and pick it up." He looked at Braemhor. "If this goes smoothly, we should know by day after tomorrow."

"Call me as soon as you know. We're at the Sleat Inn in Glencoe. And, Don, I may need you to come to Glencoe to officially bring this case to a close."

"Why, John, you seem to do very well without officialdom." Livingstone smiled facetiously.

"But I have no official arresting powers, you know, and besides, I may need physical backup when an arrest is to be made. I can count on you?"

"Of course. We'll be there, if needed. And, John, it's good to see you haven't quit yet." Livingstone rose, took Braemhor's hand and said his goodbyes.

****

Braemhor met Mary in a tea shop in the Highlander Arcade where he informed her of his meeting with Livingstone and Starkly. "What's your conclusion, John?" Mary asked.

"Still working on it. For example, if MacIain is the murderer, why are his prints not on the weapon—assuming the knife is the murder weapon?"

"Maybe he wore gloves," Mary offered the obvious.

"But if you had committed a murder and taken the precaution of wearing gloves or wiped off the weapon, why would you keep the murder weapon in your suitcase, casually stored in an Inn's storage shed?"

"Maybe he hadn't had time to dispose of it." Mary always enjoyed these intellectual exercises with her husband.

"Why not? There's a whole Loch at Glencoe where he could have disposed of it. In addition, he could have taken it with him hiking to Hidden Valley. A multitude of opportunities to dispose of it. Something about this just doesn't ring true."

"What about Inspector MacDonell?"

"Livingstone dismissed his role in the actual murder as police clumsiness, and he's probably right about MacDonell's ineptness, from what we saw of him. Still, I don't want to exclude him as a suspect quite yet."

"But what's his motive? At least with Burt, you have a motive, and a rock solid one, if the dramatizations on the telly are any indicator."

"True. True. Burt has a motive and certainly easy opportunity, living as he does at Glenlyon. But why now? Why not the week before or the week after? Why the night the MacIains visited?" He paused. "I think I just answered my own question. The MacIains visit was a fortuitous chance to commit his crime and blame it on some paranoid American who thinks he should avenge a family feud three hundred years old.... No, Burt is clever, but he's not that spontaneous...or is he?"

"Maybe Sir Robert did it," Mary said teasingly.

"You mean a suicide? The murder weapon was never found at the scene, and Sir Robert couldn't have hidden it after he slit his own throat. No, I think not," Braemhor responded. Then he turned to Mary, "I think we'd best get back to Glencoe. By the way, what did you get at the Arcade?"

Mary showed him the two beautiful cashmere scarves she had purchased for her nieces in Stirling as they settled in the Vauxhall and headed west.

****

Quickly, upon their return to the Inn at Glencoe, Mary again stood guard while John picked the shed lock and replaced the evidence he had borrowed from MacIain's bag. As they returned to the front of the Inn, a rental car drove into the car park.

"It looks like our American couple has returned from their hiking," Braemhor observed, "We might arrange to have dinner with them, don't you think?" He turned to Mary.

"That would be nice, but let's stop in the room first."

"You go ahead, I'll make our date and meet you there in a few minutes," whereupon John strode to the couple emerging from the car. "Well, how was your hiking? Did you find any of your ancestors?" He looked at Robert MacIain.

"Not yet, except for Inspector MacDonell. He's descended from the MacDonalds, too," Jean MacIain interjected. "We found that out when he interviewed us."

"We found Hidden Valley fascinating. Beautiful scenery. And easy to see why the Valley would be a place to hide stolen cattle," Robert concluded.

"Mary and I were wondering if you two would like to have a pub meal with us later. Say about seven?"

"Sounds good." It was Jean who accepted the invitation. "That will give us time to reclaim our luggage and freshen up."

"In the pub then, at seven." And Braemhor took his leave.

****

When the Braemhors came down the stairs to meet the MacIains, they found the two young people in a loud dispute with the room clerk. "What do you mean I can't have my suitcase!?" Robert shouted at the mousey clerk who was huddling behind his desk like a frightened hare.

"I'm very sorry, Sir, but Inspector MacDonell said he has impounded your luggage. You may have the lady's bag, if you want, but he was specific that I was not to give you yours. The inspector expects to be by to pick it up this evening. Perhaps you can talk with him about it then."

"My wife's bag, my wife's bag! I have no clothes except what I'm wearing, if I can't have my own bag! What is the matter with you people, anyway?" Jean was trying to calm him, but he would not be pacified. "I'll tell you what I'm going to do. I'm going to the American embassy and I'll have your G__D___ Inn put out of business. That's what I'll do!" The fire that the Braemhors saw in Daraichburn animated Robert's threats.

John Braemhor stepped in. "What seems to be the trouble?" he asked the clerk, who by now was shuddering with anxiety and fear.

"Well, Mr. Braemhor, Sir, Inspector MacDonell has impounded Mr. MacIain's luggage, and I can't let him have it. And Mr. MacIain is upset, but there is nothing I can do about it."

"Nothing you can do about it! You can give me my clothes, *that's* what you can do about it—or else I'll wring your G__D__neck. That's what *I'll* do about it!" Although the clerk seemed a little less frightened when Braemhor intervened, he was now frozen behind his counter with raw terror. "Oh, dear, oh, dear, oh, dear," was all he could whimper.

Braemhor took MacIain by the arm and forcibly walked him away from the frightened clerk and into a small alcove in the lobby.

"If you will calm down for a moment, I may be able to help you. First, there is nothing the clerk can do about the situation, so there is no sense taking out your anger on him. Second, the nearest American consulate is a five hour drive away, and they will be closed before you could get to them. Third, officialdom moves at its own pace here in the small villages of the Highlands so get a grip on yourself, stop being the hotheaded American tourist, and come into the pub and have a meal. Then maybe, just maybe, I can help you. For now you're just going to have to endure some inconvenience, like it or not." Braemhor sounded like a scolding father, but it had its effect and MacIain seemed to calm his ire, marginally.

"All right! All right!"

"I think Mr. Braemhor is right, Honey." Jean MacIain tried also to calm her husband. "Let's get something to eat."

The Braemhors and the MacIains moved into the pub, Robert MacIain wearing a petulant scowl, his wife in embarrassed, naïve wonder and the Braemhors as the guiding parental figures.

Over the meal Braemhor probed for more detailed information about the dinner at Sir Robert's the night of the murder and discovered that the ancestral chip on MacIain's shoulder had fallen victim to Sir

Robert's engaging personality and the openness with which he welcomed a descendent of the MacDonald clan into his home. In fact, MacIain admitted that he actually found himself liking Sir Robert very much and wished he could have gotten to know him better, had tragedy not struck the Campbell household. He and Sir Robert had made a good start at developing a friendship over brandy after dinner—as Burt had related to Braemhor earlier.

Initially, MacIain thought of Inspector MacDonell as a fellow clansman and attributed the latter's interview and his request for them to stay in the area for a few days as no more than a formality of his investigation. So he could think of no good reason for MacDonell to impound his luggage. He still had half a mind to charge off to Edinburgh in the morning and bring the whole weight of the U.S. Government down on MacDonell, Glencoe and the Sleat Inn. Braemhor continued to advise patience. "Let's wait a day or two and see if MacDonell actually does anything except bluster. He hasn't charged you with anything, and he can't unless he has some substantial evidence on which to base a charge. Patience is your best course for now. Then we'll see if we need turn Sir Robert's death into an international incident. Meanwhile, my advice is to lay low, see some more local sites, maybe buy some clothes at a local shop, and keep a lid on your anger. For now, the less attention you call to yourself the better. For one thing, don't accost MacDonell when he comes for your bag. Unless he contacts you, don't contact him. Agreed?"

"O.K., O.K." MacIain grudgingly concurred, and he and his wife left the Braemhors to go up to their room.

"So you don't think he did it?" Mary asked.

"Don't know yet, but I do know I can get better evidence by befriending a criminal than by alienating him," John responded. "You see, if my guess is right, there are others—besides us and Livingstone—who know the knife is in MacIain's case. Maybe the desk clerk can enlighten me. I think I'll have a talk with him before I come up. I shouldn't be but a few minutes," he said as Mary left to go upstairs.

As Braemhor approached the front desk, he found Inspector MacDonell talking with the clerk whose meekness was even more evident in the presence of a police inspector. MacDonell was in serious discussion with the clerk and had a medium-sized case in his right hand which Braemhor recognized as the one containing the suspected murder weapon.

"Taking a trip, Inspector?" Braemhor asked with a smile.

"In the first place, it's none of your business. And in the second place, I thought I gave you orders to go back where you came from."

"Now, Inspector, surely you know that in the UK the authorities cannot order ordinary citizens around without probable cause. Or is it different here in the Highlands?" Braemhor continued the MacDonell baiting he had started at their last encounter.

"I warned you, Braemhor," MacDonell exploded, his face becoming more and more crimson with each word.

Braemhor surprised even himself with his controlled response to MacDonell's bluster. "My wife and I are here on a brief holiday, that's all. I took your warning yesterday quite seriously and have not interfered with your investigation one bit. And I don't intend to. It's your investigation, not mine, but I will not be bullied about when I am enjoying an otherwise pleasant holiday. Now, can we stay out of each other's way so that I can go about my holiday and you can go about your investigation?"

MacDonell softened a bit. "All right, Braemhor, but mark my words, the minute you stick your nose in my business, I'll...I'll...." Braemhor smiled as

MacDonell walked away in the midst of his third "I'll." Braemhor turned to the desk clerk who had witnessed the exchange in stupefied disbelief.

"He's a powerful man hereabouts." The clerk nodded towards MacDonell's receding form.

"I have no doubt. Loyalties are pretty strong here in Glencoe?"

"Oh, yes, Sir, and if you please, I'd rather not be a part of any disagreement you have with the Inspector." The clerk cowered even further behind his desk.

"Of course not. Of course not. I wouldn't think of making trouble for you with the Inspector. But I do have one question."

"Sir?"

"You said that Inspector MacDonell had been in your storage shed."

"Oh, yes, Sir. Part of his investigation, he said."

"When was that? About?" Braemhor put his question as casually as he could.

"Early, while you and the missus were in the Haversack this morning—shortly after the MacIains left," the clerk paused, then looking about furtively, he continued, "Between you and me, Sir, I wouldn't be at all surprised if the Inspector suspects something. He took Mr. MacIain's case this evening. You saw him yourself. You know, Mr. Braemhor, Sir, Robert's murder is the worst thing ever to have happened here in Glencoe."

Except for three hundred years ago, Braemhor thought, as he said to the clerk, "I'm sure it has been very traumatic for the whole community."

"Oh, yes, Sir; yes, Sir. Terrible. Terrible. Terrible." The clerk shook his head as Braemhor left the desk and returned to his and Mary's room.

****

Braemhor spent the greater part of the next day pacing, first in their room, then in the lobby and finally up and down the main streets of Glencoe. Mary had seen this behavior in her husband many a time while he waited for something to happen and was unable to make it happen himself. Finally, about half past four the desk clerk came into the Haversack where the Braemhors were having tea and said, "There's a telephone call for you, Mr. Braemhor, long distance."

Braemhor jumped up so suddenly that the clerk took two steps backward toward the safety of his desk. "You...you...can take it in the lobby," he stammered, pointing the way to a telephone.

"Braemhor here. What do you have for me, Don?"

"The DNA's back and you were right. It is Sir Robert's blood. The funeral home was most cooperative. Gave us enough material for Starkly to get a match. Where do we go from here?"

"Can you and a couple of your uniformed officers come up here in the morning? We need to interview some people and the more official the interviews look, the better." Braemhor's excitement at bringing yet another case to a final conclusion animated his voice.

"If it weren't you, John, I'd say I'm too busy, but let me check my calendar." There was a brief pause, then, "About eight sound good?"

"Excellent! Meet me in the Haversack Bar at the Sleat Inn here in Glencoe, and I'll outline my ideas."

Braemhor returned to the Bar and responded to Mary's expectant facial expression with, "By noon tomorrow we should have the case of Sir Robert's death all wrapped up."

****

Eight o'clock next morning could not come soon enough for Braemhor. By six he was up and dressed after a fitful night's respite. He went down to the lobby to await Livingstone, who, as was his habit, walked into the lobby precisely at eight, followed by two burly uniformed officers. The desk clerk, who had just come on duty at seven looked with horror at this entourage of official police presence in the Inn's lobby.

"Coffee?" Braemhor greeted Livingstone, guiding him and his officers into the Haversack.

"O.K., John, what's your surmise?"

Braemhor then proceeded to tell Livingstone what he had thus far deduced from the evidence at hand— the fingerprints on the murder weapon, the relationships among the suspects and the close-knit society of the village environs. "I think we should start our interviews with Burt. He's the key to the whole puzzle. The MacIains will be here at the Inn, and we can call them later. And...it might be a nice touch to use MacDonell's offices for the interviews. Keep him off balance, so to speak."

Livingstone smiled his assent, rose and said, "Shall we start then?" He sent his two men to Glenlyon to pick up Burt, and he and Braemhor headed to MacDonell's office in the center of the village.

MacDonell played the gracious host to a superior officer until he saw Braemhor with Livingstone and the latter told him he wanted to use his facilities to interview some individuals with regard to the Campbell case. MacDonell grudgingly took the two of them to his interview space and put three chairs on one side of the table in the room and one on the other, for the interviewee. "We'll only need two chairs on our side," Livingstone intoned.

"But...but these are my facilities, and this is my case. This is very improper! It's your doing, isn't it?" He glared at Braemhor.

"I know this is highly unusual, Inspector MacDonell, but highly necessary. And there is no reason for you to feel animosity towards Mr. Braemhor. These interviews are my doing, not his. So calm down and go back to your office, and let me get my work done," Livingstone ordered.

MacDonell glowered again at Braemhor and turned to go back to his office when an expression of near panic spread across his face, for there, coming down the hall were Livingstone's two officers with Burt Marsh, Sir Robert's man, in tow.

"What?..what?" he began when Livingstone frightened him even more by saying, "Just go back to your office, MacDonell. We'll interview you later. Oh, and, MacDonell, bring me MacIain's case that you impounded, now please." He, with Braemhor, the two uniformed officers, and Burt Marsh, entered the interview room, and he quietly closed the door.

Having delivered MacIain's case to Livingstone, MacDonell crumpled up behind his desk and looked more like the frightened desk clerk than the blustering inspector he had been the day before.

****

An hour and a half later the group emerged from the interview room, Burt looking like a broken man.

"I think that wraps it up, John," Livingstone offered.

"Yes, I think so, but what about MacDonell?"

"Oh, I'll take care of him later. He won't go anywhere. He's already in enough trouble; I don't think he'll risk fugitive status as well."

"What about MacIain? He's still at the Inn."

"I thought you could take care of him. Officer McFadden will give you his bag—minus the weapon, of course—and a ride back to the Inn."

Braemhor put in a quick mobile call to Mary to meet him, with the MacIains, in Haversack Bar. He turned back to Livingstone. "I'll head back to the Inn then, and thanks for the official assist." He extended his hand.

"Always good to work with you, John. And, John..."

"Yes?"

"...I'm glad to see you haven't quit the profession yet."

"Not yet anyway." Braemhor smiled and followed McFadden to the car.

****

"Here's your bag, MacIain. You and your wife are free to go and enjoy the rest of your holiday." Braemhor put the case on the table in the booth where Mary had brought the young couple.

Jean MacIain was the first to speak. "Oh, Mr. Braemhor, we are so relieved, and we thank you so very much for all of your help. Robert and I really, really appreciate your help. We were really scared. I don't know how we'll ever thank you enough," Jean continued to gush.

"No need to thank me, but..." Braemhor turned his look directly at Robert MacIain. "...you and your hotheadedness very nearly got yourself into serious trouble. After that outburst at our B&B and at the dinner table at Sir Robert's, you both became prime suspects in Sir Robert's death. Your staying for after-dinner cordials only made matters worse because you two were the last to see Sir Robert alive—Burt had gone to bed, remember. So there we had it. A hotheaded American still ruminating over an injustice three hundred years ago, as a motive, and the after dinner opportunity... except for one thing."

"What was that?" Robert MacIain asked sheepishly.

"The weapon didn't have your prints on it."

"What weapon? What are you talking about?"

"The weapon that killed Sir Robert. The one found in your luggage. Either you were devilishly clever, or you had nothing to do with the death. I opted for the latter," Braemhor went on.

MacIain sank back in his seat in disbelief. "But I didn't kill Sir Robert; I really liked him by the time the evening was over."

"I know that, but the evidence was mounting against you. You had motive, avenging a family feud from three hundred years ago, and opportunity—as I said, you two were the last to see Sir Robert alive in the early morning of February second. But your anger at not being able to retrieve your bag last evening did not strike me as born of fear—that the hidden weapon might be discovered—but more of genuine anger born of frustration of being helpless in the face of authorities in a foreign country. So with you out of the way as a suspect, I had to concentrate on the other two who had knowledge of the weapon."

"Burt and Inspector MacDonell," Mary interjected.

"Precisely. Burt had motive and opportunity, as you, Mary, pointed out, and MacDonell could have had the same distorted motive as our young friend here." Braemhor looked again at MacIain. "Opportunity? I wasn't quite so sure on that count. Burt was still the better bet."

"So I and Mrs. Hawkins were right," Mary proudly concluded.

"Only you. Not Mrs. Hawkins." Braemhor's comment drew a perplexed look from his wife. He turned to Mary. "Do you remember when we were discussing the possible suspects?"

"Yes, Burt, MacDonell and Robert here." Mary looked across the table at the MacIains.

"There was a fourth," Braemhor quietly said.

"A fourth?"

"Yes, a fourth. You suggested that maybe Sir Robert had committed suicide, and I scoffed at the idea because the weapon was not found at the scene. Well, the more I thought about it, the more sense it made. But there was still the puzzle of who took the weapon from Sir Robert's hand. Burt was an obvious suspect since his prints were on the knife, but so were MacDonell's. MacDonell's could be accounted for by his generally sloppy police work, except, how did the weapon get into MacIain's case. The desk clerk solved that riddle when he told me that MacDonell had been into MacIain's case in the Inn's shed.

"Now, did MacDonell murder Sir Robert? He did have the ancient family feud motive." Braemhor looked at MacIain. "MacDonell is a variant of MacDonald. But there was no obvious opportunity for him unless Burt let him into the house after the MacIains left. Then the whole possible scenario struck me. What if Burt, when he found Sir Robert, took the knife and hid it to save the family the embarrassment of a Campbell suicide? Servants can be very loyal, you know. Then he called Inspector MacDonell for help. MacDonell took the knife and put it into your case and intended to charge you with murder and save the Campbell reputation. Small Scottish villages are a hotbed of local loyalties, you see. For all his dislike of the Campbells, MacDonell was more loyal to protecting the reputation of the local community, including the Campbells. Blaming the 'murder' on an outsider was the perfect solution. In addition, MacDonell had the perfect opportunity to place the 'murder' weapon in your case, MacIain, when he went into your bag stored in the Inn's shed.

"And when Livingstone questioned Burt, that is essentially the story that came out. You," Braemhor looked directly at MacIain again, "provided the two with the perfect foil by your outburst at dinner before all of Sir Robert's guests. You were the obvious suspect, and the local court might well have supported MacDonell's charges. But in the end Burt's confession of Sir Robert's suicide and his desperate hope of salvaging the family honor wrapped up the case."

"And what will happen to Burt and MacDonell?" Jean MacIain asked.

"For Burt, not much. Local loyalties will see that he doesn't suffer much. In fact, he will probably be seen as a loyal manservant who was just doing his job for a local, important and powerful family. Besides, with his inheritance from Sir Robert's estate, he should live a very comfortable retirement. MacDonell, on the other hand, I suspect will spend a good long time behind bars not only for his actions but for the embarrassment he will have caused in official police circles. I don't think he will being doing police work ever again.

"That summarizes the case of Sir Robert's death, and I think it's now time for all of us to be on our respective ways—you two to the remainder of your holiday and Mary and I to Daraichburn and our B&B. Shall we?" With that, Braemhor rose, said his goodbyes to the MacIains and directed Mary to their room to pack for the trip home.

As the Braemhors left the car park later, Mary looked at John. "Ready to go back to Daraichburn and retire?"

"What do you think?"

Mary smiled as John headed the Vauxhall out of the village and on to the highway.

Chapter 12

The day they returned to Dunmoor Cottage Mary began to get dinner together when she noted a change in the contents of the pantry.

"John," she called. "I think we have a mystery right here in Daraichburn. Do you know where my cooking sherry is? And what is this half full bottle of Dry Sack doing in the pantry?"

"I can't imagine." He thought for a minute. "Or maybe I can. When did you last use the cooking sherry?'

"Before we went to visit James and Jennifer. It's been quite some time. You don't suppose?"

"Rita???" John smirked.

"Surely she would not have drunk the cooking sherry, would she?"

"Certainly a possibility. James did say that in Rhodesia she always had either a glass of wine or beer in her hand. She must have been disappointed when all she found was cooking sherry."

"But she knows the only spirits we use are for cooking."

"Why don't you call her and see if we can solve the 'Mystery of Dunmoor Cottage?'" John suggested with a broad smile.

"I will." And Mary went to the phone in the sitting room.

Ten minutes later Mary chuckled her way back into the kitchen. "We can write up another solved case, John. Aunt Rita drank the cooking sherry and then, feeling guilty, I guess, for finishing our only bottle, replaced it with Dry Sack."

"That's an expensive exchange, but I thought you said there was only half a bottle of Dry Sack in the pantry."

"Well she did say that the sherry we had was not very good. 'Not very smooth' was her phrase. Apparently after tasting her replacement, she couldn't resist it."

"Who knows, maybe the half bottle we now have is not the first replacement." John smiled. Mary just shook her head and went about preparing dinner for the two of them.

****

After solving the case of the disappearing sherry, the Braemhors' life slowed considerably. Things were unusually quiet for a while and John's agitation was beginning to show again. Then Mary read in the newspaper of the sudden demise of one of their friends, Sally Baines, a stalwart of nearby St. David's. Hers was not a singular case at St. David's.

The beginning was insidious. Hardly noticeable. One by one they passed on. Not that they should not have. They were elderly, some very elderly. Most were infirm, but their infirmities did not threaten their lives.

The last to go was the Braemhors' friend, Sally Baines. She was a youngish widow of fifty-three with the usual complement of the beginning ailments of age, more arthritis than she cared to admit, and skin that needed constant observation lest those occasional splotches of basal cell carcinoma be melanoma instead.

Mrs. Baines attended mass regularly during the week and twice on Saturdays. During Sunday vespers she seemed as vigorous as usual, carrying on her animated post-prayers interactions with fellow parishioners, though she did remark that she was not feeling well. By Monday morning she was dead.

The Sunday afternoon funeral was packed with hundreds of parishioners in addition to legions of Mrs. Baines's secular friends, John and Mary Braemhor among them.

"Such a shame. She seemed so full of life," Mary had said to other mutual friends, "and so sudden."

"Too sudden in my estimation," John began before Mary shushed him with a meaningful look.

"You're right, John," Ian Kilhenny, a small, slender Irishman with a shock of flaming red hair and eyebrows, added quickly. "We've had a steady diet of funerals during the last six months."

John wanted to pursue Kilhenny's remark, but they were interrupted by Father Delany, who had quickly stepped between Braemhor and Kilhenny. "I don't believe we've met." He held out his hand to Braemhor. "I'm Father Delany. St. David's is *my* parish." His last sentence had an air of proprietorship about it.

The priest was a tall, slightly overweight man of fifty-seven with tufts of white hair above his ears and around the back of his head, and blue-grey eyes that pierced friend and foe alike. His physique projected a past of robust musculature that had deteriorated through the years for want of exercise.

As he took the priest's outstretched, surprisingly limp offering, Braemhor said, "Braemhor, John Braemhor, this is my wife, Mary. We were good friends of Sally."

"Ah, yes, such a shame. She was a bulwark of *my* church. Very much involved in everything; one of *my* most active volunteers. An ever present presence."

"I understand she had strong opinions, too." That was Kilhenny.

"Oh, that too, that too." The priest smiled. "But that's what makes *my* parish...lively." He paused for a moment. "Braemhor...Braemhor, your name is very familiar to me.... Well, I must talk with some of the others. Good meeting you, Mr. Braemhor, Mrs. Braemhor. Please join us sometime for mass. You'd be most welcome."

"Thank you," Mary responded as the priest walked away toward another cluster of attendees.

"You said she had strong opinions?" Braemhor turned to Kilhenny.

"Oh yes, and not afraid to voice them. Had a number of run-ins with the good Father. Didn't agree with the way Father Delany ran *his* church. They had a loud 'discussion' after mass Saturday about his decision not to offer wine at communion anymore."

"No wine at communion? Doesn't that undermine the meaning of communion?" Mary asked.

"No matter. He said it was too expensive, particularly since *his* church is about £80,000 over budget. She was as angry as I've ever seen her. But when she accused him of spending church funds to take his Filipino houseboys on trips—conventions, he calls them—he really lost his composure. The two of them stood there, both red-faced, shouting at each other in the midst of the church members leaving the mass. Quite a scene."

"Fascinating," John added. "Maybe you and Martha could join us for tea this afternoon? Say about four? You know where our B&B is," John suggested without consulting Mary.

"That sounds good." Ian looked at Martha, who nodded her assent. "We'll come by then."

John was deep in thought during the drive to the Braemhors' B&B. Finally he said, "I just don't know what to make of Ian's comment about Father Delany and Sally's confrontation. She was always so even and mild tempered, despite strong opinions. But...well, we'll see when we talk to Ian and Martha."

****

Mary set out the tea service and fresh scones on the low pine coffee table between the two divans in the peat warmed common room at Dunmoor Cottage just as the Kilhennys arrived.

I'd like to hear more about your remarks at the funeral this afternoon." John opened the conversation.

And so for the next hour, Ian Kilhenny's noticeable Irish brogue filled the Braemhors' sitting room as he outlined some of the inner turmoil of the church, with occasional additions and corrections offered by Martha Kilhenny. It seemed that Father Delany worked in the Philippines before returning to Scotland and St. David's. There he established a modest home for orphaned boys. Each year he returned to the Philippines for a short stay and brought one or two of the boys back with him for a year of education and experience at St. David's. His relationship with the boys was grist for the rumor mill that was St. David's, but most of the parishioners saw Father Delany as carrying on the mission of the church, rather than carrying on a closeted affair with young men. Sally Baines was not among this latter group and often voiced her suspicions, hence the confrontation with Father Delany a few days ago.

Similar suspicions regarding the good Father had surfaced about a year before he started bringing the boys to St. David's. The church bookkeeper, Glenn Canwell, appeared to have a particularly close personal relationship with Father Delany. So close that when the church Elders attempted to have him removed for incompetence—St. David's budget was deeply in the red—Father Delany rejected the recommendation and kept him on anyway.

Strangely, about a week after Father Delany brought his first houseboy back from the Philippines with him, Glenn and Father Delany had a falling out. Prior to that time Glenn had always been a cheerful, happy person, fun to be around. Small of stature—

some of Father Delany's detractors thought almost boy-like—Canwell's head of blond, unkempt hair gave him a youthful look that took ten years from his actual thirty-six years of age. From the time of the importation of the Filipino houseboys, however, Glenn had become noticeably morose, hardly speaking with any one, shuffling around the church halls like an angry ghost. He continued to do his job in his usual incompetent manner, but it seemed the joy had gone out of his life.

"You certainly do have some interesting interrelationships at St. David's. I didn't realize a church could be so complicated," Mary observed.

"It's worse than the secular world because the same tensions are there, but they are distorted by the level of discourse people expect within the church. It makes the usual pettiness of the world seem so much more so because the perceived gap between expectations and reality is so exaggerated. You expect better of those who profess devotion to higher values," Martha added to the conversation.

"You said that St. David's has run up a deficit of £80,000 and Sally accused Father Delany of misusing the funds. Isn't that rather excessive for a church? Has there been an audit?" John asked.

"One is in process; we—I'm a member of the Council of Elders—asked the diocese to initiate one. Very few church members know about it because we keep these sorts of things hush-hush in parish circles." Ian smiled.

"And you also said that St. David's has had a run of funerals of late." John looked at Ian. "But that shouldn't be too unusual, should it? After all St. David's does serve an older population. A constant procession of funerals would be expected, I would have thought."

"True, true," Ian acknowledged, "but their numbers seem to be picking up recently. Mostly older parishioners, of course. Nothing unusual about that, but still...."

"Still, what?" Braemhor was intrigued.

Ian continued his tale of St. David's, giving the Braemhors a thumbnail sketch of the parade of funerals. Six months ago Percival Pasley, a bedridden widower of seventy-six, was found dead in his bed one morning. Unlike the outspoken Mrs. Baines, he had been a quiet participant in things religious, never questioning the authority of Father Delany. Mr. Pasley had been reasonably healthy until a few months prior to his demise when he was diagnosed with bone cancer arising from undetected prostrate cancer. Mr. Pasley suffered greatly, until at last he was even unable to attend mass. Then one morning he was found dead in his bed.

A week and a half after Mr. Pasley's passing, a second bedridden, widowed parishioner, Mr. Hugh Riley, was found dead in the morning. Like Mr. Pasley, Mr. Riley's life was severely limited, his by Parkinson's Disease. Father Delany spoke of him often in the prayers offered for the sick and shut-ins.

A third parish death followed a similar pattern. An older member of the church, whose life and church attendance had been suddenly curtailed by severe cancer of the spine, was found dead in his bed one morning.

And so it went, elderly parishioner after elderly parishioner died of natural causes following a debilitating, activity-limiting illness. However, in each case, although the diseases that had curtailed the lives of the deceased were severe and ultimately terminal, none were in the final crisis of their illnesses when suddenly each died. At each of the celebrations Father Delany had spoken of God's mercy and benevolence in granting each person release from his or her suffering and unhappy circumstances, and the congregation uniformly nodded in agreement and bowed to the will of God. The church in general, and Father Delany in particular, were very sympathetic and thankful that their suffering had reached an ending.

"It sounds like the good priest is a very caring and loving person," Mary opined.

"Oh, he is, he is, until you cross him," Ian observed.

"As our Sally did," Mary noted.

"Exactly," Ian acknowledged. "Of course, one did get the better of him."

"Oh?" John, who had become a bit bored with the litany of church politics and funerals, perked up at the possibility of a different topic.

"Yes, the Music Minister, Alice Harwell. She and Father Delany had always gotten on so well; the argument, which took place at coffee after mass surprised everyone. He berated her for having the adult choir sing a particular hymn. He said it was inappropriate and would not be tolerated in *his* church. She stood her ground that it was part of the church's music liturgy and fit well with the lesson for the day. I have never heard him so vitriolic, but Ms. Harwell won the day when she just smiled into his vitriol and told him she would consider his suggestion the next time she prepared the music for a similar lesson. The parishioners stood by dumbstruck, though I think a few even applauded Ms. Harwell quietly as Father Delany stomped out of the meeting room.

"Alice Harwell is one of the most beloved of St. David's staff. I have never heard one person say anything untoward about her. She's a vivacious woman in her fifties, tall, willowy with long chestnut hair that she has the habit of moving from her shoulder to her back with a quick twist of her head. Always friendly, always in a good humor. She was a real find when Father Delany hired her last year, and she has built a better music program than St. David's has ever had. People couldn't image the two of them having such a public disagreement. But there it was. And she had bested the good Father. Not to his liking, I dare say.

"And one other thing, John, it has seemed to me that the age of the church's dying population has changed."

"Oh?" By this time Braemhor's interest had come full circle, and he zeroed in on Ian's narrative.

"Yes, it seems to me that in the past three months the people dying are younger than in the past."

"Like Sally?" Mary asked.

"Precisely. They have been people who, so far as anyone knew, had had few sick days in their lives. Yet on three consecutive Monday mornings, they were found dead. It was the main topic of church gossip for several weeks. You can imagine how it devastated the congregation. And now Sally."

"What was the cause of death?" John was now on the edge of his seat, and Mary could see the enthusiasm written on her husband's face.

"Oh, I really wouldn't know. But I do know it has been a pretty unnerving period. Particularly with the last one—before Sally that is."

"Yes?" John leaned forward.

"It was Father Delany's current, or most current, houseboy, Charles. Father Delany was very distraught. He tried to do the mass himself, but broke down in the middle of it, and Dr. Burns had to finish up. We were sitting near the front, and I have never seen Father so devastated. We could see the tears streaming down his face. I don't know how he ever began the service, and we weren't surprised when he couldn't go on."

"What was the reason for his death?"

"I don't know that either. We all assumed that it was from norovirus. Father Delany had had a bad bout with it a few weeks back, and the houseboy had nursed him through it. So everyone naturally thought he had contracted it from Father Delany and...."

"A reasonable assumption, I'd say. Is that what the other younger parishioners died from? It has been going around," John asked.

"I don't think so. Father Delany was the only person we heard of suffering from it."

"Did any of these last deaths have anything in common?"

"I...I don't think so...." Ian was becoming visibly uncomfortable with Braemhor's interrogation.

"Would you like more tea or scones?" Mary interjected, trying to deflect her husband's eagerness lest he further upset their visitors.

"Oh, no, thank you. We've already overstayed our welcome and should be heading back home," Martha answered as she stood and nodded to Ian.

"Right, I think we'd best be off," he joined in. "Thank you awfully much. I hope we haven't bored you too much with the inner workings of the church. You really should take up Father Delany's invitation and join us for mass sometime soon."

****

"Well?" Mary looked at John after the Kilhennys left.

"Well, what?"

"What are you thinking? You certainly seemed to regain your interest in the conversation as it progressed."

"I did that. At first I thought he was concerned about the spate of funerals at the church. But it sounded as if they were no more than expected, given the age of the parishioners, until he mentioned the apparent youth of the last four. That did strike me as a bit odd."

"Sally wasn't all that old either," Mary said.

"I've included her." John thought for a moment.

"The houseboy's death doesn't sound odd. Ian said that he had tended Father Delany through a very bad virus. Maybe you're making too much out of Ian's observation, John." Mary tried to defuse her husband's eagerness.

"Well, maybe so. Yet, according to Ian, the whole congregation was upset by the youth of the last four deaths. Now, if these events were so unusual as to alert the entire church and become the center of church gossip...."

"Oh, John, you know how people will gossip about the most inconsequential things."

"Yes, but didn't Ian say that the bookkeeper, Glenn...Glenn...what was his name?"

"Canwell, I think."

"Yes, Canwell was very close to Father Delany and had a dramatic personality change when Father Delany began bringing houseboys back from the Philippines?"

"Oh, John, surely you're not suggesting he was jealous and killed one?!!"

"You have to admit jealousy is a powerful motive." John smiled.

"In a church? Really?" Disdain clothed Mary's words, but then she added, "Perhaps we should have some supper now," and she went into the kitchen, leaving Braemhor deep in thought.

****

Next morning, Braemhor was painting in the studio room he shared with Mary's writing when the telephone rang.

"John, it's Ian," Mary called from the kitchen.

"John, we've lost our Music Minister," Ian's voice was pinched with emotion.

"What do you mean?" Braemhor queried.

"Alice Harwell. She was found dead this morning. At home. In bed."

"What happened?"

"No one knows. Her friend, Charlotte Chassie, found her when she stopped by to talk over some church business. Charlotte called the parish secretary to let Father Delany know, and she spread the word. Everyone is terribly upset. I can hardly believe it. She was such an alive, full-of-life person. Martha is terribly broken up; she sang in Alice's adult choir."

"When is the funeral?"

"Next Saturday afternoon, I believe. Why?"

"And where does—er, did she live?" John continued.

"On Mulberrry, right near the church, why?"

"Just curious."

"John, you don't think that there's anything ominous about Alice's death, do you?"

"I don't really know, Ian, but let me make a few inquiries. Maybe Mary and I will see you and Martha next Saturday."

"I really would appreciate it if you would look into the matter," Ian paused briefly before continuing. "I must admit that's why I called you this morning. I understood that you've not fully retired and continue to get involved in the unusual from time to time. Frankly, before Alice, I was ready to attribute the last three or four deaths in the church to coincidence, but now I'm not so sure."

"Nor am I. Let me look around and see if recent events are anything we should be concerned about. I'll see you Saturday." With that Braemhor finished the conversation by offering his and Mary's concerns to Martha. He hung up and turned to Mary. "Looks like we're going to another funeral at St. David's." He then brought her up-to-date on his conversation with Ian.

******

As the audit of the financial records at St. David's proceeded, both Father Delany and Glenn Canwell seemed to become more removed from the congregation, hardly speaking with anyone but the staff. Once, when Andria, the staff member in charge of scheduling events like weddings and funerals, asked the priest how the audit was going, he exploded, reminding her that it was none of her business and that if she paid more attention to her normal duties perhaps she would do a better job.

He had recently admonished her for scheduling a funeral with a family without obtaining his permission first. Since a priest who was a member of the grieving family was conducting the mass, she had not considered bothering Father Delany with the details of a funeral in which he had no duties to perform. That time, he followed up his verbal lashing with a most unpriestly email in which he admonished her: "How dare you make decisions without my prior approval!" She was very distressed to be so treated by someone she looked up to and revered. Andria dissolved in tears in Alice Harwell's office where she had taken refuge from the priest's onslaught.

All of the church staff were becoming increasingly nervous at the changes in Father Delany ever since the death of his houseboy. He had become very irascible, out-of-sorts, and most difficult to get along with. Some even felt that he had become irrational, verbally attacking members of the staff and some parishioners as well at the least provocation. His sermons, too, had become a series of free association diatribes on things secular, calling down the wrath of God on some of the major attitudes of his congregation and insisting that they were not worthy of the church's, God's or his blessings. A few parishioners had actually been so offended that they changed their membership to a nearby parish.

But none seemed more upset at the prospect of an audit than the bookkeeper, Glenn Canwell. His manner went from morose to agitated and anxiety-ridden. He moved around the church no longer like an angry ghost, but more like a frightened rabbit, avoiding contact with others whenever possible. Once when asked what was wrong, he launched into an outburst of disjointed phrases and sentences attesting to his having "done his best" for the parish and Father Delany. He maintained that he was sure the books were all right, but even if something was found amiss, it wasn't his fault. He had only done what he was told even though, he hinted, he was not always in agreement with how accounts were to be kept. His verbal defenses—and that is what they were—were an odd mixture of contrite fear and hostility seething just below the surface. At one point as Alice and Andria turned a corner of the corridor to Father Delany's office, they came upon Glenn and the Father in what briefly appeared to be another of Father Delany's now famous harangues. Both stopped their conversation immediately and uncomfortably acknowledged the presence of the two women before hurriedly retiring behind the glass enclosure that was Father Delany's office.

****

Braemhor spent the afternoon in the library reading obituaries in back copies of the local newspaper. Ian Kilhenny's observation was correct; the last five deaths occurred in decidedly younger parishioners. All were in their forties or fifties, whereas during the previous months most funerals had been for seventy and eighty year olds, one even ninety-three.

Other than that fact, the obituaries yielded little of value—the usual litany of survivors and the dates when funerals were held at St. David's. Most of the early ones did ask that the reader make any remembrance gift to St. David's. *Not unusual,* he thought. Most of the older parishioners had been with the church since their childhood and no doubt some of their family's gifts were quite substantial. *And yet St. David's is £80,000 in debt. Doesn't quite make sense.*

Braemhor resolved to hold that thought in mind for the present. But there was one fact that suddenly took hold of him as he pondered the meager data in the obituaries. Every one of the deaths of the last five parishioners—the younger ones—was discovered on a Monday morning, in bed, in their homes. Such was not the case with the older parishioners. *Meaningful? Perhaps not, and yet.* He resolved to give more thought to that datum as well as the possibility that gifts from the families of the older deceased members should have helped the financial crisis the church now found itself in. He went home to supper.

****

"Well, what did you find?" Mary asked as they sat down to supper.

"Not very much. Ian's observation about the comparative youth of the last five was apparently correct, but only two other things caught my eye. First, I wondered if the older parishioners' estates had included the church in their bequests, and second, I found that all of the last five victims were found on a Monday morning."

"Victims? You make it sound as if a crime has been committed. All we know is that a number of St. David's congregation have died and some were younger that others," Mary admonished him, knowing his proclivity for finding crime in situations others would consider commonplace.

"I know. I know. But it does seem odd that the church should be in such financial straits when in the past six months a number of older members, whom I will wager were very well-off, have passed on. It seems probable to me that at least some of their estates would have come to St. David's. And I can test that hypothesis. Remember Hugh Riley?"

"That nice man we met on the tour of the islands three years ago?"

"The same. Well, he was one of the early elderly deaths. I thought I might call his family—one of his sons lives near the church—and see what I can find."

****

Next morning Braemhor telephoned Hugh Riley's son, Hugh, Jr., and told him how he and Mary had met his father and wondered if he could spare a few moments.

The younger Riley's home was in one of the modern subdivisions on the outskirts of the village next to Daraichburn, a ten minute drive from the Braemhors. The house was modern as well, plastic and brick with a small garden in front.

John was struck by how much Hugh, Jr. resembled his late father—tall, slender, with sandy hair already showing signs of receding away from his bushy, blond eyebrows. Braemhor explained how he and Mary had met the elder Riley on a boat tour and had only recently become aware of his death. He wondered what had happened, because, "Your father seemed so robust just three years ago."

"Yes, Dad was a very active person until Parkinson's Disease took hold. At first it wasn't so bad. He was able to get around quite well using a cane, but as it progressed his mobility became severely impaired, to the point that he was confined to his house. It was so sad to see such an active man confined in a single, small dwelling."

"Did he suddenly take a turn for the worse?" John had known people who had lived for years with the limitations of Parkinson's.

"Not really. That's why his death came as such a shock to all of us and to Father Delany."

"Father Delany?"

"Oh, yes. The good Father was most solicitous. He came to see Dad every Tuesday. Said that Dad's confinement was testing his own faith, in that he could not understand why God would visit such limitations on such an active person and why God did not give him surcease of suffering. It's strange, but when Dad finally died, Father Delany seemed almost... relieved. I remember wondering at the time if he had been praying for Dad's early release. I know that's a cruel thing to say, but.... Anyway, Dad was most appreciative of Father Delany's caring. He actually left St. David's a sizable sum in his will, but most of the older parishioners do that. It's the only church they've known all of their lives, and we certainly didn't begrudge sharing the estate. It's the only church we've known all of our lives, too."

"It does seem sometimes that people suffer long illnesses unnecessarily. You said Father Delany attended to your father every Tuesday?" Braemhor asked.

"Yes, Tuesdays and Thursdays are Father Delany's visitation days. He tries to see all of the shut-ins every week, except when he's in the Philippines," young Riley replied.

"The Philippines? Does he go there often?"

"About every six months. He was there before he joined our parish. Established a school and home for orphaned boys. In fact, his houseboys are from there. He brings them over to broaden their education. A fine opportunity for them."

"I understand one of them died here?" Braemhor was now probing the whole workings of the church.

"Yes, a terrible tragedy. He was found dead the day after Father Delany returned from one of his trips. He had gotten back from the Philippines very late at night on a Saturday, and though he appeared terribly fatigued, he insisted on celebrating mass on Sunday. He was so tired that he even dropped one plate of unblessed wafers. He really should not have been conducting the mass, but Father Delany is very headstrong.

"The next morning Father Delany found Charles dead in his bed. As I said, Father Delany was devastated. He tried to conduct the requiem mass for the boy, but it was too much for him. Dr. Burns had to take over. In fact, he hasn't seemed to be himself since."

"What did he die of? Surely he was very young?"

"I really don't know, but some said it was a heart attack."

"But I thought I saw a young Asian man near Father Delany at Sally Baines's funeral." Braemhor wanted more details.

"Yes, that's William. Father Delany sent for him shortly after Charles's death. They serve as housekeepers for Father. It's nice. They get to broaden their education and the parish doesn't have to hire a housekeeper for the vicarage. You know, you and your wife should really consider joining us at St. David's. It's a very caring congregation."

"Thank you. Father Delany suggested we do the same when we met him at Sally Baines's funeral. Perhaps we will stop by from time to time, but I see I have taken enough of your generous time. As I said, we did enjoy your father so much on that trip, and we wondered what had happened to him. Well, I'd best be off." With that, John rose to leave.

"Glad to be of help, and do consider joining us for mass sometime." Riley shook John's hand.

"Perhaps, perhaps." And with that Braemhor left.

His thoughts drove him home. *Let's see now. All of the deaths at St. David's in the last six months have been discovered in the morning and the last five—the younger ones—on Monday mornings. At least one of the older parishioners, Hugh, left the church a sizable—I presume—sum of money. I wonder if that was true of any of the others. Probably. But nothing unusual about that. Still the church is in financial difficulties. Well, the audit Ian mentioned should clarify that problem.* He decided to let these thoughts work on his unconscious until the next day. "Nothing like letting the brain work on a problem while you sleep. By next morning you have a new perspective and, hopefully, a new solution," was what he used to tell young DIs he was training as a DCI in Rhodesia, before he and Mary retired to their B&B in Daraichburn.

****

Tuesday morning Braemhor rang up Ian.

"Hello, John, what have you discovered so far?" The anxiety in Ian's voice was palpable.

"Not much yet. You were right. The last five to die were younger than the previous sixteen."

"Sixteen?! I hadn't realized there had been that many. This is just over the last six months?" Ian was shocked.

"Oh, yes. And—this is curious—all of the last five occurred on Mondays. Mean anything to you?"

"Not really. They all attended mass the day before, as they had always done. That did call their deaths more to attention. All of them, including Sally and Alice, seemed to be in good health at the service, although I think I did mention that Sally complained of not feeling quite right. Come to think of it, Alice complained of the same thing last Sunday, at the coffee following mass. John, what do you think is going on?" Ian's concern was mounting.

"I don't know that anything untoward is going on, Ian, not at this point, but can you help me?" Braemhor tried to ease Ian's apprehension for the moment.

"Be glad to. How?"

"I'd like to talk with some more of the families of the older parishioners who recently passed away."

"I have a copy of the full membership list, complete with family members, addresses, whatever you want."

"Maybe I could stop by and look over the list, say in about an hour?" Braemhor asked.

"That would be fine. I'll see you then."

****

Andria was headed for Father Delany's glass enclosed office to go over the week's scheduling with him. Even before she turned the corner in the corridor that led to the large atrium into which all of the staff offices, except hers and Glenn's, opened, she could hear the raised voices. She and Glenn had maintained side-by-side offices down one of the wheel spoke corridors that led to the more public atrium. Both insisted that they needed the quiet and lack of traffic their remote location afforded so that they could concentrate on their jobs, hers the scheduling of almost all the church functions and his, the keeping of the financial records.

As she turned the corner, she recognized Father Delany and Glenn in the priest's office having an animated, if not violent, discussion. Both were gesticulating wildly and apparently throwing verbal thunderbolts at one another. The glass walls of Father Delany's office—installed to protect him from accusations of abuse or other unpriestly behavior when he interviewed Sunday schoolers or other vulnerable individuals—muffled the argument just enough that Andria could not quite understand the basis of their confrontation. She was able to make out just enough to know that it involved financial records and the ongoing audit, to which she was privy as part of her staff position.

Andria was about to turn around and retreat back down the corridor when both men simultaneously saw her and abruptly brought their dispute to an end. About a half hour later Father Delany appeared at her office and delivered another of his now famous tongue-lashings. He accused her of spying on him and trying to undermine all he had done for the parish. He even suggested that the financial crisis in which the church now found itself, could be laid, if not directly, at least indirectly at her doorstep. He said he knew what she had been doing and that he was not going to take the consequences of other's sinful behavior. When she tried to defend herself, he shouted at her that she was to speak only when asked and that her presumptuous behavior was putting her on the path to mortal sin. He concluded with the threat to fire her on the spot if she mentioned to anyone what she had seen in his office.

After Father Delany stormed out of her office, Andria crept next store to Glenn's office for consolation, but none was to be had. Glenn was huddled in the large soft rocking chair he had next to his desk.

"I've got enough problems of my own without hearing yours," he hissed. "Go away and leave me alone."

"Worried about the audit?" She tried to sound concerned.

"Aren't you? It could ruin all of us, the *good Father* included," Glenn sneered his last sentence. "I'm so...I'm so... I just don't know what to do." His sneer had melted into a whimper, and he began softly to cry.

Andria left Glenn curled in a fetal position in his comfy rocking chair.

Chapter 13

Armed with Ian's list of the St. David's parishioners, Braemhor spent the next few days attempting to interview the families of the sixteen elderly parishioners who had died in the last six months. He was able to reach seven of them. In every case Father Delany had been most caring, coming to see them on a weekly basis, either on Tuesdays or Thursdays as the young Riley had mentioned. When he was in the Philippines for a two week period, he sent his brother-in-law, Dr. Burns, to visit and administer the Eucharist, as he had done on each of his weekly visits. Dr. Burns, it turned out, was Father Delany's younger brother-in-law who had left the priesthood to minister to others through medicine.

The families told Braemhor that Father Delany was very solicitous and loving of their elderly family members and seemed to be very concerned lest their suffering be too prolonged. When their misery was finally over, he thanked God for their release. As with Hugh Riley, each had remembered the church in their wills, some with quite substantial bequests, a point not lost on Braemhor.

After he returned home from his queries, Braemhor again rang up Ian.

"Ian, if I want to know more of the inner workings of St. David's, who should I talk with, besides you, of course?"

"I'd say Andria MacDonald, John, why?" Ian's curiosity radiated through the telephone.

"Just a hunch. Where would I find her? At the church?"

"Yes, she is usually there all day from about eight on. Anything I can do to help, John?"

"You've already been a big help, but can you do one other thing? I'd like you to smooth the way with Ms. MacDonald for me, so that my queries can be very discrete."

"That won't be a problem. What if I tell her you're making some private inquiries for me as a Council of Elders member and that she should keep your conversation in the strictest confidence?" Ian relished being a part of Braemhor's investigation.

"That would be perfect. See if you can arrange a time tomorrow morning."

Five minutes later Ian called back to confirm an eight o'clock meeting for the next morning.

****

Early Friday morning, Braemhor entered St. David's front office and quietly asked the secretary where he might find Ms. MacDonald.

"And who may I say is calling?" she asked as she picked up an internal telephone.

"Braemhor, John Braemhor."

"About?"

Braemhor fumbled for a brief moment and then said, "I have an appointment; I may need to schedule an event." He smiled.

"A Mr. Braemhor to see you, Andria." She turned to Braemhor. "Down the first corridor to the right. Third office on the left," she pointed.

Andria MacDonald was a short, rather plump woman in her mid-forties with coal-black hair which encompassed her pale white features. She extended her hand. "How may I help, Mr. Braemhor?"

Braemhor took her masculine-like grip, "I need to get a sense of St. David's. Know how active the parish is, how active Father Delany and the staff are. Comings and goings. That sort of thing."

"Ian said this was all to be very hush-hush. Is it about the audit? That's what is on everyone's mind right now."

"Well, I'm not really at liberty to say, but I would appreciate your keeping our conversation between just the two of us for the time being. Maybe I can let you know more later." Braemhor remained circumspect. "Would it be possible to see the schedule of activities for the last six months or so?"

"Easily. My job for this morning is to bring it up-to-date. Where would you like to begin, March, April?"

"March would be fine."

Ms. MacDonald laid out the large annual schedule book before him on a side table and opened it to the March entries. Braemhor quickly scanned the schedule, jotting down hasty notes on funerals, weddings and other special events, paying particular attention to Father Delany's visitation schedule, who he visited and when. "I notice that there seems to be a gap in some events in the middle of July?" He looked at Andria.

"Oh, yes. That was when Father Delany was in the Philippines."

"But there were three weddings. Do you have another priest at St. David's?" Braemhor had taken note of the lack of funerals during that period.

"No, not officially, but Dr. Burns, Father Delany's brother-in-law, helps us out in busy times or when Father Delany isn't available."

"I see," Braemhor said, wondering if he were seeing more than he wished to in the emerging patterns.

"You know, there is no reason for you to take so many notes. I can just copy the pages for you if you like," Andria offered.

"That would be a big help."

Ms. MacDonald photocopied the last six months' pages from the schedule book, put them in a large manila envelope and handed them to him. Thanking her profusely, he reminded her of the confidentiality of their meeting, "If anyone asks, just say I was exploring possible wedding dates for my niece."

"I'll pencil in some possible dates," Ms. MacDonald said.

"Good thinking," Braemhor commented and then proceeded back down the hall toward the secretary's area and the exit. Unknown to him, however, Father Delany was watching him exit, through the glass wall of his office on the other side of the secretary's space. Braemhor headed back to the public library where he had started his inquiry.

****

"Who was that?" Father Delany accosted the secretary.

"Mr. Braemhor."

"What did he want?" The priest was becoming increasingly worried and agitated.

"He asked to see Andria."

Father Delany left the secretary's office abruptly and headed down the hall to Andria's office. He burst in, "What did that Braemhor want?!"

Andria MacDonald was so startled she nearly told the priest the truth, but was able quickly to compose herself and say, "He...he...he wanted to know about possible dates for scheduling his niece's wedding. Why?"

"Don't lie to me!"

"I'm not lying! Look here!" She showed him her schedule book with 'Braemhor wedding' penciled in three consecutive Mondays in November.

He narrowed his eyes on her as he still tried to assess the veracity of what she said. "I don't like strangers snooping around *my* church." With that he exited her office slamming the door behind him, and Andria sank back into her chair in relief. *What is going on here?* she thought.

****

Mary recognized the signs. There was a spring in John's walk and an excitement in his conversation that was only there when one of his investigations was going well.

"What have you found, John?"

"Some patterns. Some possibly very disturbing patterns," he said as he spread his notes and a chart on the kitchen table, "but I still have a few details to work out; however, that can wait for awhile. What are we having for dinner?"

****

The funeral for Alice Harwell was even larger than that for Sally Baines. The sanctuary was overflowing; extra chairs had to be set up in the entry hall so that all the mourners could be accommodated. John and Mary sat with the Kilhennys, Mary trying to console Martha particularly. It was a sad, sad scene, with many of the parishioners dissolved in tears throughout the mass. *Strange,* thought John, *Father Delany does not seem very moved by the gathering.*

Father Delany's conduct of the mass seemed perfunctory and even his specific remarks about Alice struck both the Braemhors and the Kilhennys as if taken out of a book of "nice things you say on occasions such as this," things a priest might say about a person who was not a part of the congregation much less for a person who was universally loved by almost all of the parishioners. There were none of the personal touches to be expected about someone who had been such an intimate and integral part of the church and its congregation. It was a flaw in the service that was not lost on most of the attendees, as parishioners could be heard discussing the impersonal nature of the mass considering the acknowledged admiration the membership had for Alice Harwell.

"What a strange mass," Ian noted, as they moved from the sanctuary to the entry hall.

"Father Delany seemed so cold and distant," Martha added, "as if he didn't care about the person he, himself, had hired."

"Maybe that's the way he shows his upset, by retreating into a personal shell," Mary offered.

Ian smiled. "Not Father Delany. He wears his emotions on his sleeve, if anything."

The four strolled amongst the parishioners, the Kilhenny's introducing the Braemhors to others. Then Father Delany approached them.

"The Braemhors again, I see. Friends of Ms. Harwell, also?"

"Not really, but the Kilhennys have told us so much about her that we almost feel like we knew her. We came to pay our respects and offer what comfort we could to Martha. She was especially fond of Ms. Harwell from singing in the adult choir, you know," Mary responded.

"Yes, of course." His eyes riveted on John. "And why were you here yesterday?"

"I needed to talk to Ms. MacDonald. See what dates might be open in November for scheduling our niece's forthcoming wedding."

"Why here?" the priest's hostility was thinly veiled, "Doesn't she have a parish of her own?"

Though taken aback at Father Delany's brusqueness, Braemhor tried to keep the conversation light. "Oh, you know young people, always looking for new venues for everything they do, and St. David's does have a very fine reputation."

"Yes, I suppose." With that the priest turned abruptly on his heel and walked briskly toward the main entrance. Then, even more abruptly, he turned to Braemhor, "I know who you are, you know. I said before I had heard your name. You were involved in the investigation of that gruesome murder down by the Wall, weren't you?"

"I did help out the nephew of an old friend on that one," John admitted.

"Sort of a private investigator, aren't you?" Father Delany's whole attitude was accusatory.

"Not really," John responded. "I once worked for the constabulary in Rhodesia, but that was many years ago. I understand that you have an affinity for the Philippines?" John tried once again to keep the conversation light.

The priest would have none of it. "Well, *my* church doesn't need investigating. Good day to you." Off he went, out of the main entrance.

Ian was dumbstruck and allowed that he had never seen Father Delany in such a mood, but also told the Braemhors that he was never one for staying long after a mass to mingle with the parishioners. He always left very quickly as if he had fulfilled his obligations and did not want to spend any more time at St. David's than he absolutely had to.

At that moment, Glenn Canwell strolled by walking toward the exit. Ian stopped him and introduced him to the Braemhors. Ian thought John might be curious to meet the person at the center of the financial turmoil at St. David's. Canwell struck his usual frightened rabbit countenance, saying very little and looking as if Ian had snared him in a trap from which he wished desperately to escape.

John made matters worse. "Are you the one I should speak with about the financial arrangements for my niece's wedding?"

"Yes, yes, I suppose." Canwell struggled for an easy exit.

"Maybe I could stop by and see you on Monday?" John asked.

"Yes, yes, that would be fine." And off he scurried without so much as the pleasantry of saying goodbye.

Ian shook his head and said that Canwell had been acting like that since the audit began, and wondered if his change in behavior was related to St. David's financial woes. "First, he acted like an angry ghost after Father Delany started bringing Filipino houseboys back with him from his trips to the Philippines. Then when rumors of an audit being needed arose, he turned into the skittish hare you see now." He shook his head again in embarrassment.

****

Father Delany caught Glenn half an hour before mass the next day, grabbed him roughly by the arm and pulled him into an empty classroom across from Glenn's office.

"Why were you talking to that Braemhor person?" he asked accusatively.

"He...he...he just wanted to discuss financial arrangements for his niece's wedding. Andria had mentioned it to me, also," Canwell stammered.

"Do you know who he is? Do you know who he is?"

"A...a...a friend of the Kilhennys, I believe."

"Oh, yes...*and*...someone with a reputation for freelance investigating! Do you know what that means?!? Do you? Huh? Do you?" Father Delany was in high dudgeon by then. Canwell's face blanched and he cowered back against a chalkboard. Again he looked like a trapped hare desperately trying to disengage its snared foot from the steel vice of fear that held him fast. He fled the room, unable to respond to the priest's rapier-like questions. Father Delany's words followed him down across the hall to his office, "If you know what's good for you...!"

At mass Canwell sat hunched over in his usual chair, near Father Delany's ambo. Father Delany served communion first to the Elders then to those who either helped with the Eucharist for the congregation or were part of the service itself. So when it came his turn, Glenn quietly took the wafer, placed it on his tongue and let it dissolve while he silently asked God's forgiveness. He returned to his seat and did not participate this Sunday in the administration of communion.

****

Braemhor arrived at St. David's at eight Monday morning and inquired at the secretary's office for Glenn Canwell. He was directed down the same hall he had traversed on his way to Andria MacDonald's office a few days ago. The secretary had told him that she had not seen Mr. Canwell yet but he could have come in when she was away from her desk.

Braemhor knocked, and receiving no answer, gently tried the knob. It was open so he decided to look inside. He entered and then took a quick step back in disbelief. He was not expecting what he saw. There in the middle of the room was Canwell hanging from a stout rope tied to one of the open rafters above. A tipped over chair lay just beneath the body.

Though startled by what he saw, he quickly ascertained that Glenn Canwell was beyond resuscitation and then picked up the telephone on the desk and called for police and medical assistance. He notified the secretary to keep everyone out of the hallway to the offices and classrooms and asked her to contact Father Delany, who had not yet arrived at St. David's. While he waited for the constabulary to arrive, Braemohr made a quick inspection of the office. Nothing looked particularly out of place, save the chair Canwell used to gain height. The office was a model of obsessive-compulsive neatness. *What I'd expect of a very careful bookkeeper,* Braemhor mused. More importantly, there did not appear to be a note left by the deceased. *If he did commit suicide, why no note?* Then Braemhor noted something that put in jeopardy the whole idea of suicide. As far as he could see by looking up at the hanging body, there were no signs of a struggle and no apparent rope burns or hematomas about the neck. *Canwell was dead before he was hung from the rafter,* Braemhor thought.

About that time, the local DI, his sergeant and two other officers arrived. "Rafferty? What are you doing here?" Braemhor exclaimed as the four officers entered the small office.

"Mr. Braemhor! This is a surprise!" Rafferty, a burley, solid build EastEnder, said as he looked up at the hanging body and extended his hand to Braemhor. Rafferty had been a sergeant in London working under DCI Killmart the last time Braemhor had seen him. Now, apparently, Rafferty was working as a DI here in southern Scotland.

"I went about as far as I could go in London, so I came up here to take over for a retiring DI. Struck out on my own, you might say. Learned a lot from DCI Killmart, but it was time to move on. So here I am. What do we have here, a suicide?"

"I think not." Braemhor took Rafferty aside and quickly told him about the church's financial troubles, the ongoing audit of the books, and his reasons for thinking the hanging body may not be a suicide. "But that determination will be up to your coroner, of course," Braemhor concluded.

"Of course. He should be on his way by now." With that Rafferty had his men cordon off the hallway, gather together all of the staff that were in the building for questioning and gave them instructions to let nobody enter the hall except Father Delany when he arrived. A medical team, including the coroner, Dr. Burns, arrived and ascertained Braemhor's diagnosis that Glenn Canwell was indeed dead and beyond resuscitation. They cut down the body and took him off to the morgue for further examination as Father Delany arrived.

"What's going on here?" the priest asked as he entered the scene of commotion. Rafferty took him a few yards down the hall where they could speak privately and explained what Braemhor had discovered. To Rafferty's surprise, Father Delany took the news calmly, almost serenely. There seemed to be no shock, no real concern over the death of one of his staff members. He told the officer that Canwell had been terribly upset by the audit and seemed to get increasingly morose as the audit progressed.

"It would not surprise me if Mr. Canwell were at the bottom of our financial difficulties here at St. David's. Did he commit suicide?" Father Delany offered.

"Well, we still have to determine how he died," Rafferty said. "Dr. Burns will confirm the cause of death when he files his report. If you'll excuse me, Father, I need to talk to some of the other staff members." He walked back down the hall and past where Braemhor stood.

"Braemhor! You here again?" Father Delany strode up to Braemhor.

"Yes, I found Mr. Canwell when I came in for an appointment with him."

"I see! You seem to have an inordinate interest in the affairs of St. David's. Why would you want to see Mr. Canwell?"

Braemhor maintained his composure in the face of the priest's onslaught. "To arrange finances for my niece's wedding, of course. Why?"

"I don't think it appropriate for you to be constantly snooping around *my* church. Disturbing *my* staff. And now this! Finding poor Mr. Canwell hanging in his office. I suppose it will now be all over the news reports."

"Certainly not from me. I have no intention to report what I found other than to the local constabulary." Braemhor still held back his mounting irritation with Father Delany's mounting paranoia.

"Well, maybe you should consider coming in the front door of St. David's instead of sneaking in through side doors for whatever evil plotting you are engaged in. Attending mass for a change might help you to cleanse your soul. When was the last time you came to confession or took communion?" With that Father Delany strode on down the hall in the opposite direction toward a side exit from St. David's.

Well, the good priest certainly has a temper to match his Irish background. I must have touched a raw nerve or two for him to get so irrational. Now I think I am really getting somewhere! Braemhor mused to himself as he drove back to his B&B.

****

Later that morning, Braemhor called Ian to inform him of Canwell's suicide—he did not want to share his other suspicions as yet. "Oh, my God! You don't suppose he really was involved in the financial troubles of the church, do you?" Ian exclaimed.

"I'm sure that is what most people will assume. Father Delany implied as much to the police."

"Oh, this is terrible, terrible for Glenn and terrible for the church. I'll get the Council together right away." With that, Ian rung off to make other calls.

Two days later, Rafferty called at the Braemhor's B&B to bring John up-to-date on the Canwell death. Dr. Burns had rendered his verdict; Canwell died of asphyxiation, the official report said. "I just don't think so," Braemhor offered. "Could we...eh, you get another opinion?"

"I've already put in a request for a nearby coroner—a friend of mine from Melrose—to give us a second opinion. We should have his report in a day or two." Rafferty smiled.

John returned the smile. "What prompted you to do that?"

"Well, your suspicions made me look closer at the body and I saw what you saw, no struggle and certainly no signs of hematomas around the neck.

"Rightly so, rightly so." Braemhor noted Rafferty's astuteness. *Killmart trained him well*, he thought. "So do you think the priest is involved?" Braemhor looked for confirmation of his own suspicions.

"Probably not directly involved, but maybe knowing more than he's letting on. I just don't know.... Well, I'd best be off. The Canwell affair is not my only case. If you have any more ideas, I'd be glad to hear them."

"I may have, I may have. In the meantime, will you let me know the results of the second autopsy when they come in?"

"Certainly. And, Mr. Braemhor, it's good to have you helping out again." With that Rafferty shook Braemhor's hand and left the cottage.

Braemhor sat by the peat fire contemplating what he knew and what he did not yet know about St. David's and Father Delany. Mary joined him and when it was clear to her that he was ready for conversation engaged him in a long, detailed discussion of what he had concluded.

****

Saturday morning Mary answered the phone then turned toward the sitting room, "John, it's DI Rafferty."

"What have you got?" Braemhor asked as he took the receiver from Mary.

"Canwell died of Ackee poisoning."

"Ackee poisoning? That's extreme hypoglycaemia!"

"Just so," Rafferty confirmed. "Canwell didn't die of asphyxiation. He was dead before he was hung from the rafter. You were right; this is no suicide; I'll keep you informed."

"Right," Braemhor said and hung up. Then he rang up Ian and asked him to let Father Delany know that he was going to attend Sunday mass with the Kilhennys. "But, Ian, make it a casual remark, so he doesn't think we're deliberately letting him know? OK?"

"Sure, I'll see him tonight at the church dinner. But, John, what's going on?" Ian asked.

"Just trust me for now, Ian, I'll tell you all about it in a few days. I'll see you and Martha tomorrow at mass. And, Ian, don't mention this to anyone else."

Braemhor then explained to Mary that he was going to attend mass at St. David's tomorrow with the Kilhennys and why. When she heard the why, Mary said, "Don't you think it would look more natural for the two of us to attend? Father Delany may be quite suspicious if just you show up. If what you assume is going on, it would certainly put him on his guard. No, I think it best if we both go with our friends. It will be out of the ordinary enough for us to attend a mass at all."

"You're right, of course, but if you go, you must follow my instructions explicitly and do absolutely, exactly as I say. I am not at all comfortable placing you in possible harm's way like this, but I will agree to your going only if you do as instructed," Braemhor spoke as a domineering father might.

Though offended by his tone—they had always shared equally the dangers of his sleuthing—Mary realized that it was only out of desperate concern for her well-being that John was acting as he was. She also knew that the extent of his concern indicated how serious he thought the situation to be. She listened quietly as he outlined, in detail, what she was to do and not do during the mass. That night they both slept a troubled sleep, anticipating the adventure which faced them the next day.

****

Sunday morning dawned in the usual Scottish leaden grey. The clouds blotted out what might have been a lovely autumn sunrise and coated everything with a fog of mist, broken only by an occasional harder rain shower that caused rivulets of water to cascade down the lane by which the Braemhor cottage rested. John and Mary were in the sitting room before six, having soft-boileds and toast. John reviewed again what Mary was to do during the Eucharist, so that there would be no misunderstanding of her role and actions. Mary listened quietly, marveling at the simplicity, yet complexity, of her husband's plan. When both were satisfied that all was in readiness, they dressed for church, he in his blue Harris tweed and dark grey pants, she in a stylish woolen matching pants and cardigan, and got into their dark Vauxhall and headed down the Melrose Road to St. David's.

The Kilhennys met them in the car park and the four friends strolled into the entrance to the church. As they entered, Father Delany called out to them from where he was putting on his vestments, "Ah, the Braemhors, I see. So, you decided to accept my invitation to mass to cleanse your soul." He looked directly at Braemhor. "St. David's is happy to welcome you," he said, a sardonic smile flickering on the corners of his mouth. "Why don't you sit in the front with the Kilhennys and the other Elders, the better to hear my homily."

"Most kind of you," Braemhor responded and moved forward with Mary and Ian and Martha Kilhenny to the front row of seats. St. David's was a modern structure without the usual rigid alignment of pews, but instead had rows of freestanding, cushioned chairs.

"This is quite an honor," Ian said as they took their seats. "Father Delany, himself, administers the Eucharist to those in front. He usually reserves these seats for visiting dignitaries and members of the Council of Elders."

"Excellent," Braemhor commented as he caught Mary's eye in a prolonged and meaningful stare.

Father Delany's homily was a strange mix of decrying the waning influence of the gospel in everyday life with a diatribe against politicians and overly influential business men who are more focused on maximizing profits than on the compassion which should emanate from the teachings of the church. Then came the moment Braemhor awaited. The entire congregation rose, and then Father Delany blessed the wafers and proceeded to distribute the host, first to those on the first row himself, then to those members of the congregation chosen to distribute it to the rest of the parishioners. When he came to John and Mary, he smiled at each, "The body of Christ." With that he placed a wafer in each of their crossed hands and proceeded to Ian and Martha.

Braemhor looked at Mary though his head remained bowed to ascertain that she was doing as he had instructed her. With a quick glance of her eye, she confirmed that she had dutifully followed his lead, and then they and the Kilhennys sat back down in their chairs.

Once the mass concluded, Father Delany mingled much longer with the parishioners at coffee hour than was his usual wont. When he came up to the Braemhors and Kilhennys, he seemed almost giddy as if he had suddenly had a great weight lifted from his frame. For the first time, Mary thought, he seemed like a real person rather than an emotionally distant symbol. Mary began to wonder if John's suppositions had been wrong and the priest was not the villain her husband had carved him out to be.

On the way home, John turned to Mary and handed her a small plastic bag containing a single wafer. "Put yours in here and seal the top of the bag. I was very impressed with your sleight of hand. You know, you could have had a career as a stage magician."

He smiled and for the first time since they had gotten up that morning relaxed. Mary noted the change in her husband, as she had so many times before when he was about to put the finishing touches on a case. She looked at him with a mixture of loving care and admiration. "I suppose you'll want to see Rafferty right away?"

"Right. I'll drop you at the cottage, then I'll hop over to Melrose to see Rafferty. I shouldn't be long."

Braemhor found Rafferty at home, expressed his regrets at intruding on his Sunday and said, "Have these analyzed for Ackee poison." He handed the DI the sealed plastic bag. "If I'm right, you'll have all the evidence you'll need."

Rafferty took the bag, looked at Braemhor and smiled. "If you're right, Mr. Braemhor, I am in your debt."

****

Next morning Mary again handed the telephone to Braemhor, "It's DI Rafferty again."

"Braemhor here."

"Mr. Braemhor, I *am* in your debt. As you suspected, the wafers were laced with extract from unripe *Blighia sapida* fruit. Father Delany and his brother-in-law, Dr. Burns, are both in custody. Did you know Dr. Burns is Father Delany's brother-in-law?"

"Ian told me."

"Well, we've got him as an accessory and we found a drawer full of red-dotted wafers, just like the two you gave me, in the good Father's desk and several unusual potted plants also in his office. We're having them analyzed today."

"I think you'll find them to be from the Ackee tree, known to grow in the Philippines. Very toxic. It seems Father Delany was importing more than just Filipino houseboys into the U.K."

"Well, thanks to you, we now have enough evidence to prosecute both Father Delany and his brother-in-law for the murder of Glenn Canwell."

"And the other twenty-one parishioners over the last six months, I suspect," Braemhor added.

****

No sooner had Braemhor finished talking with Rafferty than the telephone rang again. It was Ian Kilhenny. "John, what's going on? The police have arrested Father Delany and his brother-in-law, Dr. Burns, and carried off almost the entire contents of his office including some houseplants he kept there. Did this have anything to do with your inquiries?"

"Yes, it did. Why don't you and Martha join us for some tea and scones later this afternoon? I can tell you what has transpired," Braemhor suggested.

"That'll be fine. We'll see you later." And Ian rang off.

That afternoon Mary brought the cozy-covered teapot and scones into the sitting room filled with the aroma of peat where John and the Kilhennys had settled themselves into the overstuffed settees. John began, "When you first told us about the numerous deaths at St. David's, my curiosity was aroused, but Mary and I put them off to the increasing age of your parishioners, as I suspect others did also. But then when you told me about Alice Harwell and asked me to look into the matter, I found patterns in the deaths and in Father Delany's behavior, pointing to something far more sinister.

"First, I interviewed a number of the families of the deceased. According to them seven of the sixteen elderly parishioners who recently died left sizable gifts to the church. I knew that St. David's was in dire financial straits so I began to wonder if the deaths were hastened to salve the needs of the church. Father Delany had been visiting each of them on a weekly basis, and each one was found dead the morning after one of his weekly visits. If he visited them on a Tuesday, they were found dead on Wednesday. If it was on Thursday, they were found on Friday morning. I rechecked the obituaries on the other nine and cross-checked them with Father Delany's visitation schedule I got from Andria MacDonald, the woman who keeps the church schedules, as you know. The same pattern was there. Visited on Tuesday, found on Wednesday; visited on Thursday, found on Friday. Still, all I had was a correlation. I couldn't pin down any cause and effect. It was only when I found a hiatus of funerals for two weeks in July that the things began to fall into place."

"How so?" Ian was fascinated by Braemhor's exposé.

"Those were the two weeks Father Delany was in the Philippines. His brother-in-law, Dr. Burns, covered the visitations for him during that period. No Father Delany, no deaths. Now I had a demonstrative connection between the elderly deaths and Father Delany."

"Wait, John. Are you suggesting that a priest of the church is murdering his parishioners? I find that very hard to believe. Maybe priests do that in mystery novels, but not in real life." Martha was incredulous.

"Almost half of the elderly church members left St. David's sizable bequests. Money is always a powerful motive, even in a church."

"But what about the last five? If your 'murderous priest' idea is right, what's the motive? I don't think Sally had much money, and I doubt a church Music Minister would be exceptionally wealthy." Martha Kilhenny sounded like a defense lawyer.

"That was one of several gaps. I still haven't worked out the motive for getting rid of the younger victims yet. What did they have in common?" Braemhor spoke as if he were musing to himself.

"I think I can supply that," Ian interjected. "All five had had very loud, unconstrained public confrontations with Father Delany in front of almost the entire congregation."

"Just so. Thank you, Ian," Braemhor continued, "And another thing, all of the last five deaths—including Sally and most recently Alice Harwell—were discovered on Monday mornings, the mornings following mass on Sundays. But I still had only circumstantial hunches to go on. No solid evidence. I needed to understand the delivery system. If he did it, how was he doing it?

"And how did he keep from getting caught? Then I realized his brother-in-law was the coroner. Dr. Burns could have easily covered up any non-natural cause of death with his official reports. And who would be the wiser?

"But things really began to coalesce when, after I discovered Glenn Canwell's body, Father Delany remarked that he was not surprised that Glenn had hung himself. You see, Glenn's body had been taken down and was headed to the morgue *before* Father Delany arrived that morning. How could he have known? That, for me, confirmed that Father Delany was the 'murderous priest'." Braemhor looked directly at Martha.

"Yet his method and his delivery system still eluded me until I remembered that one of his houseboys also died mysteriously, found on a Monday morning."

"Yes, what about the houseboy? What was the motive there?" Ian interjected.

"That was a mistake. Hugh Riley told me that Father Delany insisted on conducting mass after he returned from the Philippines terribly fatigued. He even dropped a plate of wafers. The plate of wafers and the houseboy were another key. I concluded that Father Delany was poisoning the members with the wafers, but he was so fatigued that Sunday that he got confused and gave a tainted wafer to his houseboy, causing his untimely and unintended death.

"Finally, during my rather bizarre confrontation with Father Delany after I found Glenn Canwell's body, he made a point of inviting me to mass again and emphasized my taking communion to 'cleanse my soul.' It was an invitation to death and confirmed for me that the communion wafers were the means of delivery."

"But you came to mass yesterday and took communion, knowing that you suspected Father Delany of poisoning parishioners with the Eucharist!" Ian exclaimed. "Wasn't that rather dangerous for both you and Mary?!"

"Yes, but I...we," Braemhor looked at his wife, "needed hard evidence of Father Delany's involvement. Sometimes, Ian, detective work is not all thinking and pondering. At times it takes action, rather drastic action. At any rate, by palming and not eating the wafers, we got two to give to Rafferty for analysis. Sure enough, they, and the others they found in Father Delany's desk were highly toxic. That and the fruit found in his office and the vicarage wrapped up the case for Rafferty. Father Delany and his brother-in-law will be spending a long time in prison." Braemhor concluded.

"Fruit?" Ian asked.

"Yes, the fruit they found was from the Ackee tree, which grows in the Philippines as well as South and Central America. When it is ingested it causes extreme hypoglycaemia and liver failure, and death within twelve hours. I had a similar poisoning case once in Rhodesia many years ago."

"So he really was a 'murderous priest'," Martha shuddered. "And to think I took communion from that man."

"Well, I suspect that the whole escapade may have started out rather benignly," Braemhor allowed. "It could have been that he thought he was helping the sickly, elderly parishioners by hastening them out of their misery. But then the possibility of raising the church out of its financial difficulties moved his actions on to intended villainy. And finally, under the strain of his conscience and the tragedy of the death of his beloved houseboy, he broke and used his poisonous skills to avenge himself on those he felt had embarrassed him before his flock. It's very sad that evil grew out of what he may have originally meant as acts of benevolence."

"More tea, anyone?" Mary concluded.

Epilogue

The next day John and Mary busied themselves with their B&B, John tending the landscaping and his apple trees and Mary putting clean linens into the rooms in anticipation of incoming guests that evening. Two rooms were already let and by late afternoon both couples had arrived and were directed to the nearby Inn for dinner. John and Mary relaxed in front of the small peat fire in the common room, John reading his paper and Mary reading Durant's *The Story of Civilization.*

John, have you read this third volume, *Caesar and Christ?"* Mary asked.

"Not yet. I read the first two volumes, but I want to finish Gibbon first so I can compare the more modern version with the older. Something special?"

"No, not really. It is just that I am so struck by how modern the Roman culture and system of society was."

"I thought the second volume, *The Life of Greece,* had the same impact. We are just not so far removed from our ancient forbearers, are we?" John mused.

Mary smiled, always pleased to share the intellectual with her husband. It is what made their life together so comfortable and stimulating. *Maybe now with his painting he will finally be able to relax more into retirement,* Mary thought. After finishing the illustrations for her book of poetry, John had started a series of small portraits of famous artists like Dürer, Bernini and Riemenschneider. With the thought of no more adventurous investigations, she went back to her book.

Suddenly John sat forward in his chair.

"What is it, John?" Mary was shaken from her involvement in the governmental system of Rome.

"Look at this!" He held his paper out to her and pointed to the article on page ten, titled *Police Baffled by a Series of Strange Occurrences.*

Mary quickly recognized the signs and could see that their B&B respite was to be short lived, and that she had overestimated the importance of John's painting. She knew it by her husband's renewed alertness. His eyes literally flashed with excitement. Mary knew another adventure was not far off.

THE END

ABOUT THE AUTHOR

 Owen Magruder is the *nom de plume* of a retired college professor. He has authored three professional books and a small volume of remembrances of the American Civil War. In addition, he and his wife have co-authored a brief biography of a little known abolitionist from upstate New York for the National Abolition Hall of Fame. From 1989 to 2005, the couple ran a small publishing house that specialized in original letters and journals from the American Civil War.

Magruder's ancestral home is in the Scottish highlands, hence the Scottish link to his mystery novels. *The Feud at Glencoe and Other Adventures* is the third of the John and Mary Braemhor mysteries. Owen Magruder resides in upstate New York.

www.Ingramcontent.com/pod-product-compliance
Lightning Source LLC
Chambersburg PA
CBHW050418260626
47156CB00003B/1060